MW01118221

Two Sweeties

by

Norman S. Giddan

authorlink press
www.authorlink.com

Published by Authorlink Press
An imprint of Authorlink!
(http://www.authorlink.com)
3720 Millswood Dr.
Irving, Texas 75062, USA

First published by Authorlink Press
An imprint of Authorlink!
First Printing, July 1999

Copyright © Norman S. Giddan, 1999
All rights reserved

Without limiting the rights under copyright reserved above, no part of this book may be reproduced, or introduced into a retrieval system, or transmitted, in any form, or by any means (electronic, mechanical, photocopying, recording, or otherwise) without written permission of the publisher and copyright holder.

Printed in the United States of America

ISBN 1 928704 10 7

Dedication

This novel was quite a learning experience for a novice.
My geriatric patients taught me strength and hope.
Susan Malone taught me technique and style.
Sharon Williams taught me computer literacy.
Doris Booth and Jeffrey Bloom taught me
that my writing had possibilities.
My family taught me love.
To all, my sincere thanks and appreciation.

Author's Notes

This is a work of fiction. All the names, characters, organizations, and events portrayed in this book are either the product of the author's imagination or are used fictitiously for verisimilitude. Any other resemblance to any organization, event, or actual person, living or dead, is unintended and entirely coincidental.

PROLOGUE

January, 1996

Doc stared solemnly out the window. Snow fell, quiet, soft. His thoughts turned, as they often did with the silence, to Myra and Margaret. He smiled. How badly they had wanted to visit the cemetery *together* during the last warm weather of summer. The sharp contrast of the current bitter-cold streak failed to mask the recollection, now burned into his memory. That cemetery trek seemed like only yesterday.

Uncertain as to the merit of such a trip, he wanted to be realistic, but still hopeful for both ladies. Time dwindled for Myra. Acutely ill, her chronic problems growing more insidious by the day, the old woman still smiled. And Margaret wanted to visit her burial site, where she and James would be laid to rest in the family plot.

The two old women's insistence continued until Doc agreed to lead the tour, so to speak. Myra had become more awake and talkative those past few days, a sign that could not be clearly interpreted as positive. The calm before the storm? Part of her preparations to die? She could slip back into a coma at any time.

Doc sighed heavily and shook his head. Margaret identified closely with Myra's dying, her own depression increasing with the impending loss. The arrangement of the million-dollar transfer from Myra's to Margaret's children and grandchildren and great-grandchildren had been completed. An odd request, and one about which Myra's own daughters would scream. Margaret just clutched Barry the Bear even closer to her bosom–hanging on to life, to Barry, to love, and to Myra at once.

Margaret had told Doc that she felt horrible about her lingering desire for a new roommate, her desperation for someone to be near, to love, and hopefully for whom to help tend. When Myra lay awake, this need for a replacement receded, but never entirely disappeared. It became shadowy and vague, just as Myra's dying weaved more like a spider web than a single strand of silk.

Doc agreed to the cemetery visit, after consulting with other mental health professionals. He had helped patients write notes to the dead, or tell stories about them. As a psychologist, he had taken patients to cemeteries to speak to departed relatives, to express vehement anger or crippling guilt, but he had not visited burial sites with patients in advance of death.

Nursing home residents such as Margaret and Myra proved surprisingly realistic in this regard. "Don't you want to see your new house before you move in?" Myra asked. Margaret added, "You don't buy a car without driving it around the block, do you, Doc?"

The preparations included a van and driver, as well as an aide to provide any nursing or medical assistance.

Margaret needed her portable oxygen tank, while Myra needed extra medication in case her diabetes acted up. Prone to falling asleep, she had to be very securely strapped into her chair so as not to slip out since she had lost so much weight. Both needed sweaters, shawls, and lap robes in order to go from an air-conditioned van to the outside heat, then return to the van.

Under the blistering sun, they were rolled down the ramp and loaded up as they chatted away. Myra was more articulate than in weeks, although her hollow cheeks and sunken eyes produced a ghoulish look that fooled no one. Even so, all around her momentarily smiled at this burst of energy.

The tom-boy inside of Myra surely saw the trek as the final five yards of a hundred yard dash. Margaret surely thought so, too, but she wouldn't say so or admit it to him. She did, however, bounce in her chair.

"Well, okay, I'll take it. The lawyers can give it to my kids. James and I don't need it." Margaret giggled. "Who needs a million dollars, you silly?"

"I'm glad. You know how I feel about you, the love. I want you and yours to be taken care of. There's plenty left. You'll miss me, but the money will remind you of how much I love you and your family. You'll remember Myra."

"It won't happen for a long time. You're like a new person, now eat more and get better, dammit."

"I'm dying. You know that, Meg."

Margaret asked for the van's shades to be pulled down to block the bright sun. Except for the Bar-B-Que, or a trip to the hospital, neither woman had been outside of

Golden View for months. Doc turned around to study them. The outside world proved a shock. The forty-five miles per hour speed of the van unsettled them, although little traffic passed and virtually no road noise sounded or horns blew. The oppressive sun and heat hit senses generally exposed only to air conditioning, artificial light, and a myriad of unpleasant odors.

Margaret said, "I like the car smell. There's no paint or urine smells in the van."

Myra, always the more blunt of the two, answered, "I'm so used to it, I almost miss it." They both chuckled.

Doc sat in front with the driver while the nurse Jeremy sat in the jump seat next to both residents in their wheelchairs. No one had yet mentioned burial, coffins and urns, infinity, eternity, or that great abyss everyone reached at some point. Doc thought how death had such different meanings or salience at different points of one's life. When young, talk of death was easy; remote and unthinkable; an interesting philosophical concept. Older people talked of impending death, its closeness and reality. Too close sometimes. Yet, as the gap closed over the years, with the inevitable illness or pain, death became that long-awaited comfort and friend. It might not be close enough. Margaret and Myra would surely have no trouble with it when they reached the cemetery. Death was so familiar to both of them, if not yet a friend they were ready to meet.

He found it nearly impossible to remain focused on the needs of Myra and Margaret. But he had to do just that. Time enough later to process the experience, to search out the meanings for himself and his life. At first, he wanted to hurry through the cemetery episode, hurry back to life, live it to the hilt. He grabbed hold for the moment, then an overpowering emptiness and loss covered him–of his own failed marriage, one not really strong or good enough to sustain itself through the loss of their daughter, Frannie. Dead at eight and one-half months; his love and hope for the future. Her planned-for brother became an obsession, but not a reality. Both hopes–son and daughter–disappeared in a flash with Frannie's crib death. To not know what had happened proved especially terrifying. Were Myra and Margaret replacements for his own family, his children?

Margaret said, "It's very beautiful here, Myra. The lawn is green, and there are no dandelions. There are flowers and floral arrangements on a lot of the graves. Beautiful shades of yellow, red, pink, and orange, bright and so beautiful."

"Is it quiet?"

"Yes, very quiet. Can't you tell? Don't tease me. You know you can hear."

"Do you think it's peaceful?"

"Oh yes, very peaceful."

"Are we near your grave site? I wish I could see."

"Yes, there's our plot. I can see it. It's for James and me, and we bought sites for our kids. I don't know if they'll want them. I never realized how many grandchildren there would be. Didn't think of it then."

"Any trees?"

"Yes, tall poplars in the driveways through the place. Big oak and maple all over. Nice shade. And some small hills in places."

"How far away is the mausoleum? My urn will go there with John's. Our children didn't want to be cremated. I want Jeremy to take me inside. I want to touch the marble slabs. Our urns will be in a little cubby hole like my books and snowshoes were in when I was in grade school."

"And you can't get in or out," added Margaret. They both laughed.

One day Doc had wheeled Margaret to see Billie the Bird. She described a huge white eagle with broad and powerful wings, all white with smooth, soft feathers. A mature bird with dark, intelligent eyes, just about to fly away. It held a shimmering silver fish in its mouth. She wasn't sure that eagles really ate fish, but this one did. It flew with tumultuous flutter and precise strokes that put awkward airplanes to shame. Margaret had been poetic. Such power and precision formed the exquisite perfection of nature.

Now, *that* kind of bird took charge, protected its family, had freedom and power. No bird in a cage, it could soar to the heavens. Margaret couldn't keep it any longer in her mind's eye and said it flew away.

Margaret surely had not felt so powerful, so ready to assert herself for a long time. Strange that just the promise of visiting the cemetery, observing the resting place for herself and James, would put her in such a state of serenity and calm, balanced by an outward sense of freedom and strength. Certainly she could survive Myra's death, and cope with her own, too. Her husband James was virtually gone since his last stroke.

The van eased to a gradual stop. Doc pulled the empty wheelchair up the stairs backwards. Jeremy carried Myra, then seated her in the chair and left. They went into the mausoleum.

"I know who you are. You've been down home with them. I wanted to kiss you, but John wouldn't let me. I was loyal." Periods of confusion and delirium had become more frequent for Myra.

"Have you got me mixed up, Myra? It's me, Doc."

Myra's thin lips pursed. "I know who you are. You're the only man I wanted to kiss. Did you go see her? Did you sleep with her?"

"You're part in the present, here at the cemetery with Margaret and me, and part in the past with John."

"I know it," said Myra. "I'm not stupid. It's just that there's so much there, I get mixed up. I can't keep it straight all the time." She began to cry.

Doc patted her bony shoulder. "There's so much on your mind. It's a burden, isn't it?"

"Will you kiss me goodbye?"

"You know I can't do that. It's against the rules. I'll blow you a kiss," said Doc. He reached out and held Myra's hand. He then blew her a kiss and made sure she felt the air from his mouth.

Myra blew him a kiss back after kissing her own hand first with a real lip-smacker.

Doc smiled. "We're close to each other. We feel close. I'll read you the Lord's Prayer again, okay?" He read it very slowly.

"Yes, good. I love the Psalms," she said. His reading them always helped Myra to settle down. She loved the imagery.

The mausoleum, damp and chilly despite the warm and sunny day, was quiet. Voices echoed inside the twenty by thirty foot building with its twenty foot ceilings. Doc read the words aloud from the outside of their crypt, the place where John's urn sat: "John Gronbeck, 1908-1985, beloved husband of Myra, and loyal father of Ursula and Trudy. A truly good man."

Myra asked, "Could you wheel me closer so I can touch the marble? I like to run my fingers over the wording." Doc did it.

"Yes, that's good," she said, moving her fingertips lightly over the remembrance of John. "I'll be there soon with you, my dearest. Very soon."

Doc began to tremble.

"Kiss me, Doc. I know you've loved me since high school. I remember that hayride. You felt my breasts. Kiss me, Doc."

"Jeremy! We've got to go back to the van," yelled Doc. "Please come help get Myra's chair." This time, Doc carried Myra, holding her frail body close to his chest. Jeremy took the chair, its wheels squeaking as he pulled it up into the van.

Once inside, Myra fell into a sound sleep. She snored. Jeremy sat unusually quiet. The driver said nothing.

Margaret asked, "How did it go?"

Doc replied, "Fine. We found John's resting place. It's very still and peaceful in there. A lot of marble."

As they drove the van to Margaret's site, she began to fidget. She wanted to get out of the van, touch the ground of the plot, and examine the grass, trees, and surroundings. She wanted to be buried on the left side of their plot, with James on her right. She had no idea of and felt completely indifferent to protocol. James couldn't care less in his current condition and wouldn't even understand the question. She still wanted to be buried in a coffin, embalmed, made to look pretty, so all the kids could "ooh and aah," and say, "She looks so lifelike." She got a kick out of thinking about it sometimes.

Now they'd have her genes and influence inside of them, their memories of her, her looks, her ideas, but they'd also have more money than she could have dreamed of leaving them. The only thing Medicaid had let them keep was a small savings account and the life insurance policies of twenty-five thousand each, which she and James had paid up years ago. Had they ever told the Medicaid people about the insurance? Maybe they didn't care about insurance. They took the house. That should be enough for the government. Rich people didn't lose their savings and their houses when they got old and sick. Now she'd leave a million. No wonder she felt powerful. She was a white eagle ready to fly away after feeding and nurturing her brood to maturity.

Jeremy faked a deep, theatrical baritone voice as he spoke to Margaret. "'We'll be the last to let you down.' You know who says that?"

"Who?"

"The undertakers. They are always the last to let us down. Very old joke." Low-key chuckles filled the van.

"I remember that one," said Margaret, nodding. "And I've got another. When you pass a cemetery, you ask 'How many dead people are in there?' and the answer is 'All of them'." They all laughed quietly. Myra slept on.

As her chair was lowered onto ground level, near her plot, Margaret said, "Just wheel me over there and let me sit alone for a moment." Doc did as requested, while Jeremy got into the passenger side of the front seat and waited.

Margaret liked it. Plenty of shade blocked the bright, hot sun. Someone tended the section well. A nuclear attack or an earthquake could shake it up, but little else. James and she would be happy there.

She said a silent prayer for forgiveness with a touch of surprise. She told James how much she had loved him, how much she had loved the kids. He had been a good husband, and very loyal to her. Disappointment and sadness over something always lay between them. Something had been missing. She'd found it with Myra. Their comfortable intimacy meant another kind of love. She asked James to understand and forgive her. She asked God, too.

"Doc, I'm ready. I mean, I'm ready for you to come over here. I'm not ready to die. Got it?"

"Yes, I do." He came closer.

"The main thing is that I don't want to be a burden to the kids. I don't want it to be difficult or costly for them to visit me at Golden View. I don't want them worried to death over me or James. Myra's kids should be worried to death now, but they're not. They should be."

Jeremy and Doc brought her into the van and Doc said, "I understand, Margaret. You don't want to be a financial or emotional burden on anybody."

Jeremy smiled and said, "You're a burden on me, yes you are. And so is Myra. And I'm here to tell you, girlfriend, listen up. I'm here to tell you that I love it. Be as big a burden as you can be. I love it. I love you both. I love my two burdens, my two sweeties." Everyone laughed, even Myra who had awakened briefly. But Margaret knew he did mean it; he loved them.

The van glided away, quiet and slow. Inside silence descended softly. Margaret glanced back and thought she saw two tiny white butterflies near her plot. Nah, probably the sunlight playing with her tears.

She shut her eyes, remembering her first meeting with Myra, smiling.

Chapter One

To Staff:

January 27, 1995. Weather report is for snow, cloud cover, and continued cold. Lo 22, Hi 33. Census is 175. Two admissions, one discharge home, one expiration. Administrator and assistant administrator in today.

JA

Doc stepped from his car and crossed the parking lot, the red-bricked Golden View Rehabilitation Center spreading before him. This one, like all nursing homes, scared people. No one wanted to be there. It proved the end of the journey for most residents. Technically referred to as residents, not patients, their families and doctors seldom visited. The nurses and aides engage in very exhausting and low-paid work. Senility, disease, and death remain constant companions of the residents. Old men occasionally grabbed an attractive rear end, while elderly women screamed and yelled with seldom a "thank-you."

Today's nursing homes had plenty of medicine. The ordinary resident took at least seven or eight pills, several times a day, plus the big, rough-textured diapers which elicited one's deepest fears of dependency and being a child again.

Even the newest of the new nursing homes, euphemistically referred to as skilled-care, long-term care, assisted-living, or independent-living facilities, eventually smelled. Urine, feces, blood, infection, and vomit played no favorites, forcing new buildings, freshly painted with wide hallways and quiet background music, to eventually stink. Sooner or later, the stench of the human body overwhelmed any new facility, however inviting and beautiful, even if it overlooked a quiet Florida harbor whose sailboats lined up in neat rows parallel the tankers and yachts several miles off shore.

In a clinical sense, Doc knew that most people did not want to die. They just didn't. Even when they said so. They often took a long time to do it. Or, did it erratically, raggedly, getting better and then worse in fits and starts, and claiming that they'd done everything and been everywhere, that their kids and grandkids were all that mattered. Then they lay in bed for weeks or months, possibly wheeling themselves around pretending that the effects of the stroke, cancer, or leukemia had magically disappeared, at the same time claiming to be ready for the Lord.

He took one more deep breath, and then stepped through the double doors.

Margaret thought she smelled foul vomit. Hers?

Her new roommate's eyelids fluttered as she was wheeled into the room on an ancient, creaking gurney by two nurses. The old woman mumbled weakly, "Where am I? What happened? Am I . . . ?"

Beds and chairs, pictures of children on wallboards, and several IVs crowded Margaret's room. A loud air conditioner's rumbling (even in the dead of winter) masked the humming of the oxygen machine and the voice of the woman raising herself up slowly in the bed by the opposite wall.

"Who's this?" Margaret finally asked. She smiled and looked at Myra, then glanced away as they moved her gently into the other bed. "What's wrong?"

Myra shut her eyes, held the lids tight until they hurt, like a child's game of hide 'n seek. "I'm cold. They cut off my leg. Nothing's wrong. Who are you?" A nurse put an extra blanket on her, then left the room wordlessly.

"I'm Margaret Princeton. Why don't you look at me?" She was slightly annoyed, but secretly overjoyed at the prospect of a new roommate. She'd been alone for too long.

"I'm blind, you silly, but I can see plenty. I don't need sympathy either. My name is Myra Gronbeck, and I'm eighty-two."

"I guess they put you here 'cause I've got eyes enough for both of us," answered Margaret. She slid the nosepiece out and put on her glasses.

"They cut off my other leg last week," explained Myra. "At least they won't do that again. Both are gone now."

Margaret's pulse quickened. "Let me know when you're ready to go to the bathroom to pee. I'll guide your chair. I can get you there, but you'll have to do it by yourself."

Both laughed. “Will you straighten the things in my chest of drawers, too?” asked Myra.

“I’m not a maid, you know.” Margaret finally sat upright in her bed and looked directly at Myra, admiring her beautifully coifed, curly, silver hair. Did Myra have a husband? Children and grandchildren? Where did she live? What was she like? Margaret closed her eyes and imagined Myra and herself as elegant white swans skimming along the surface of a peaceful pond on a hot, bright summer morning.

Myra pulled the covers up to her chin. “What do you look like? It’s not fair. You can see me plenty good, can’t you?”

Margaret answered, “The medicines bloat my face and lips, so my tongue is more outside of my mouth than inside. It looks like my face has been injected with air. Sometimes I wear sunglasses with huge dark frames that hide me from me. I don’t like to look in the mirror. Well, my eyes used to be a pretty shade of brown.” Margaret slid from the bed into her wheel chair, wanting to get closer to Myra, having been alone in the double-room for several months since her roommate had died.

Myra’s delicate face tilted upwards at the rustling of the sheets and Margaret’s robe brushing against the corduroy chair cushion.. “What are you doing?”

“I’m in my chair now. This place is not bad. A lot of people die here, but that doesn’t scare us.” Margaret paused and then asked, more frankly than usual, “Do you want to live or just die?”

A knock at the door announced a visitor. “Hello, hello, it’s Jeremy, your friendly nurse. How are you, girlfriends? Are you receiving?" He strutted in with a flourish, immaculate in his white shoes, white slacks, and starched white shirt open at the neck. "Well, who do we have here? Could you be Myra? At least I can see a face. Peek-a-boo." He fluttered the fingers of both hands in front of Myra's head. The air hit her skin.

Myra half-smiled, but only moved her thin lips. "I had asked for a single room, but I like it here. I decided I want to stay."

"Oh good, good, very good. Very lucky, too," replied Jeremy. "I'm here to tell you that Margaret's the most wonderful, the absolute greatest. Also, no more singles. You're stuck here. Who wants what? Coffee, tea, milk, or water? Gin or vodka?" He cackled like a mother hen.

Margaret laughed softly, but sensed that Myra wasn't quite prepared for the easy familiarity or the constant jocularity of Jeremy. She still looked a bit groggy from all the pain medication and the antibiotics after the surgery.

Jeremy quickly checked Margaret's oxygen tank, adjusted her nosepiece, and then moved to Myra's bed. "I'll just take a quick peek." He briefly examined the most recently operated on stump, checking for bleeding or infection. "Looks real good, Myra, fantastic. I'll be back soon, girlfriends, with caviar and champagne. The service here is better than on the *Queen Mary*. Aren't I an absolute hoot, admit it," he added, breezing away.

Margaret wheeled her chair to the air conditioner. "I'm turning the AC down so it won't make all that racket. We can talk better, okay?"

"That's fine. He's quite something, isn't he?" Myra lifted her hands and arms out of the blankets so that they lay in full view. Purplish blotches covered them where numerous IV's, shots, and shunts had been located before and after the surgery. She was still hooked up to two IVs.

Margaret moved closer. "The other nurses aren't as good as he is. They may strike. You know, stop working. They want more for what they do."

"What kind of place is this?" asked Myra. "Don't they care?" She put her hands and arms under the blankets again. "If they leave us, I'll just go home. I miss it so much. I don't know where anything is here. It's all so strange. You're the only one I know. I can't see anything or anyone. Maybe I'd better go back to the hospital." Tears began to form in her eyes. She blinked quickly.

A stab pierced Margaret's heart. Myra needed her. "I'll help you. We'll find things. You'll see. Your personal things are in a box. I'll put them in the cabinet near your bed. Your clothes are already in the closet. We'll eat soon."

"I can't go to the dining room for a few more days," explained Myra as she tried unsuccessfully to turn on her side. "I've got to heal more, the doctor told me."

Margaret moved her chair within inches of the bed. "I've got a secret. I've got my own names for things here. I call the dining room the restaurant so that I feel like I'm going out to eat when I go there. I call the gift shop the drug store. I always loved drug stores as a kid. Gift shops are for the sick, they belong in hospitals."

Myra smiled wanly so Margaret continued, "There's a place where all the nurses and doctors sit and write. They call it the nurses' station."

Myra nodded.

"I call it the post office 'cause all of our mail, reports, and letters go there first. So, to me, it's the post office."

"Do they sell stamps?" asked Myra. They both chortled. Then Myra dozed off, and Margaret knew she could trust her with secrets.

Margaret whispered, "It's how you think about it that matters. We'll have fun. You'll see. We'll have some fun. We'll get our hair washed and set for three dollars, and they'll polish our nails cherry red for free. We'll put on bright red lipstick. Better days ahead. Better days ahead. You'll see. Sleep well. Sweet dreams."

But Margaret's smile faded. Golden View faced an uncertain future, the union for the nursing aides and maintenance staff trying to decide whether to go on strike. Nurses and doctors would not strike, only the nursing aides, activity staff, and those involved in food preparation. The strike could affect well over two hundred workers and staff in the two-hundred-bed facility. Most felt severely overworked and underpaid, living from paycheck to paycheck. But what would the residents do?

"Is this a good place? I wanted to go to hospice so I could die there." Myra awakened the next day feeling stronger and wanting to talk.

"Why didn't you?" Margaret inched from her bed to move her wheelchair.

"Well." Myra opened her pale, sightless eyes. "They said I'd recover. So, I said I wanted to go home. My furniture, my pictures, my rugs, my TV, my bathroom. I know it all by heart, the feel of everything, even the smells and sounds. It was my house."

"So, why don't you?"

"They said it wouldn't be safe. How do they know?"

Over the loudspeaker came John Anderson, the chief administrator: "Good morning, everyone. It's a beautiful day outside. The sun is shining, and we have so much to be grateful for. To be honest, there may be clouds and snow before the sun peeks through again later today. There are more rumors of a strike. I hope not. If the staff has one, we are prepared. Your quality nursing care will continue here at Golden View. New nursing aides have been hired temporarily. You may therefore see new faces in the halls, but they will provide you with the same quality care you've been receiving. Not to worry. This is Mr Anderson signing off for now. Please enjoy card bingo and the sing-along with the activity staff this morning."

"What do you think?" Myra asked, fully alert. "Does it matter?"

"Well, it does to me. I'm used to the aides and assistants. Been here in this room for two years. I love them. Even if my oxygen tank gets messed up," answered Margaret.

Myra sighed. "I hope I feel the same way soon. I can imagine it would really hurt some people. Especially if they don't like change. You get used to a place, to the staff, the routine." Myra slowly pulled out her headphones. Her eyes closed and her face relaxed. The skin from her chin to her chest hung slack. "There's a story on CNN about right-to-work laws. People don't have to be in unions, do they? They could work anyway, couldn't they?"

Margaret said, "Why wouldn't they be in it? The union helps them get more."

Myra replied, "The announcer says not always. Says they should decide for themselves. Maybe they don't want to."

"Well," Margaret answered. "I always thought that unions get people better salaries and benefits."

Myra nodded. The flaccid skin on her throat wriggled. "I did, too. This guy says they're full of gangsters. They cheat workers. They don't do what they promise. People can lose jobs."

Margaret's breathing became more rapid and shallow. She moved slowly to reach for a tank and a nosepiece. "I need my oxygen."

Myra said, "That's fine. Just tell me, then I understand. I just wonder if the staff knows about this right-to-work stuff and that unions do bad things."

"Do you think they need advice from two eighty-some biddies like us? Do you?" Margaret asked. Laughing out loud used too much oxygen but she did it anyway.

Myra put on her headset and joined in the infectious humor.

Jeremy returned later to report a phone message. He stood in the middle of the room and cupped his hands in the shape of a megaphone. "Girlfriend, got some news. Myra, your daughter called to remind you that she'll be going to Europe. She didn't know if you'd remember."

Myra tried to pull herself up to a sitting position, but slumped down instead. "Yes, yes, I remember. She was going to come here to discuss life wills."

"You mean *living* wills, don't you?" asked Margaret. "It's a way to say don't try every darn new gadget to save me. I don't want those gadgets."

"Yes, that's it. I'm competent. I know I am. I want the machines to keep me alive. Well, I'm not sure."

Jeremy propped Myra's back with pillows so she could sit up before leaving.

Margaret strained to move too quickly to her bedside. "I'll brush your hair. Do you want your glasses?"

"Thanks. Please give me my sunglasses. Covers up a lot of my sins."

Margaret found them in the drawer. "I'll put them on you. Want your hair combed?" She found Myra's comb and brush, then stroked the lustrous silver hair slowly as she spoke. "You may not want a living will, but don't let any of your kids have Power of Attorney, so they control things. You do have kids?"

Myra nodded. "Yes, two. Ursula and Trudy. Never see one and hardly ever see the other these days. Trudy is the one going to Europe. Used to be in touch all the time. Guess she's sick of me. That feels good. I need a shampoo, too, don't I?"

"I'll do it later, if you want me to."

"You have kids?" Myra asked.

Margaret smiled warmly, and answered, "Yes, several of each. They give us lots of attention. I wish we had more to leave them. Did our best." She stopped stroking Myra's hair. "Want lipstick or rouge?"

"No, not now," answered Myra. "But you said we. Who is we?"

"Well, my James is here in this place with me," explained Margaret. "We couldn't live in the same room anymore. He's sort of out of it. Can't talk much. Never did, come to think of it."

Myra came as close to a belly laugh as she could. She continued to laugh until she finally spoke. "Mine, too. My John's been gone for years. He never talked much either, even before he got sick. Such is life."

Doc, the new kid on the block, a consulting psychologist who worked with the elderly, had just signed on to perform evaluations and psychotherapy with the residents in the home, and also to do some consulting with medical and nursing staff. Nearly forty-five, his grey hair framed his oval-shaped horn rim glasses. A bushy grey mustache split his round face. He tried to exercise and watch his diet, not always successfully, often saying that a three hundred pound wrestler inside kept struggling to come out of his five feet ten, one hundred seventy-five pound body.

The chief administrator warmly welcomed him during a fifteen-minute chat, and then the assistant director of nursing, Maria Rodriguez, RN, showed him to his office. They stopped at a door.

"Well here it is. Very quiet, but very small. You'll do most of your work out in the rooms and lounges. It's all we have now."

"Thanks, Maria. It'll be fine." Doc admired her deep-set, flashing black eyes. He opened the door into the ten by twelve office, painted white enamel with one overhead fluorescent light fixture, one desk, two chairs, and one window without blinds or drapes. The room smelled of fresh paint and strong deodorant soap.

They sat and Maria said, "Good. You've already got business. Two women in the same room. Margaret is already referred, and chances are good that her new roommate, Myra, will be too."

"That's fine. I'll find them," Doc responded.

Maria continued, "Margaret and Myra are loved by staff because they have not given up. The cardinal sin here is to give up. If you do, specialists are called in to treat every exotic malady. If staff are sure you've given up, they give up on you in their own way. Death has few friends. Because Margaret and Myra haven't given up, they're called 'sweeties.' I shouldn't tell you this, but we always have a betting pool on the residents treated by psychiatrists or psychologists."

He started to stand and then sat down again. The walls of the small office closed in a hair. "What do you mean, a betting pool?"

Maria touched her necklace. Then she smoothed her dark hair even more tightly at the nape of her neck. "Well, you see," she hesitated, "we sort of bet on when your patients, the residents you see for therapy, will expire. You know, die."

"Just for *my* people?" Doc asked. He shuddered, wanting out of the office.

"No, no. We have betting pools for cancer, for emphysema, and for cardiac cases. Different pools for different problems. We don't single out one disease or disorder, or one medical specialty. We don't play favorites."

"How does it work? What do you do? It's sort of morbid." Doc's eyes flitted over the room.

"It's easy," answered Maria. "For psych, we each put in a slip of paper with the day, date, year, and time of day we predict the patients will die. We put our name on it and staple a ten dollar bill to the paper. Only nurses, nursing assistants, and dietary staff can be in the pool. We had some problems with the maintenance people. They talk too much. When the person dies, we see who's closest to the 'time,' and they get all the money. We figure if they need a psych consult, they're pretty nutso or downright depressed, maybe even ready to give up and die. We've got three hundred dollars on Margaret already. We love her. She has not given up, but no one thinks she'll make it to summer."

Doc stood, accidentally banging his chair against the table. "That's a new one to me, but I appreciate your honesty,"

"You're welcome. We used to have a pool on how long, days, weeks, or months, a resident would see a shrink before the therapy was completed. It didn't work out because they usually died during the counseling, before the shrink was finished. So we changed the bet to death itself."

Doc prodded half-seriously, "Now the nurses don't try to do anything to make sure that they win the bet, do they?" Rats, he shouldn't have said that.

Maria's cheeks reddened. Small beads of perspiration formed on her lips. She pulled her chair toward the desk as she jumped up. Shaking ever so slightly, her dark eyes piercing Doc's, she spoke in measured tones, very slowly and quietly. "Just what kind of a place do you think this is, Doc?" Then she turned and stomped out.

She left the door wide open and Doc said, to no one, "Indeed. What kind of a place is this? Plenty of contradictions. It's fair game to bet on death, but no implications, even embarrassing half-jokes, about poor-quality nursing care are permitted, at least not with the assistant director of nursing." He'd have to find out if she even *had* a sense of humor. At least she loved to gamble.

Maria seemed to down-play her natural vitality and exuberant sexuality. Her full, red lips wore no lipstick; her lustrous, curly, and long black hair was done in a tight bun with pins in it; and her gorgeous full-breasted body was virtually hidden at every curve. She wore something to flatten her bust line. Her baggy uniform looked at least one size too large. Wonder what she hid in her past?

Chapter Two

To Staff:

February 12, 1995. Weather report is for clouds with fog and sleet turning to snow in the afternoon. Lo 20, Hi 38. Census is 172. Three expirations. Administrator at a conference all day. Assistant Administrator in charge.

JA

The plane had just taken off and was still in a climb that would take it to approximately thirty-three thousand feet for the initial part of the journey between New York and Berlin. De-icing of the wings had taken nearly forty minutes. The delay had only heightened Trudy and Helmut's anticipation. They pressed their seatbelts tight, feeling comfortable in the textured seats–a relatively plush addition for airlines these days. Warm and cozy, they sat in first class in a 747 Lufthansa and headed for the lounge as soon as the captain allowed movement in the cabin.

Trudy turned to Helmut, looked dreamily into his eyes, and smiled. She spoke softly. "You know, I'm so happy we're making this trip. I know Mom won't like it, but I needed to get away from her. She is so selfish. So self-centered. She's ended up right now with all this money. And now she's old and sick and barely hanging on."

Helmut was reading an overseas copy of the *New York Times*, in German. Several German newspapers also lay in his lap. He slowly took off his glasses, rubbed his bright blue eyes, scratched his grey crewcut, and nodded. "We've got to do something. There must be some way to handle this that will be fair for us and allow us to go on with our lives the way we should." Reflectively, nibbling the frame of his glasses, he said, "As long as you mentioned your mom, I suppose I should let you know that you give her way too much attention. You see her once or twice a week. You call her every day. And of course, it's that nurturing that helps keep her going. I would like some of that time and attention for myself."

Trudy glanced out the window. Myra had once taken her to an amusement park where they rode an elephant together–very frightening–and then a camel that had the strangest and most uncomfortable gait and stride. Myra had been an attentive and creative mother. Trudy had been her favorite. As Helmut was wont to remind her, though, that was then and this is now. Still, it was her mother, not his.

A steady hum came from the Boeing 747 engines. People moved about in the relatively quiet cabin. Still in an ascent mode, they slowly climbed to cruising altitude of forty thousand feet. The plane did not shake or rock, staying literally as stationary as their living room. A pale blue sky stretched as far as the eye could see. Truly felt as though floating on puffed up marshmallows as she eyed the clouds below. Dishes clattered in the nearby kitchen area. Coffee, tea, and wine, or soft drinks, would be served with snacks.

Trudy said, "We can have some wine here, or we can go up to the lounge, if you'd like. Maybe we will meet somebody interesting."

This was the first overseas trip they had made in about three years. Now that their children were old enough to stay with a housekeeper while they traveled, Trudy wanted to take more trips. They had budgeted carefully.

Helmut nodded. "Let's have some Rhine wine, maybe a drinkable 1987 Liebfraumilch, the kind we like. Wouldn't it be nice to have some potato pancakes or schnitzel, if they've got it?"

They stepped slowly down the aisle and up the conservative navy blue with a grey striped carpet of the stairs. Both wore designer sweat suits, hers a bright red and his black and white, and sports shoes. In a discount mall Trudy bought Gucci and Polo. They liked to travel this way. The only thing more contemporary would have been for each to have on a white baseball cap turned backwards, but Trudy wanted to maintain some semblance of maturity, even though she felt more alive and free than in a long time.

In their mid forties, neither looked it. Trudy was addicted to the treadmill and weight machines at her health club, while Helmut cycled, kayaked, and played soccer as often as he could. They could easily pass for two examples of Hitler youth who had reached middle age.

They eyed the other travelers. A youth group going to visit Auschwitz. Several businessman in loosened their ties, many already asleep with ear phones playing music or the sound track to the movie. A young woman discreetly nursed an infant who gurgled with self-satisfaction; one of the best ways to overcome the inadequacies of airline food. Trudy hoped that they could find like-minded travelers with whom they could share the journey.

In the lounge, they went to a banquette area near one end and took a small table in front. The spicy aroma of the buffet greeted them. A very attractive, sophisticated-looking European couple, probably in their early to mid sixties, sat at another booth-like table. The man nodded and though seated, performed a half bow of greeting. The woman nodded and, ever so slightly, lifted her glass. Both drank from large steins of dark beer, and a bowl of pretzels sat in front of them, as well as a plate of sausages and boiled potatoes cut up as hors d'oeuvres that emitted a tantalizing smell. The gentleman unbuckled his seat belt, arose, and walked over to Trudy and Helmut. He wore a dark suit, a white shirt with a starched widespread collar, and a dark tie. Very thin, steel-rimmed glasses covered his grey eyes.

He stuck out his hand to Helmut. "Please allow me to introduce myself. I am Professor Heinrich Hohl from the University of Berlin." He then turned slightly and pointed to the woman. "This is my wife, Heidi. She is a nurse."

Heidi smiled and nodded.

Helmut shook his hand and started to rise, but his seat belt still strapped him in. He awkwardly unbuckled it, stood up, bowed slightly, and shook hands again with

Professor Hohl. "I am Helmut Schmidt, and this is my wife, Trudy. We are from the United States, and we are traveling to Germany to see friends."

Professor Hohl said, "Please permit us to buy you a drink, and we would enjoy the chance to visit with you and your wife."

Trudy nodded, and Helmut said, "Fine, that would be wonderful." Trudy and Helmut walked to the Hohl's' table and took the other two chairs. The flight attendant brought a bottle of cold white wine and the table shook ever so slightly, though not enough to stir up bubbles in the wine. The pretzels didn't move.

Helmut asked, "What sort of professor are you?"

Hohl replied, "I'm a professor of sociology at the Institute for the Study of Euthanasia at the University of Berlin. My particular field of interest is the elderly, especially individuals over the age of eighty, and all of the issues that surround euthanasia, even what you Americans now call assisted suicide."

Heidi beamed and said, "Yes, Heinrich is very famous and has studied this all of his life. I am a cardiology nurse at the hospital, and we have four grown children." A striking woman in a white turtleneck and black slacks, Heidi wore just a hint of makeup.

The red light indicating seat belts went on. The captain spoke briefly over the loudspeaker to indicate minor turbulence ahead. He thought he could fly below it soon. The blue sky had turned dark. Rain and hail were very heavy ten thousand feet below.

Trudy said, "My mother, Myra, is in her eighties. She has no legs, and now she's blind. She lives in a nursing home that is very expensive, and she really doesn't have much of a life."

Dr Hohl leaned back and rubbed his chin. "Yes, yes, the very old, they need a lot. We don't help them very efficiently. When they get over eighty, they lose certain intellectual and cognitive abilities. Some develop Alzheimer's and lose their memory. And especially in our developed countries, it costs a fortune to keep the elderly and the extremely sick alive."

Trudy answered, "Yes, we wonder about the same thing. Sometimes I wonder about the young. I wonder what would happen if we redirected our spending toward all their problems: drugs, crime, and their medical problems."

Professor Hohl fidgeted, then sat still and replied, "Yes, that is an issue, how society wants to allocate its resources, and what kinds of costs it can bear, for both the young and the extremely aged. There is also the currently popular philosophical and practical question of whether people have the right to choose their own death, and whether they have the right to say to themselves, to the world, and to their maker, 'I want no more pain. I want it to stop. I want to cross over.'"

Helmut shrugged and reached for the pretzels. "That's the situation we see Trudy's mother, Myra, in. There is really no quality to her life. In addition to what Trudy said, she has other illnesses. At times, she is very depressed, and perhaps even a bit cuckoo."

Professor Hohl looked at his wife, then at Trudy. "Yes, of course, you understand that women live longer than men, but if both do live into their eighties, women deteriorate more in terms of their physical and mental functions than men do. It sounds as if Myra has deteriorated considerably at this point."

Trudy rolled her small hazel eyes upward and spoke as if to no one in particular. "Yes, I really think mother should have the right to die if that's her choice. She's blind. There is not much quality to her life, and I think that if she wanted assistance with suicide in order to end her pain, suffering, and depression, that should be permitted. But of course, Professor Hohl, you know that euthanasia and the concept of assisted suicide are extremely controversial in the United States right now." She admired the color coordination of the lounge, the muted blues, black, and grays which contrasted nicely with the royal blue of the attendant's uniforms. She couldn't help but think of the blood, feces, and vomit of Myra's abode.

Heidi said, "What's the movie today? The scenery doesn't get interesting until we hit the continent. I love flying over France."

Professor Hohl ignored her as he gathered steam. "Yes, controversial in many other countries also, although in reality, physicians and nurses have been practicing euthanasia, and in many cases assisted suicide, for many years. They just don't acknowledge it, and it is usually done with the permission and consent of the surviving family members."

Helmut said to Heidi, "As you can see, those escape doors at either end of the lounge are the best in the business. The best accident rate is from sliding down them, of any jet."

Trudy paid little heed, responding to the professor, instead. “Exactly. And speaking of family members, what about the rights to a full and happy life for the survivors? In our case, my father’s will left almost everything to my mother. My sister and I fought it, and my mother bought us off, tried to shut us up with a little bit of cash, but almost all of the money, property, and cars are still controlled by her. Don’t we have the right to a good life? Helmut and I have a decent income, but we certainly could use the resources and the property left to her. No one seems to think about our rights.”

A flight attendant brought a second bottle of wine and opened it. Helmut sniffed the cork this time and sampled the wine. “This is delicious, very delicious. Thank you so much, Professor and Mrs Hohl. It’s a pleasure talking to you, and we very much appreciate your inviting us over for a drink. Please be so kind as to be our guests for dinner in Berlin this week.”

The Hohls both nodded. Heidi said, “Please share the sausages with us. There’s so much of them.”

Tears formed at the outside edges of Trudy’s eyes as she picked up her wine glass. She speared a piece of sausage with a toothpick. “I am ashamed to say this, and I know it’s a horrible thought about one’s mother, but I almost wish she could find a peaceful end soon so that we could get on with our lives. I’m afraid that Helmut’s right about me. Everything I do, the incredible amount of attention that I pay to my mother, only serves to keep her alive. Since her condition is so bad, and her quality of life is so poor, I guess I’m really not doing her a favor.

Maybe I ought to handle my relationship with her in another way."

Maria appeared at the door and knocked. "Hello, may I come in? I'm Maria, assistant director of nursing. I've got a lunch tray for Myra. Is that you?"

"Yes, please come in." Myra smiled. Higher-ups bringing her tray. "I'm blind, so you'll have to guide me. What have I got?"

Maria gently put the tray on the nightstand. "It's all soft. Jell-O and consommé and–"

"I want candy. I want chocolate. Or licorice. I need something sweet."

"Myra, you know you've got sugar. What do you want to do while you're here at Golden View? Margaret can tell you about all of the activities in detail."

Margaret spoke up as she wheeled her chair close to her own TV at the foot of the bed. "I'll tell her, but I still won't go much myself, Maria. Never was a joiner."

Maria glanced sternly at Margaret and then said briskly, "Well, maybe Myra will be more of a joiner than you are. We'll have to wait and see."

Myra immediately joined forces with Margaret. "No, not me either. I like TV, especially CNN. I want somebody to wheel me somewhere after I'm myself again. I can't stand being cooped up."

Maria, one of the head nurses, whose job was to promote activity and involvement, trembled slightly as she spoke again. "We've got games, music, outings or trips, movies, church services. You name it, we've got it. Please think about it, Myra. Stay busy, keep happy."

Myra smelled the bland soup. "May I have my tray in front of me, please? Also, Maria, no offense, but I miss my home. I miss it terribly. When can I go home again?"

Maria answered, "We'll see. We'll see how things go. Bye for now." She walked out quickly.

Margaret said, "You know, she doesn't wear much jewelry, but gold and silver would look beautiful on her light brown skin. She has short nails with clear polish. She doesn't smile much, but she has perfect white teeth. She looks like a model. Something's wrong with her."

"She doesn't wear perfume or cologne either," added Myra. "They're afraid we won't like their choice, but anything's better than what we usually smell."

Much later, unsettled by the discussion with Maria and sure she'd dream about it, at 3:30 a.m., Myra awoke with a start. "What's that sound? That thumpy thump–thump–thump." Myra screamed, "Do you hear it?"

Jeremy knocked and came in the room. "It's the middle of the night, girlfriends. The old lamplighter is here. What's happening? Sleepy time."

Margaret, half-asleep, said, "Be quiet. It's the middle of the night. Go to sleep."

Myra knew she was groggy and angry and would not get up. "Don't you hear it? Was I dreaming?"

"It's the rain. Lightning. Thunder," said Margaret.

"No, that's not the thump–thump–thump. I'm scared," said Myra.

"It's hail," explained Jeremy. "No problem. Go back to sleep. Sweet dreams."

Affairs of the heart were mystifying, but attempts to understand them could be instructive. Margaret was Doc's first case at Golden View. A clinical psychologist, specifically a geropsychologist who performed evaluations and therapy, Doc had built up a good reputation from his university-based work as a therapist. He studied the nursing notes, which stated that Margaret was depressed, and in a long-term care environment, that means "really, really, really, really depressed." Normally, everything moved more slowly in a nursing home, so clinical depression often meant actually "giving up," not eating for weeks on end, perhaps even planning a suicide with the specifics of when, where, and how laid out in grim detail.

Doc knocked on their door, walked in, and introduced himself. "Hi, I'm Doctor Norris Gordon, a psychologist here. I'd like to talk to Margaret. May I come in?"
Margaret looked up, squinting over the top of glasses that were halfway down her nose, her face puffed like a "Doughboy" pastry ad on TV. She eyed him carefully, with a trace of a grin. She straightened her back just a tiny bit in her wheelchair and said, "Well you're already in, so come on the rest of the way."

On the other side of the room, Myra laughed as she lay stretched out in a recliner, her two scarred stumps exposed, tinted glasses covering her sightless eyes. She explained, "Don't mind her, Doc. She's a spoiled brat, sometimes. But she's not a bad person underneath it all."

Margaret laughed, coughed, and wheezed. The bells sounded when her breathing apparatus fell out of her nose.

An aide appeared and, without saying a word, put the breathing tube back in her nose and checked the tank. The aide, puffing a bit himself, said with a huge chuckle, "Would you two behave? I've got sick people to look after."

Doc had heard that Margaret had reasonably good "eyes," while Myra had super sensitive "ears." Margaret refused to wear her new Beltone because it "made things sound funny, and it looked funny even when I put my hair over my ear." This Beltone was not the tiny "hidden in the ear" type that they constantly harped about on TV. Margaret's Beltone was flesh-colored and "big like the old days."

Doc tried to begin his work. Margaret wore a blue flowered house-dress and support hose. She wheezed against the background noise of the TV, oxygen tanks, a radio, a large standing fan, and an air conditioner that needed its fan system oiled. He talked too loud. "They say you're down in the dumps, and they want me to see you."

Margaret turned away from her crossword puzzle, gazed quickly at a family portrait on the huge TV, and said "What?" to no one in particular.

Doc talked louder. "Which ear is better?"

She pointed to her left.

He leaned closer, maybe a foot from her left ear and said in a normal voice, "I'm here to help."

Margaret jerked away, put her hand over her left ear, and shrieked, "Not so loud!"

Myra laughed. "She'll drive you crazy, Doc. She hears what she wants to hear. Stop it, Margaret. Give the guy a break, why don't you."

Margaret looked over at Doc with a half-smile, her blue-brown eyes still twinkling, despite being bloodshot and swollen. She said, "Yeah, I'm pretty sad, but who isn't in this place? You'd be sad too, wouldn't you?"

Myra laughed again. In this small, cramped, hot and steamy room, the window did not open, so they had turned on the air conditioning. The mid-February wind blew the snow around outside, while the boilers rumbled full blast. Doc took off his Shetland sport coat and rolled up the sleeves of his blue button-down dress shirt. He loosened his black knit tie.

Margaret opened up a little, too. "You know, it helps me to help Myra. She can't see, and she can't walk. How do you think she pees?"

Doc knew he should play dumb. "Beats me," he replied.

"I guide her. I tell her where to wheel her chair, how far, how to open the John door, how close to get to the toilet stool, how to raise and lower herself. The whole shooting match. Do this more to your left, a little higher, and so on."

Myra said, "Yeah, but you don't control the pee itself or number two either, do you big shot?" They both howled. So did Doc.

The nurse, Jeremy, passing in the hallway, looked into the room. "Everything okay?"

The three of them howled even longer and louder after the nurse left, without getting a polite reply.

Folie à deux, hand in glove, peas in a pod, two to tango–whatever way one expressed it, Margaret and Myra made a matched set. When one itched, the other scratched.

Doc took out his pad and Margaret said, "I want you to know about my James. He had a massive coronary and two strokes. One morning, he was strapped into his wheelchair. He was still salivating a bit. He'd had a huge breakfast of fried eggs, juice, milk, toast, coffee, sausage, ham, and bacon. Both of us were wheeled by him with two student volunteers pushing our chairs."

Doc said, "Must have been hard on you to see him like that."

"Yes, we'd been married sixty-five years, and I was planning our sixty-sixth anniversary party. I didn't really care if we were both tied up in wheelchairs. James was dozing. The aide put my chair by James' face. I whispered, 'I love you. How are you, honey?'"

Doc cocked his head. "How did he respond?"

"He snored and, with his eyes closed, he sort of gurgled a word or two. He never was one for much feeling. Worked hard at the machine shop. Gave me his check and never drank or whored around. He bowled and danced because I liked it. Never did say much."

"What about Myra? She was with you, wasn't she?" asked Doc.

"Myra asked the aide to point her chair at James' good ear. She leaned over and in an Ethel Merman type voice, yelled at the top of her lungs, 'Tell her you love her, you son-of-a-bitch. Tell her you love her.'"

Doc barely held back his laughter.

"Well, James opened his eyes momentarily. He moved his lips. He looked at me, well really at my shoulder, since he couldn't lock eyes anymore. His speech was slurred, still out came, 'I love you . . .' Big hurrahs and loud cheers came from everyone in the hall. A crowd had gathered. When James spoke, all listened. He didn't really say much more on our wedding night." Tears filled her eyes. "Of course, Myra was not there to prompt him."

Doc wished he could magically transport Margaret to a spacious, comfortable, private office. He felt the need for privacy, if not the true confidentiality that belonged to Margaret by virtue of law, precedent, and professional ethics. Staff read the case notes and reports, but he wanted to talk to her without others listening. In long-term care though, someone always stood by: a volunteer, a doctor, a nurse, a nurse's aide, an administrator, a specialist, a maintenance staff worker, a family member, a psychologist, or a minister. And then there was all the equipment needed to breathe, for the heart, the eyes, and the mind or the equipment needed to walk or simply something always beeping, whirring, whooshing. Crowded, noisy, privacy-less.

Doc asked "Could I wheel your chair to a lounge so we could talk more easily and in private?"

Margaret looked at him, over her glasses and said, "Yes."

As they left the room, an aide changed Margaret's tank to a portable oxygen one. As they left, Myra, immobile in the recliner, her eyes still closed, asked hurriedly, "Is she going to talk about me some more? Where you going?"

Margaret replied, "Out for a walk. We'll be back soon."

Doc asked, "Can we do anything for you?"

Myra shot back, "You two be careful out there. Come back by midnight. Don't keep her out past her curfew, and both of you–I said *both* of you–behave yourselves. Don't do anything I wouldn't do, or didn't do."

They all laughed again, Doc finally saying, "I promise."

How deep was Margaret's depression? How long-lasting? Was she contemplating suicide? Was there an underlying anger or hostility? What would help? Who could know better than these two women? They defined mental health in long-term care, a pair of relatively bright-eyed, relatively bushy-tailed survivors taking care of themselves and each other. What on Earth did he think he could do for them? Both women were there to teach *him.*

Chapter Three

To Staff:

February 28, 1995. Weather report is for continued rain and fog throughout the day. Lo 26, Hi 43. Census is 170. Two discharges to hospice. Both administrators out today. Director of Nursing in charge.

JA

Rumors flew about the strike. The word said soon, perhaps in days or, at most, a few weeks. When Doc reached the door to their room to say goodbye, he overheard Margaret speak. "Yes, and we can leave here, too. You know that."

He knocked and entered, then spoke to no one in particular. "Who's going where? Please don't leave me. I'll be so alone".

Both Margaret and Myra chuckled quietly. Up, recently washed and fed, both were almost ready for another nap. Margaret's pain was worse, and Myra's stumps itched to high heaven.

Both women worried about the effects of the strike. Margaret's eyes were darker and more penetrating than usual. Myra's face was red, and the lines around her mouth quivered. "I don't care. Yes, I do. Well, I don't know if I do or not," she said.

Doc tilted his head and asked, "Not care about what, Myra?" He put on his glasses, took out his note pad, and sat on the edge of Margaret's bed.

She answered, "Whether we have Jeremy or the other nurses. I do like that Rodriguez woman, too."

Doc replied, "It's like changing an important part of your daily life. You get used to them, and they know your needs. You can count on them."

The med.'s cart squeaked by in the hallway. Someone argued with Jeremy about taking some pills.

Margaret said, "Well, I heard it could be bad. Myra had CNN real loud. At a nursing home in Cincinnati, there was a move from one part to another. They fixed up the old part, and people had to move their stuff to different rooms. Two women went crazy. You hear that? Two went nuts because they changed rooms they'd been in a long time, and they moved into a different building. So there." Breathless from this outpouring, her head slumped.

She had a good point though. "You're really scared of what can happen to you and Myra, aren't you?" His pager trembled, but he ignored it. The emergency bell had not sounded, and the pager sometimes played an old song he couldn't stand.

"Me too, Doc, me too," added Myra. "Maybe we should move and be done with it." Lines bunched on her forehead.

Doc squinted slightly. "What do you mean exactly, Myra, move and be done with it?"

She turned her head to Doc slowly, unseeing eyes blinking behind some old tortoise-framed black sunglasses that Margaret had given her. "I mean this. We can take our insurance, our money, and our clothes and move. We can go elsewhere, and you know it."

A housekeeping aide knocked softly, looked into the room, saw Doc, and quickly left.

Doc agreed. "Of course, it's possible to move to another facility. There *are* beds available most places. But there is a lot to consider. Margaret has been here several years. You like it. You're both great together. Her husband is here. Some of the companies that manage these places are too cost conscious. The services and food may not be as good, and so on." He'd said too much too quickly, afraid of losing them and they knew it.

Margaret nodded. "We've got it good. We don't want to lose you either, Doc, not at all."

Doc replied, "Given your feelings, you don't like what might happen, and so you're thinking of leaving. That would be pretty unsettling, too, though. Whether they unsettle you, or you do it–either way." The meal cart rumbled by in the hall. Something for lunch smelled spoiled; a familiar foul odor.

"Well," said Margaret, "is there anything else we can do? You're right, Doc. If we leave, or they change our nurses, it hurts us. We have to deal with new people, maybe new places." She warmed her hands by moving them under the blanket on her lap.

Myra added, "Yeah, can we do anything else?"

Doc replied, "Residents have a council. You have representatives. You have a voice with the administration."

"Gosh Doc, the representative of the home's residents is Mabel. She can't remember what she had for breakfast most days," said Myra.

Margaret added, "And she never does remember when you play cards with her the night before."

"And she's got different words for everything. She learned them from Margaret, but she doesn't know the difference. The lounge is the living room. The nurses' station is the post office. The gift shop is the drug store. The dining room is the restaurant. Does she even know where she's living? If she can't remember, she should have the decency to just shut up. That's what I often do."

Laughter died down before Doc replied, "But you could give her a note, and she'd give it to the council. You can talk to other residents, and they can do the same. We could make sure the council members get the information."

"We could run for president of the United States, too. Want to buy some land on a river in Arkansas, Doc?" Myra listened to CNN at least fifteen hours a day and was very up-to-date on Washington politics.

Helping Margaret and Myra mobilize their reactions to a potentially disruptive personal event was within the bounds of his profession. They might leave. He had an almost overpowering impulse to hold them both, to hug them into staying.

"Okay," Margaret began, "we could get a few others to say they'd leave. They'd have to listen to us. Without our money, there's no facility, and no jobs for any of them. I feel more powerful than I have in years. We're in charge."

Myra buttoned the top of her new nightgown. "Why don't you run for president? You're so powerful."

Doc added, "The uncertainty here is unpleasant. You don't feel you have much control over it. Who wouldn't want it to stop? If residents band together and tell the administration they don't like it, and would consider leaving, that provides some control, some degree of influence. You can tell your friends and families, too."

"Well, yes, if those strikers at automobile plants when I was young carried on long enough, they wouldn't have made cars, and the public couldn't have bought them. If they carry on here, maybe we won't buy what they've got," Margaret concluded.

Myra added, "I just wish Mabel had a better memory. Maybe we could work through somebody else on the committee. This is more important than what they usually deal with, the Saturday night movie or the music at lunch."

Margaret agreed. "I hear they're trying to decide the menu for this year's Bar-B-Que. We may not be here for one." She was instantly asleep in her chair.

She slept lightly, but with a slight, irregular snore. A certain peace fell over Doc as well, though trouble rumbled in his belly. Golden View was not in touch with the unsettled feelings of the residents. If Myra and Margaret felt this way about the possible events at the facility, so did others. He knew that other staff were disturbed, too, but little inclination existed to provide a forum, or services, directed at the mounting level of uncertainty and strain. As Doc tiptoed out of the room, he whispered good-bye to Myra. He had reached the door when Margaret awoke suddenly to Myra's voice.

"Is there some soap that smells like cabbage?" Myra whined loudly.

"Are you kidding me?" Margaret's question came out in a cranky, irritable tone.

"Well, then it's the real thing. It stinks," said Myra.

"We're too close to the kitchen. It must be on the trays. I always hated cabbage. We had it when we were broke. Almost never with the pork ribs that I loved."

Back in his office, Doc reviewed the social service information and background data on Myra. As he worked up some preliminary ideas on her situation, he noticed the generally supportive, attentive role of her daughter and son-in-law. Recent sharp changes had occurred, however.

As Myra was moved from the Sub-acute Center, following the second leg amputation, she developed a low-grade fever and an infection in the top of the stump. That same week, leaving Myra's two young grandchildren with their college-age sitter, Trudy and Helmut flew off to Germany for almost two weeks. The trip had been planned for months, and they chose not to cancel it. In all fairness, the nursing notes *did* mention that Myra's daughter had called every few days from Frankfort and Berlin. On the other side of the ledger, when they returned from Germany, a week passed before they visited. This whole episode seemed uncharacteristic of her daughter. Just as they returned from Europe, Doc was finishing his psychological evaluation of Myra, who had already moved back into the long-term care section of the home to room with Margaret. He asked to meet the daughter and son-in-law, and they complied.

Doc led them into his tiny, cramped office. They took off their winter coats and each took a chair. Doc hoped that the modesty of the surroundings would not lead Helmut and Trudy to minimize his role, or the significance of his work with Myra.

"Thank you for seeing me. I'm the psychologist seeing your mother," Doc began.

Trudy, short and muscular, wore a severe blue suit, cut in a mannish style, with a yellow button-down shirt and a blue and white polka-dot bow tie. Not much over five feet tall, she surely weighed one hundred and fifty pounds. She resembled an athletic trainer gone to seed, the kind who wore tights and hawks treadmills or exercise steps on TV in the middle of the night. Her skin was pock-marked and weathered by the sun, making her appear older than her husband.

Helmut, about forty-five with prematurely white hair in a short crew cut–definitely a military type–said, "You're welcome, Doc. I'm Helmut, and this is my wife, Trudy. Everyone thinks we're awful. We left while mom was in the hospital here. We'd planned the trip to Germany to see old friends for a long time. We took our chances."

Quickly, Trudy added, "We *do* care, but we had to get our priorities straight. Mom is old and very sick. What could we do?"

Doc said, "Yes, well, I think I understand. But your support–you are her family–is quite important to her."

Without warning or explanation, Trudy said, "No med.s, Doc. Take her off the antidepressant. It caused hallucinations when she was in the last hospital."

"I don't prescribe," answered Doc. The skin on his neck tightened and grew hot. "I'll mention it to her medical doctor. In my experience, though, her medication would help control the hallucinations, especially those associated with extreme depression, not cause them."

Commotion came from the hallway. A physical therapist loudly warned a resident to use the walker. Doc tried to ignore it.

Trudy said, "We'd rather she were depressed than crazy. Please make sure, no depression med's."

Helmut said, "And we're still anxious to see if Myra is able to comprehend her husband's will. Her mother took everything and gave Trudy and her sister their father's Seiko watch, his Mason lodge ring, and some cash. Sometimes we get annoyed at all that. It should have been more fair, don't you agree? We don't want anyone to think we're trying to make her look crazy or incompetent. Know what I mean?"

Helmut rose and picked up their coats. After donning his, he put Trudy's around her shoulders. The room was too cold, but Doc didn't apologize or explain.

Doc imagined Helmut in an SS uniform with highly polished boots, cleaning his Luger before going out into the open pit in the forest to continue his assigned military duties. This fantasy was very extreme, even for Doc. He had to overcome these feelings in order to be helpful.

"Of course, I'm here to help your mom with her depression. We have no evidence of hallucinations. I think the med.s are part of what's helping, to tell the truth. How can you folks help? Ideas?"

"We'd like to do more, but we're so busy," Trudy responded. "We don't want her to die. We've never really been close emotionally. We usually see her or talk to her daily. But we don't want her back with us, and we don't want to baby her. She's blind and a double-amputee. We can't take her anywhere. People stare."

"Sure, I see," added Doc. "That's really some situation you face with her."

"And she's got over two million bucks, or at least she had it. We only earn one hundred thousand a year between the two of us. So, life just isn't fair."

Doc couldn't think of what to say. Finally he answered, "Well, well, well. Some kettle of fish." The heating hissed on again.

"And you know she is so different now," Trudy complained. "I don't mean to say weird or kooky, but different. She nurses a bear doll and pretends to be a mother again."

"Yes, I see," Doc replied. "It must be a comfort to her."

Trudy upped the ante. "Sometimes she doesn't know what is real and what isn't. She thinks she can walk."

"Don't you mean 'fly,' not walk?" Doc was immediately sorry he'd said it. But these people were getting to him.

"Very funny," said Trudy. "Mom thinks she can *really* walk. There was never a prosthesis that worked. Crutches didn't work either. She's too old and weak. She really thinks she can walk. That's not really crazy, just kind of a white lie she tells herself. Something to help her make it. It doesn't sound good, though, if you say both things. She is a mother nursing a doll, and she thinks she can walk when she has two legs amputated at the knee."

Doc toyed with his pencil. "What do you want me to do? It's not unusual for elderly patients to get some unusual ideas. Sometimes they last for awhile, and sometimes they go away. Sometimes these ideas are part of a pattern of the beginning of senility, sometimes not. Sometimes, it is just the depression. I'll try to stay alert to these things, observe them, and see what's going on."

Helmut rose. He rubbed his hands furiously (Doc wasn't sure if he clicked his heels together or not), and then spoke quickly and authoritatively. "We think her mind is going, Doc. We are concerned. There are important financial and legal matters here: a large home, investments, several Japanese automobiles." The latter must have been a bone in his throat. He finished with, "We need answers and we need help. I'm glad your office doesn't stink like the rest of this place." He sat down again, with his back very straight and knees together.

Doc drew back a bit and started to rise then didn't. "Perhaps you need a forensic psychologist or psychiatrist to declare Myra legally incompetent. Then have a hearing with a judge and your lawyers and all that stuff." Neither answered that question.

"Mom's gotten difficult–sort of impossible. I wouldn't want to live like she is. She wants to live on machines.

She has kept the Power of Attorney. She won't face things."

Doc said, "Yes, Trudy, I understand. We're all different when it comes to health, sickness and death. If you were in her place, you'd do it all differently." He twisted slowly in his swivel chair.

Trudy spoke with conviction. "I know the doctors think she's sane and competent. But they don't know her like I do. Her values and beliefs were that life should be lived. She was active. She did things. She didn't want to lie around blind listening to TV. She never lived that way. I wish the doctors would take matters into their own hands."

Helmut said, "Perhaps that's enough, dear. Doc understands. Your mother can still decide for herself. Maybe they'll help with the depression. You must admit it though, Doc, for us to stretch our budget and our precious time off to try to keep Myra alive, well does it make sense?"

Doc cocked his head. "We had a cat at home. It got very sick. Then one day, it simply went to the neighbor's house, curled up in a basement window well and died. It was an old, sick cat."

"Yes, exactly," said Trudy. She excitedly nodded in a jerky manner. "Yes, yes, that's what we want Mom to do. Exit gracefully, and generously now. For us and for her."

Doc had had enough. Were they just brutally honest? Was some vital empathy missing? Sweating, he took off his sportcoat and rolled up his sleeves.

"You know, Doc, our plate is really very full. Mom is here. We've got one son and one daughter at home–"

"Both of us work full-time," Helmut said, sliding his fingers along the arms of the chair, then grasping it tightly. The skin on the back of his hands was taut and white.

Doc looked at first one, then the other. He should dredge up more concern. They were raising children and trying to monitor Myra's life in the nursing home. His coffee pot gurgled. He didn't offer any to his guests. "The modern dilemma," summarized Doc. "Raising a family and caring for aging parents. More than most of us can handle." He felt ashamed for them.

Trudy nodded. "Our daughter is fourteen, and has gone boy crazy. I found her with a Planned Parenthood pamphlet. I guess I should be pleased that she wants to be careful. She's busy at school, is a cheerleader, and is on the school paper. I'm plenty worried about her."

Doc asked, "And your son?"

Helmut straightened as he answered, "Well, he's very active in our church youth group. He's twelve now. Beautiful, big, strong, blonde boy, Strong soccer player. Loves to hike in the hills. He's life and strength, itself. The embodiment of our ideals."

Trudy reddened somewhat and nearly nudged Helmut, but didn't. She squirmed in her seat. "Yes, of course, but he's so typically American. Trying to become an Eagle scout and loves hamburgers, fries, and chocolate shakes. An All-American boy."

"What about his friends?" asked Doc, for no particular reason.

Trudy sighed. "Well, that's a big worry for us. They aren't the right kinds of boys for him. Several have had minor scrapes with the police. A few use drugs. You know the type. Very diverse."

Doc's pager went off, but he ignored it. Myra's people deserved his undivided attention. He said, "So there isn't much time or energy for Myra, is there? Not for either of you, or the kids, who sound as if their lives are very busy also." But time always existed for what one really wanted to do.

He wrote furiously on his note pad in order to hide his growing anxiety. He wouldn't get far with these people today. He had to try to reach them, but avoid the risk of pressing too hard, maybe even making matters worse for Myra. They weren't ready for a commitment to change.

Trudy finally stood. "We want you to counsel Mom with her depression. Then we'll see about the rest of it. By the way, we're going to Argentina for a week or ten days on business. Helmut has a big deal. We'll call when we return."

Doc tried some levity. "Don't cry for Mom, Argentina." But both already marched in unison down the hall.

A week later, Doc reviewed his last progress notes on Margaret:

Goal(s) for this session: To assist Margaret in identifying one irrational belief, related to her depression, which influences her remaining in bed throughout much of the day.

S (Resident subjective report): "I'm not good for anything anymore. I'm just a burden, might as well stay in bed."

O (Current psychosocial stressors): Family reportedly visiting less and may be pulling away from resident (per nursing staff, social services' reports, and Margaret's comments on same).

Doc then skipped to the bottom of the page.

A (Prognosis/need for continuing care): Making good progress in CBT, reporting decrease in depressive symptoms, considering spending more time out of bed. More activity. Good prognosis.

P (Plan/goal(s) next session): Resident will monitor (and work on modifying) the faulty belief above during this next week. Review next session and proceed with other unhealthy beliefs.

Doc also wanted to consult with Dr Arun Ramantha, the local physician and medical director of the home. Consults between two professionals usually took place when they parked their cars and walked into the home, or, if they needed a lengthy conference, then they stood in the hallway while dodging med. carts, wheelchairs, and well-meaning volunteers kibitzing with everyone who could talk. Dr Ramantha, tall, slim, and dark, had bad teeth, but a huge oiled mass of curly black hair. He looked like an Indian movie star, which his brother actually was.

"You asked about Margaret," said Ramantha. Concrete and specific, he stuck to the facts. "Her primary diagnoses are cerebrovascular accident, essential hypertension, angina pectoris, cancer of the bladder and liver, myocardial infarction, depression, and emphysema.

She takes Rocardoc, Zestril, Dolobid, Ditropan, Norm-a-dyne, Monopril, Adalat, Buspar, and Prozac."

Doc swallowed. What a fantastic memory. Dr Ramantha had one hundred and twenty patients in this home, another eighty at a different assisted-living center, and a flourishing small-town private practice. He also did some surgery.

Doc said, "I'm doing some cognitive-behavioral therapy to try to reduce depression with Margaret. I have added Myra too."

Dr Ramantha rolled his dark, sexy eyes. "That's fine. I'll do the order each month for both of them."

"What about Myra?"

"She has diagnoses, if I recall, of gastritis, dehydration, hypertension, pulmonary disease, arthritis, hypothyroidism, urinary tract infection, depressive disorder, ulcers, and adult-onset diabetes. If I recall, she's taking some med.s like Cipro, Catapress, TTS, Zantac, Synthroid, Betoptic, Nicotine patel, Ativan, and Zoloft. I'll up the Zoloft, and you continue to see her."

The conference had taken ninety-three seconds according to Doc's sports watch. Time was money among the service providers in nursing homes. They tried to be efficient. Doctors wore old clothes, played down their fees, acted as though they were keeping Medicare costs under control, and only showed their wealth in the parking lot, crammed with Mercedes, BMWs, and Porsches, ornamented with antennae for everything that involved communication: satellites, cellular phones, faxes, or computers.

A general unspoken agreement existed among the professional service providers to maintain distance–not to talk of feelings or reactions to the residents and to try to avoid the sadness, the impending losses, and the relentless pain of here-today-gone-tomorrow situations. They stuck to the facts, the cumulative diagnoses, the matching set of cumulative medications, treatments, and ancillary orders. Psychological evaluations and counseling were ancillary in this environment of severe medical conditions and prescribed pills, shots, IV's, patches, vents, tanks, and feeding tubes.

Doc wrote up his new psychotherapy progress notes on Margaret. As he punched the three holes on the top of the note and slipped it into the consults section of Margaret's medical chart, Dr Ramantha walked back into the nurse's station.

"You know, Doc, my memory is failing me. I said that ulcers was a diagnosis for Myra, your new patient, and it should be ulcerative colitis. I'm giving her Azathioprine, Imuran. So, we have to monitor WBC and platelets and do liver function tests, total bilirubin. Then we have to watch out for some side effects, too, and you can help me do that. They include dose-related myelosuppression mainly, leukopenia and thrombocytopenia; nausea and vomiting, which is uncommon at low doses; cholestatic hepatitis; pancreatitis; restrictive lung disease; infection; and secondary malignancy."

Doc didn't fully understand what he had been asked to do. "Thank you, I will try. Appreciate you filling me in."

Dr Ramantha's feats of memory were, indeed, legendary at the facility, but his medical degree from

India made him a second-class citizen in the local medical community. He still had an accent, and despite its attractive upper-class British quality, it was frowned upon. Occasionally, one of his patients couldn't understand him. He and his wife were Hindu, and their beliefs, if exposed, would have clashed with the beliefs of the Christian nursing home residents, as well as those of his private practice patients. He loved fresh fish, braised with exotic spices and curries, not fried or baked. He had an acquired taste for vodka and scotch, both on the rocks, and Doc had occasionally seen him do the unthinkable and mix them.

Personal arrogance sometimes overrode his self-contempt for an MD degree from the University of Calcutta. After all, he had done his work in cancer at Sloan-Kettering and his work in endocrinology at the University of Chicago. His son was at MIT after achieving almost perfect College Board scores.

The sun had broken through the fog for a brief fling with hope, but the morning dawned otherwise dark and overcast. At 8:00 a.m., Doc found Myra and Margaret still in bed.

The nursing staff had several emergencies, causing a delay in their early morning clean-up. The medication cart hadn't gone around yet either. The strong, pungent odor of urine and feces filled the room. Breakfast would only last another forty minutes, so Margaret and Myra needed some help soon. They were each scheduled for a bath and shampoo before breakfast. Since this event occurred only three times per week, residents eagerly anticipated it. Downright excited, they chattered away about all kinds of gossip.

Doc greeted them with a smile. “Good morning. What are you two up to?”

“Hi, Doc. How’s the weather?” asked Margaret, struggling to sit up and then propping herself up with several pillows. She turned down the loud TV a notch.

Myra said, “You know, Doc, my daughter brought me some old notes last night, about my husband, John. You know, he died ten years ago. Well, he had rheumatoid arthritis, and he had ulcer problems, too.”

Myra seldom mentioned her husband or described her experience as a widow. Doc perked up. “What kind of notes?”

She replied, “Copies of nursing notes. I got a lawyer when he got sick. Then he died, and I dropped the whole idea of a lawsuit.”

“You had a lawyer? What happened?”

A nursing aide knocked before walking slowly into the room. She cleaned Margaret’s area and changed the linen. Then she said to her, “Okay, let’s go. You clean up good. So let’s get that bath.”

Margaret looked at Doc. “Be back in a few minutes, Doc. Will that be all right with you? Looks like Myra’s caught your interest anyway.”

“Fine, Margaret,” replied Doc. “I’d like to hear Myra’s story.”

“Look at these.” Myra handed him a sheaf of paper.

Doc read the first note outloud:. “February 12, 1992. Patient discharged on February 14, 1992. Planning with

Social Services two times per week. Evaluate medications: Methotrexate and Cyclophosphamide for Rheumatoid Arthritis and Omeprazole for Acute Duodenal Ulcer and Gastroesophagus Reflux. Likely Long-Term Care." He paused to look at her. "Yes, that was the nurse's progress note, or maybe the nurse's case manager's. Is that it, Myra?"

"Yes, we found those notes later. I remember the details like it was yesterday. John came here to this place on February 14, and he got very, very sick. By the seventeenth, they were ready to send him back to the hospital to figure out what had happened. His medical condition had been managed fairly well and, when he came to this place, they expected a two to three month rehabilitation period. They said he would gain weight, get his strength back, walk better, and maybe even go home. Who knew for sure?"

Doc leaned against the wall near Myra's bed. The steady buzz of the humidifier and fan distracted him, and the extra heat in the room made him fear he would lose concentration. He pulled up a chair and stretched and twisted before sitting. He sometimes stiffened when he kept one position for more than five or ten minutes. "What had happened? Did they figure it out?"

"Yes," replied Myra with a huff. "Yes, they got their act together. He went back to the hospital. They put him in ICU. He had the last rites of the Church. They told me to be brave, that he was on his way to a better place." Nothing moved but Myra's lips. She stretched out the story. She often did that. "He had tremendous pain and swelling in his joints, his knees especially. It was the worst pain of his life. His ulcer bled, and they could not stop the internal bleeding. They thought that maybe it was cancer. Then some big-shot chief nurse called me. She wanted to know where his pills were, especially the stuff for his arthritis and for his ulcer. I told her I didn't know. No one else did either. They finally went back and reread all of the notes in his chart. Most of it was in the records office at the hospital."

"Yes, yes," said Doc. "Go on. What did they discover?"

Myra paused, in no hurry. She did a thing that Margaret called a BSS, a "bilateral stump scratch." She reached down with both hands and scratched the terrible itches on the tips of both of her stumps. The scar tissue almost always itched like this after she awakened and then again just before sleep. Margaret told Doc she often heard Myra's unusually loud, continuous, nail-to-skin scratching. When they did not want an outsider to know what they were talking about, they used the code "BS" with the second "s" silent, as Margaret would say.

Finally, Myra said, "Well, the medical geniuses figured it out at long last. John lived."

Doc said, "Yes, go ahead. May I hold your hand while you tell me the rest?" Fearing what came next, he stroked her hand slowly.

"Yes, please do. Well," Myra went on, "they had read the nursing notes too fast at first. They had been too sloppy. Somebody thought the D/C meant 'discontinue' not 'discharge.' So they discontinued all of John's medications at the hospital. No pills here either. He was very sick. No one noticed. They just stopped all of his medicine and the chemo for days. He almost died." Myra scratched intensely for another few seconds. Then she stopped and lay back exhausted. Tears streamed down her cheeks. "He died many months later. At least, they brought him back from the D/C stuff."

She concluded, "I hated them, but I got over it." Her blindness and inability to walk had taught her patience, self-control, and the futility of unnecessary emotion. Doc marveled at her strength.

But her story got to him more than he realized. Later, in his office, he drifted back to his own marital woes. What once had been good finally died a slow, tortured death. Before he'd obtained his doctorate in California, Doc married Tannie and became involved in college campus mental health. A self-styled expert in the psychology of late adolescence and early adulthood, he became a decent therapist for the students, and was popular and well-received on campus. Tannie had her MS in health care and an excellent management position in long-term nursing home administration at a local facility. They planned a family of five, loved life in California, played tennis, walked and jogged, drank California jug wine, and slept on the beach at Carmel. A daughter they named Francesca came into their idyllic existence, their main concern merely how soon to have another.

Her parents had been musicians with the Chicago Symphony, her mother a cellist and her father a violinist, both deceased. She was pert, bright, motivated, sweet, somewhat argumentative, and as she put it, "Doc, I'm not going to take any extra shit off you cause you're getting a doctorate." Attractive, she took good care of herself, without being overly fastidious. Doc had waited for marriage, fearful of a commitment that wouldn't work out, unsure of his own value.

They almost bought a houseboat in Sausalito, and then they found a romantic cottage near campus. A half-timbered ceiling topped the living room over a full wall of bookcases with a rough stone fireplace in the center. Old, but not antique, European furniture filled both bedrooms. Doc became a weekend outdoor-grilling chef.

In 1983, little Francesca arrived. She was bright and energetic like her mother. Tannie and Frannie, he called them. He couldn't wait to get home at night, and they teased one another about names for a boy. Manny? They would decide later.

When she was eight and one-half months old, they found Frannie dead in her crib. She had not been sick, not even had the sniffles. She had not been to the doctor. She had not taken any medicine or received any shots or inoculations. She was not near any sick animals, or any epidemic. She was not around any children or adults who were sick or infected. She simply died. She hadn't choked, fallen, or hit her head. They found her curled up with a tiny plastic rattle in her right hand and her left foot outside her blanket, lying on her back in the corner of her crib.

Doc and Tannie had just finished making and painting her "big girl" furniture, a bedroom suite they had designed especially for her with a block letter "F" in the headboard. A child's table and chairs and a small dresser had been finished, painted, and ready to use.

Frannie had been asleep for four or five hours. At eleven p.m., Tannie had gone into her bedroom to check her and maybe put on a blanket since she often kicked it off at night. Her body was already slightly cool to the touch. No breathing. No pulse. Her skin had a strange translucence. Early rigor mortis showed up in her neck and jaw.

Tannie screamed, "She's dead! My God, she's dead!" and collapsed on the floor, one hand slipping down through the crib's side slats.

Doc ran in. "What did you say?"

"She's dead," she sobbed hysterically.

Frannie looked bluish and waxy. He reached toward her tiny wrist to feel for a pulse. None. He ran to the phone, and called 911. Then he went back and sat on the floor, one hand on Frannie's foot and the other arm wrapped around a shaking Tannie. She had vomited on the carpet, and it dripped down her nightgown. Beads of perspiration dotted her forehead. She was going into shock. He should raise her feet and cover her with the blanket. Or was it lower her feet? He couldn't recall.

The fire department life squad took them to the hospital where Tannie was treated for shock and acute depression. The medical description accepted by the coroner's office stated the cause of death as SIDS, Sudden Infant Death Syndrome. An autopsy found no disease of the heart, aorta, blood vessels, respiratory tract, brain, meninges, kidneys, or intestines. Had she suffocated? No one knew. And Doc wondered if even God did.

Why? What? How? Their doctors, friends, fellow therapists, and nurses rushed to their aid. People made food for them, cleaned the house, and never left them alone. They had a funeral, but they couldn't stop thinking about the autopsy. Nothing. Frannie was completely normal. No bizarre virus appeared. No, their friend who had gone to Africa for two weeks had not infected her. No parasites surfaced.

Tannie couldn't eat. Doc couldn't sleep. He'd walk all night long around their neighborhood and through the city parks, then he'd take long drives for two or three hours. They went over everything time and again, cried, and sobbed, and held each other. Then Tannie began to eat. Did she want to eat herself to death?

They became stuck in profound melancholic grief. They didn't know what do to. They talked to two Rabbis, three therapists, and two psychiatrists. They went to a support group for parents of children who had died. But three of the six couples in the group had a child abducted and murdered, and Doc and Tannie became even more depressed there. Everyone said "keep busy," "don't stop life," and "time heals" and reminded them "how well" they were doing. In some vague and irrational way, they blamed each other. They couldn't find acceptance, couldn't heal, and couldn't forgive themselves, each other, or God. Their daughter lived on, in their ragged emotional foreground.

Sitting around the fireplace one night, they decided to burn the furniture they had so carefully crafted for Frannie's next stage. Doc went to Sears and bought a saw. He cut up the furniture. They burned it all, the fire going until five a.m. The paint sparkled in the flames, blues, pinks, reds, and even yellow.

"Are we burning our marriage, maybe ourselves, Doc?"

He was tired and had drunk a bottle of undated Beringer Burgundy. "Maybe we are." It felt like a cremation.

"Should we keep going like this?"

Doc didn't know what to say, felt like maybe he didn't even care very much at that moment. He half-joked, "This paint really stinks, doesn't it?"

Tannie asked, "Well, we don't seem to help each other much, do we? Should we try it apart? Would that help?"

He got up and put on a windbreaker and cap. He thought of buying a simple gold band to wear, to remember Frannie always.

Tannie said, "I never want to have another child. Yesterday, I did, but not today. Not ever. I just want to be Tanya Rosenzweig-Gordon."

"I'm in no hurry. We could always adopt if it got too late for you." Doc said, just restating what others had repeatedly said to them. He started for the door and then paused, holding on to the back of a chair.

Tannie said, "My director of nursing has a spare bedroom since her roommate got married. Maybe I'll try it, sharing her apartment for a few months."

He nodded

"Doc, the empathy makes it double, mine and yours. And I know it's the same for you. Without meaning to, we make it worse. We both hurt too much."

Doc had been waiting for the right mental health practice, and it came, in Ohio of all places. "I'd be going back to my midwestern roots. I'd be working primarily with kids and families, part time in nursing homes, more of the real world stuff."

She whirled around, moved to the window opposite Doc, and buried her face in her hands. "You're leaving for good. I'll never see you," she said slowly.

"No, I'll make enough money that we can get together whenever we want. I'll come here, and you can visit me. We're still married."

But Tannie had been right. The marriage was over.

Chapter Four

To Staff:

March 8, 1995. Weather report is for overcast conditions with brief overnight snow flurries. Lo 25, Hi 37. Census is 168. All administrative staff will be in today.

JA

Doc sat stiffly in a straight back chair facing Myra. He rotated his shoulders several times. Margaret wheeled herself into the room, her hair wet and combed straight back. Her skin almost glistened from the moisture, and she wore cologne, some exotic, spicy aroma. How seldom residents wore perfume or cologne, the men almost never using after-shave. Was it the money? Or did the scent have no more meaning for these elderly folks?

Myra noticed too. "God, Margaret, you smell good. Trying to get a man, are you?" She rubbed her two forefingers together, as if to shame her.

The three of them chuckled. Doc never knew for sure what was going on. So much was understood at another level between Margaret and Myra. They might have been referring to another time, another place, a guy Margaret dated in high school. Who knew? Their communication was instant, complex, subtle, and did not always mean what one thought it did. They meant what they said and usually so much more. Doc tried to fit in. "For me, Margaret?"

Margaret snapped, "If *that*'s what you want, Doc, try room 212-A. A Chinese doctor who loved old people started it." She gave a high-pitched, adolescent screech. The ex-medical director, Dr Donald Lee, had started Room 212-A. Still on the medical staff, he had several facility residents as his personal patients. He no longer had any administrative responsibility, but needed the income from those responsibilities when he started his private practice ten years earlier. He liked the elderly, learned from them, and appreciated their struggles. A second-generation Chinese-American, Dr Lee had a natural, culturally based respect for the wisdom and knowledge of the elderly. It had taken him awhile to get used to nursing homes and assisted living in the states. His elderly and revered grandmother had come from Beijing to live with his parents when he was still a small child.

"And why would I try Room 212-A, Margaret?" Doc asked as he returned a chuckle and added a smile.

Myra warned, "Better not, Margaret." She lifted both of her hands, palms facing Margaret.

Margaret went on anyway, intent on teaching Doc something, teasing him, or tricking him. Who knew. "That is where you 'get it' Doc. Know what I mean 'get it' or 'make out.'"

Doc played dumb, afraid he was misunderstanding, but also very curious. The more he knew about the place, the residents and their families, the administration, the nursing staff, and so on, the better job he could do in individual therapy.

Margaret began to blow dry her thinning hair. "Doc, when residents come here to the home, some of them are used to a drink now and then. You know, a cocktail before dinner, or a six-pack for football games on Sunday afternoon. Some drink, some smoke, and some do other things. Follow my drift?"

Doc ran his hand through his thick hair. "I wasn't born yesterday. Is that what Room 212-A is all about? Is 'A' for alcohol?" They did not laugh. He did, though very, very briefly.

Margaret went on somewhat didactically. "Well, we have rights to live a little, too, even with our sickness. We need our doctor's say-so, and our Power-of-Attorney's, if we have one. We have rights. We are not prisoners or in the army. We had lives. We had children. We had grandchildren. We had jobs. We were people before here." She teared up and slumped a bit in her chair, then put both hands over her face and covered it.

Myra took over, without losing a beat. "What Margaret is trying to say is that some of us smoke and drink now and then. If we have the green light, we smoke in the lounge or outside of the building if we've been here a certain number of years. And on Friday at four o'clock, we have a TGIF in Room 212-A if we are allowed to drink. We cannot drink much. You know, my med's. If I had three drinks, I would die. Margaret has one glass of wine, usually white, usually Chardonnay. I have a rum and Coke, because my husband, John, liked that drink. He always made me one before he lit the Bar-B-Que and made his own Martini." She sighed several times and then started to cry.

Margaret had recovered and took back over. "So Myra has her drink, and I have mine. Most of the people have a beer. The smokers smoke, and the drinkers drink, and if you do both, you are called a 'double-header.' I think it should be a 'double-dipper,' but they say double-dipper means you have two pensions. Anyhow, we have music. We have chips, nuts, or popcorn. A few times, some people tried to dance, but their canes or walkers got tangled up, and one fell, hurt herself, and sued the place. Most of us are in chairs, and it really doesn't matter. For just a brief moment, we have a drink, smell smoke, hear Sinatra sing, or Lawrence Welk, and see people try to dance, and we feel like, we're young again. Any idea what that feels like, Doc? It's magic. To be alive, to take it all for granted. To think you have plenty of time. That time is all there is. How's that, Doc? The Golden Years. So, Room 212-A is a special place, a place we revere, and if you want other stuff, we've heard that's possible, too." A dreaminess covered her tear-filled eyes.

Doc was near tears himself; the loss of his own youth momentarily so vivid. Still, the possibility of some good years existed before being in this place, or one like it. He couldn't resist the question, "What more is possible? What is the rest?"

Margaret repositioned herself in her chair, first her slacks, and then the big diaper she wore. "You know, it's the 'S' word. Sex."

"Tell him, Margaret. Go ahead. He may as well know it all," urged Myra. She adjusted her glasses.

"Well," said Margaret, and her blue-brown eyes flashed. "We don't usually do this, but the word is that if you want to miss dinner on Friday, you should stay in the TGIF after five o'clock when it's over. If you want something exciting, and you know my meaning, then it could happen. So we stayed once, and we pretended to be with each other. I wanted to watch. They turned the lights off. I couldn't see much, but we could hear plenty. If we'd wanted to, we could have touched and so on, too. It reminded us of bumper cars in the carnival because chairs occasionally collided."

"Yes, Margaret, go ahead," Doc said.

Myra said, "Tell him, Margaret. It's okay. It's in confidence. He won't tell anyone else."

Margaret continued, "Well, Doc, I saw it *all*. There were four or five couples in the room, and there was one group of three people. I couldn't tell who was who, and I didn't try to see who they were. I could see outlines, a little like seeing people in a poorly lit room with a sheet hanging between you and them. One couple was on the couch actually 'doing it.' At least it looked like intercourse." Both Myra and Margaret giggled again. "But the most interesting stuff was not on the couch. It was where people had pushed their chairs together. The threesome looked like they were doing a dance scene from an old Busby musical. Some shadowy movements. Muffled sounds. A few names mentioned. Quite a time. People groped. Squeals, snickers, and small laughs came from them. And there was one really loud groan of pleasure. Hands were everywhere–inside clothes, outside clothes, and tangled up in the wheels and padding on the wheelchairs. There wasn't much hugging because it's so hard to do unless you have the chairs fit together. But there were a few heads bobbing up and down." Margaret sat motionless.

Myra giggled. "Like bobbing for apples, Doc, in the old days. You wouldn't believe it, would you?"

Doc thought he'd better say something. "Well, I guess there's no reason to deny folks in a place like this some of their normal pleasures. So many widows and so few widowers to go around, right?"

Margaret went on. "I saw two women with their chairs close together. One of them had a hand inside her own dress and her other hand inside the other's dress. What do you think of them apples, Doc?" Her arms quivered slightly, and she lifted one leg under the lap robe.

"Well, you know . . ."

Margaret saved him. "We thought it was all fine, normal, and natural, just not for us. We haven't stayed after five o'clock again. But old timers haven't all forgotten about sex. The text books don't tell you everything. Some day, when we trust you completely, we'll tell you about the resident who sells it. Yes, she sells her body right here in a nursing home. We don't want to shock you too much this morning; then you won't come back to see us again."

Doc stood and stretched again. Merriment lit both women's eyes, even the pair that could not see.

As part of his practice in long-term care of the elderly, Doc routinely met with family members. He wasn't looking forward to meeting with Myra's daughter, Trudy, once again, or her son-in-law, Helmut, either, but these family counseling sessions came with the territory. He even rearranged his schedule to accommodate Trudy's visit to Myra on a Saturday morning. They were supposed to meet at ten a.m. in a small lounge adjacent to the cluster or rooms in station three. The wood was covered with a very light coat of polyurethane, and the fabrics were slick and shiny, some kind of mysterious plastic-like stuff that was washable. Everything had to be washable and easily cleaned. Staff and visitors constantly washed their hands to prevent the risk of infection, and housekeeping continually wiped up spills, scraped the floors and tables, and sprayed the tables, chairs, lamps, and bedsteads with disinfectant. Cleanliness, at Golden View, got much more attention than godliness.

Crisp and fresh, Trudy and Helmut walked into the lounge. Doc jolted. He'd been looking out the window at the sunny, clear, blue, early spring sky and rehearsing what he wanted to say. The weather forecast had been wrong again.

"Good morning, Doc. Good to see you," said Trudy.

They both leaned over to shake his hand. Then Trudy and Helmut pulled up high-backed armchairs so that the three of them sat in a triangle.

"Mom looks awful. Is she wearing a lot of mascara?" Trudy asked.

"No, I don't think so," answered Doc. "She's not sleeping or eating very well."

Helmut said, "Should we call in that specialist again? Didn't do squat last time, and it cost us a fortune."

"*No*," Trudy answered. She showed no emotion, except certitude. "Maybe we're an anachronism, Doc, but in our tradition, the old are allowed to die."

Helmut added, "But here, in this country, we Germans must be careful. Feelings still run high. Any talk by us of euthanasia or assisted suicide could lead to gossip or accusations. We are careful who we talk to and what we say."

Intrigued by the implication of their openness, Doc said, "Yes, of course."

Trudy spoke quickly. "We don't want mother to suffer. We don't want her to face months of horrible pain, or be bedridden and fed by tubes. You know what we mean. You've seen it."

"Sure have. You don't want her to suffer needlessly. But it's not our decision, is it?"

Trudy moved around in her chair and re-crossed her muscular legs, clad today in black tights. "Mom is so depressed. Can she really decide what's best for herself? Don't we have a voice in the fate of such a sick, old person? Don't we count?"

"Yes, of course you count." Doc stood and walked to the window. "You count a lot. That's why I wanted to see you. You only call her once a week or so now, and you don't see her frequently like you once did. Is something wrong?"

"We're very busy," explained Helmut, running his hand through slicked-back, thick hair. "Very busy, and we can't come out as often as we used to. Mother looks very, very ill to me. It's scary."

"Your visits, your calls, your notes and flowers, and your kids', too. That's what helps her keep going," replied Doc. "Surely, you understand that. You are her lifeline. If you cut the line, you kill her."

"Stop it. Halt!" yelled Trudy. "How *dare* you lecture us. Who do you think you are, anyway?"

"I'm sorry if I got carried away. But you must reconsider your behavior. Please." Doc knew he was arguing for the very existence of Myra Gronbeck. He went on. "If you don't visit and call, it's like spreading a virus. There is no treatment for it."

Margaret's and Myra's favorite male nurse, Jeremy Johnson, twenty-five, attended the local community college to become an RN. He finished a two-week course in basic nursing care, and made six dollars and seventy-five cents per hour as a nurse's aide. He made beds, bathed and cleaned residents, and assisted them when they could not get out of bed, sit up, or get into their wheelchairs.

"Hi, girlfriends," he said with a smile.

"It's about time, Jeremy. Didn't you have your *Wheaties* today?" asked Myra.

Margaret snapped, "Or couldn't you do it last night?"

"You girls should *not* talk that way. You just shouldn't. I could press charges, you know. You can't treat the help this way. I won't have it. I just won't." His slight lisp, swirling head and neck, and limp wrist belied his words. He went on, "If you abuse me this way, you'll wait and be last. And I won't give you a bath. And I won't do your hair. So there." He threw his hand from the elbow. "And I'll never ever tell you a joke again."

"What about the strike?" Margaret asked.

"Oh yes, you might not have me. Well, there's a big union meeting." He pursed his thick lips with a frown. "I'm mixed up. I want to help. But I want health insurance. I'm good at my job. I deserve more pay. If we strike, they'll have good people here."

Margaret said, "I want *you*."

Myra added, "Me, too." Then she cooed, "We've gotten used to you. We couldn't talk this way with a stranger, could we?"

An alarm went off at the nurse's station, and Jeremy turned and ran out without a word. Somebody needed him immediately. He had tears in his eyes.

The loudspeaker in the hallway came on again, and the assistant administrator spoke. "Good morning. This is Susie Wilson. I've got a reminder for you. This morning, we're taking a bus load to the mall for shopping and lunch. Don't forget to sign up, and be sure to bring money for lunch. You'll need money for shopping, too. There's room for eight people on this trip. It's your individual responsibility to check the tires on your chairs and be sure all of the moving parts are in good repair. If you don't tell us there's a problem, we won't know. Then we can't fix it. And you won't be happy when your wheelchair breaks down on the trip, and we have to take extra time to fix it, because that will mean that others can't have a good time or do their shopping."

Margaret retorted, "God, she goes on. What's her problem? She sounds like a worried mother trying to make her kids feel guilty about everything. Who becomes head of these places anyhow?"

Myra chortled. "Yeah, all we really need is the nurses and the pills . . . and the food."

Myra sighed. "Should I go; I can't see. I'd take the place of someone who could see and really appreciate the mall."

"Sure, go. There's nothing to see anyway. All the stores are the same in all the malls. Grocery stores sell clothes. Clothing stores sell machinery. It's all everywhere. It's all the same."

"Okay," Myra gave in easily, "I'll go, too."

As they prepared to go on the bus trip to the mall–preparations which began at six-thirty a.m. for a nine-thirty a.m. departure–the mail-lady, Betty, knocked at the door.

"The animal people ~~are~~ here. Want one in the room?"

Once a month, the Visiting Pets Association provided live creatures for the long-term care residents to snuggle, touch, stroke, admire, talk to, smell, hear, love, or complain about. Visits from cats, dogs, and birds were common. Raccoons or mice were occasional guests, but snakes were not welcome. One had uncoiled out of a box with netting over it at one home, then wreaked havoc. No more snakes.

Margaret asked, "What's the menu? A meow or a chirp? Anything to smell?"

"It's a puppy today, a little Scottie, and it's nervous and it pees," answered Betty.

"Well, we'd never smell it in this place," Myra rationalized.

A tall, bony woman, Betty stood in stark contrast to the squiggly, nervous, black, furry critter she rocked as she entered the room. "This is Scottie. We call him that. Of course, he is a Scottie, too. He's a month old. We found him near the veterinary hospital."

"Hi, Scottie. How are you? Let me hold him," said Margaret.

"Me, too. Hi Scottie. Aren't you a darling?" cooed Myra as Betty placed him in her arms. "What a sweetheart." She considered bringing out Barry the Bear as a playmate, but rejected the thought. Betty would think she was a kook–the idea of a toy bear playing with a live dog.

Scottie twisted and jumped out of Betty's arms as she tried to hand him back to Margaret. His fur was damp and slick. He landed on her bed, slid to the side table, and then to the floor. Her china lamp fell and broke. Her picture of all of her grandchildren fell from the table, and the glass front broke into three large shards. Scottie paid no attention, and Betty slowly got down on all fours to get under the bed and try to pull Scottie out. He went into the corner by the wall, the longest reach for Betty, and hunched up, shuddering. He did his business, both one and two.

Betty simply said, "We'll have to move the bed to clean up after Scottie. He's young."

Margaret responded, "We do the same. We're old. We understand. Get him back out here. We want to enjoy him now that he's more comfortable."

Betty got Scottie out somehow. The aides moved the bed and cleaned up the mess. Margaret and Myra held

Scottie, petted him, smoothed his curls, oohed, and aahed, dried him with a towel, brushed his coat, and passed him back and forth. Scottie squealed and squeaked a high-pitched bark and finally stopped his nervous twitches and jerks long enough to be comforted by the residents. The fifteen-minute episode gave them a weekend of gratitude.

"We love you, Betty. Come back soon," said Margaret.

Myra handed Betty paper money, not knowing if it were a one, five, or ten dollar bill. "For your volunteer program. I wish it could be more than this. God bless you, Betty."

The van had lowered the elevator section to hold one wheelchair at a time. Loading the chairs and then assisting residents to the van's bench seats took thirty-forty minutes. A full complement of eight women sat ready for the mall, lunch, and shopping. At an average age of seventy-nine years and eleven months, they composed the survivors at Golden View. They had been in nursing care for an average of two years and three months, and took an average of eight different medications per day, with two also on portable oxygen tanks, one on a feeding tube, and one blind. They were the sprightliest and most adventuresome from the facility. These trips highlighted the month, providing a time of independence and exploration, continuing concrete proof of how they were beating the odds. The average nursing home resident died within three months of admission.

Occasionally, one even sensed a feeling of cocky pride. No hints of survivor's guilt surfaced this morning.

At ten thirty a.m., and the van moved slowly through the heavy fog and constant light drizzle. The gentle bouncing from the oversized tires actually proved therapeutic. Margaret and Myra sat on the rear bench seat along with a new resident they had not met. On these ventures, Margaret guided Myra, often holding her hand or elbow when moving from van seat to her chair, and when getting in and out of a restaurant. She described the outside world to Myra. Myra then dozed, tired from the effort involved in dressing up a bit and then moving down the hallway in her chair to the activity area, waiting over an hour, and then being placed in the van. "Hurry up and wait," like in the military.

Margaret stored up her impressions: the aide's smile of encouragement when told they were going on a trip out of the facility; the smooth, soundless flow of her new chair; the nurse's statement that Myra's sugar looked good; the peach and violet flowered dress Myra wore; Margaret's powder blue shirtwaist that highlighted her silver ringlets; the overly bright, shiny, cherry-red nail polish that the volunteers had plastered on both of them for the trip; and the assorted colors and fabrics of the dresses each resident wore. Bright silk, wool, poly, chiffon, and velvet. Two slightly short skirts, one long "granny" dress, and five just below the knee. Two used walkers, one a cane, and five sat in chairs when entering the van. Most would be in chairs at the mall, an easier scenario for the staff. If staff did their own shopping, they didn't have to worry about a resident wandering off very far. The chairs also provided a built-in security system, though they were offensive to the three women who did not really need them, at least not for a trip to the mall and lunch. Staff needs sometimes outweighed other considerations.

Myra awoke with the van's sudden, creaky stop at a railroad crossing. The guardrail noisily lowered, and a loud train whistle came in the background. "Is that the emergency siren? Is the home on fire?"

Margaret reassured her. "No, no, silly, we're at a rail crossing. We're on the trip. We're driving."

"God, yes, I forgot," said Myra. "I just forgot. Did I fall asleep? I'm no fun. You can't take me anywhere."

"Well, I'm a little weary, too," Margaret said. "It's grey and chilly, and there's a light drizzle. Maybe forty degrees with overhead clouds and no sun 'til noon. Could I work for CNN? Can you hear the raindrops?"

"You're better than CNN because I know what you look like. CNN is just voices, and I don't really care all that much about the weather in Atlanta all the time," Myra stated. "By the way," she whispered, "Who's next to me?"

Margaret whispered back, "Don't know her yet. She's got her head down, and she's asleep; fairly new, I guess."

Myra whispered a little louder this time, "Well, let's find out soon because her hand is on my behind. I hope it's accidental." She gurgled, trying to choke back her laughter.

Margaret did the same, truly hoping the slight was unintentional and had happened while the woman slumbered. Otherwise, it was no laughing matter.

While the van lumbered over slick city streets toward the mall, Margaret remembered what Agnes Williams had told her the day before. Agnes had been beside herself, although she was kind of hyper anyway. At ninety-three, she felt she'd lived too long. She'd say to anyone, in her own inimitable, cranky, commanding style: "I've had enough, lived too long, overstayed my welcome. That's my only problem." Agnes had gone on to describe her complaint about the trip to the mall. "I wanted to go on the trip. I signed up. They took my name off of the list."

Margaret asked, "Why? That's not right."

"I know, it's not. I complained, but they still wouldn't let me go."

Margaret asked, "Did they say you couldn't handle it? Maybe too old in some way?"

"No, no, none of that stuff," Agnes responded. "They said I spend too much money, and that I wouldn't have money left for extra Kleenex and to have my hair done. I love to have my hair done here."

"That's your choice, isn't it?" Margaret asked. "If you run out of money, you wait 'til next month. Or, you can ask your son."

"They said I didn't plan very well. They said I spent my money too quickly each month. They said I didn't know how to budget. My husband always handled the money. He gave me plenty of cash every Friday night for everything. If I needed more, I asked." Tears dripped down her sagging cheeks onto her perpetual smile.

Margaret patted Agnes. "You better tell the administrator. You have rights. They can't keep you from a trip. It's your right. It's good for you to travel." She added thoughtfully, "Travel broadens you, doesn't it?"

Agnes finally understood the joke and stopped crying. The half smile grew wider. She chuckled. "Even to a mall like we go to. Maybe I won't really miss much. Seen one mall, seen them all."

"You complain though. It'll do you good," finished Margaret.

She told the whole story to Myra, who loved gossip. Margaret tried to recall things exactly–who said what, and when. Margaret milked the story for ten minutes with interstitial comments and critiques on the facility, and of several of the young administrators who were arrogant, smug, and "know it alls."

Myra grew thoughtful at the end of the story. "It wasn't fair to Agnes. She could have spent some of next month's allowance. Can we resign from this dump we live in?"

"Why don't we?"

"Speaking of stories," Myra began, "you know that Dorice Eriksen opened up to me. She's nearly blind, so we have something in common. She likes to confess, but she won't go near that young priest who comes on Friday morning."

"So, what'd she confess?"

They had both been moved into their chairs and lowered slowly to the ground by that time. Aides pushed them through the mall entryway into the hallway. They sat parked together waiting for the rest of the van to be unloaded and the driver and staff to park the van and return. Staff arranged the chairs in pairs in the hallway, a few feet apart, like clusters of lily pads in a pond.

In hushed tones, Myra began, "It's about her husband. He's still alive."

"Yeah, I know that. Talk louder. The noise in this place is terrible."

Myra said a hair more loudly, "Well, she always says how much she loves him, how much he loves her, and how she wants to get out of here and go back to live with him. You know . . ."

Margaret fidgeted. "Yeah, yeah, so what did she confess?"

"Stop hurrying me. I didn't hurry you. I'll get to it. If you push me too fast, I won't tell you, so there." Myra pursed her thin lips.

"Okay, sorry–don't be so touchy," Margaret said. "Tell me the rest."

"Well, you know Dorice. She always wants to tell you that she's a good wife, a good person."

"Yes." Margaret nodded vigorously. "So?"

"Well," said Myra. "Dorice let her hair down. After her husband leaves on Sunday afternoon, she does something she shouldn't."

Margaret almost felt like pushing Myra's chair out of the door and into the traffic, she was so antsy, but just bounced slightly in her own chair.

"Well, after her husband leaves," Myra apparently decided to put Margaret out of her misery, "she wheels herself down the hall to Ralph what's-his-name's room . . ."

"Go ahead!"

Myra leaned toward Margaret and whispered, "She told me she goes into Ralph's room, makes sure his roommate isn't there in the other bed, wheels her chair up to Ralph's bed, puts it sideways to the bed, lifts up Ralph's sheets and blanket while he pretends to be asleep, and she does you know what."

"Oh my. My. My. My."

"And then, he pretends to wake up, but only afterward, and he gives her ten dollars. 'For luck at bingo,' he says, 'for luck.' That's what Dorice confessed. Maybe she should see a priest."

"That would be awfully embarrassing to tell a priest. And she'd have to say the word masturbate." Fighting off faint jealousy over Dorice's behavior, she went on, "Women with husbands are lucky. They don't always act like it. Even if there's only a million-in-one chance that she will go home with her husband, Dorice should do that. She shouldn't fool around with Ralph at all. My guy has had some strokes, so he wouldn't know what I did, but I still wouldn't fool around. But you're single now, so you can do what you want." Their shrieks of hyena-like laughter rolled down the hallways, so overpowering that it brought tears to Myra's eyes, and Margaret began to cough uncontrollably.

A uniformed security guard hurried to their chairs and asked, "Everything okay, ladies?"

Myra retorted, "Thank you, sir. Everything's fine so long as your name isn't Ralph. We were just sharing a memory or two."

A bit later, as they "walked" through the mall entryway into the food court and to the shops, Margaret asked, "Can we eat now? I want Chinese."

Her aide, Johnnetta, said, "Not for an hour."

Myra asked, "What's the food?

Quickly, Margaret replied, "Chinese, deli, pizza, and big cookies is what I see. It's pretty, too. Overhead skylight. Tables with ice-cream-shop chairs. The floor is made up of reddish blue tiles, maybe marble, but I doubt it. What do you want?"

Myra stared silently for a moment and then spoke. "You know, John and I always ate pizza once a week before I had the sugar. We'd have beer with it, and I'd serve a chocolate ice-cream cake for dessert. Then we'd watch *All in the Family*. He didn't always realize it was a comedy. He usually agreed with Archie Bunker. I think I'll have pizza today, with a kiss to John. He was for whites. I didn't agree, but I loved him."

Margaret responded, "Okay, okay, old home week. Stop it. We're here to enjoy and shop."

Myra's aide, Jeannette, asked, "Didn't you want some buttons for that robe of yours?"

"Yes, I did. Glad you reminded me. Please walk me to Sears."

"Sears is all right with me, too," said Margaret. Then she added, "Where is everyone else going?"

Johnnetta answered, "Well, those who can walk themselves are going to some stationery store way down to the other end. They wanted cards."

"I want buttons and pizza," Myra reminded them.

"Just don't eat those buttons, Miss Myra," Johnnetta said. Everyone chuckled politely because Margaret's friend at the home ate a large brown button, thinking it was a cookie. Emergency colon surgery was successful, but cookies, even large ones, were never served again, only pies, cakes, and large brownies with ice cream. In fact, whole beets were also eliminated, so to speak, by the dietitian in order to be on the safe side.

In the fabric and button section. Myra wanted to touch and feel things, so she was rolled through the rolls of velvet, corduroy, wool, tweeds, and heavy silk shantung. "God, I love the feel of fabrics."

As they neared the button and zipper section, her hand hit one of the large old-fashioned cookie jars that held a potpourri of "one of a kind buttons." The jar fell and broke, and hundreds of buttons spilled out.

The clerk was apoplectic. The aide was ashamed. Myra was guilty.

"I'm sorry. I'm blind. I couldn't see the jar." She began to cry at once.

The clerk came over quickly. "It's fine. We'll clean it up. You didn't know."

Margaret tried humor with, "Buttons, buttons everywhere, and not a drop to drink."

"Stop it, Margaret," Myra said. "I'm sorry it happened, so just let it be. Find me three pearl buttons the size of a quarter. That's what I need for that grey silk robe."

The scene attracted about seven or eight patrons, looking on and gaping with surprise, condescension, pity, and humor.

Margaret suggested, "Let's come back when things quiet down. I'm starved. And I want one of those cookies, those big chocolate chip ones. I don't care if they don't serve them at our place. I want a big cookie."

Myra said, "And I want pizza, and my buttons, but I'll take pizza first. Then you can get me the buttons."

The two aides, Jeannette Newsome and Johnnetta Thompson, glared at each other. Myra's aide obviously felt some shame, since she should have been more careful. Margaret's clearly saw the humor.

"Miss Myra, you sure did make a big mess. Yes, you did," Jeannette said.

Margaret had regained her composure. "God, Myra, we can't take you anywhere."

Myra replied, "Get me my pizza please, and I'll be fine. Cheese, tomatoes, green peppers, and sausage. I don't care if I have to take extra *Pepcid*. I want pizza."

The aides looked glum. They couldn't afford to eat out. They had taken apples, rolls, and some cheese from the kitchen and had them in their coat pockets. Buying cigarettes consumed their lunch money.

The pizza took forever. Margaret was almost finished with her full plate of Chinese noodles and broccoli with oyster sauce. The aide moved the pizza in front of Myra and slid the diet coke to her left.

"It's cut in pie-shaped slices, so dig in."

As Myra reached for her first piece, her right hand quivered. "I feel like I'm ten years old at a party. Why can't they make pizza like this at our place? Oh well, here goes." She chewed carefully, savoring every morsel, in olfactory, gustatory, and tactile heaven. "I don't need to see this stuff. It's fabulous. When our children were little, we always had birthday parties at a small pizza shop called Tony's. They had thin crust, more like you see in Europe, and wonderful pasta that wasn't overcooked like Chef Boyardee's." Myra went on as she chewed, "The children were so young. My husband and I were so full of hope. The world was ours, if you know what I mean. I thought it all went on forever. The kids, our two daughters, would argue like sisters do. But they were close. They were two years apart, and they were about the same size. They shared clothes and dolls. Later, they even shared boyfriends. It was almost too good to be true."

Myra had eaten three pieces already but still chewed carefully. Margaret sat in wide-eyed wonder, as did the two aids.

"You've got good memories of pizza, don't you? No wonder you insisted on it. Chinese was good, too, in case you were wondering."

Myra sat straighter. "Sorry, I got caught up in my pizza and in my memories. The noise here, all the different sounds, the talk, the shoes clicking on the floor, and all the smells and odors reminded me of the kids. Why couldn't it have stayed like that? Why did the girls have to squabble after John died? There was plenty, but the older girl wanted more since her sister had used more money for college and travel. They fought like jungle cats."

"How'd you handle it?" asked Margaret.

"The lawyers couldn't bring peace. I was the executor of his estate. It went on for months. I couldn't believe it.

I was grief-stricken, but nearly blind, so I finally put a stop to it. I gave them each twenty-five thousand dollars. I sold the house and most everything else. I gave half to the church and the rest is in trusts set up by a fancy lawyer in Cleveland, so I could come here on Medicaid. They don't talk to each other now, and I don't see either of them as much as I used to. The early days were great, but the pizza wasn't any better than this. Not one bit."

The aides searched their bags for the noon medication. They handed their charges small cups loaded with colored pills of different sizes, and wordlessly encouraged compliance. Myra and Margaret each picked up their respective glasses in unison and quickly and quietly swallowed nine pills between them. With that thrice daily ritual concluded, the aides settled back in their chairs to finish their lunches and smoke. Both too heavy, they chain smoked long, slender "generic" lights.

Johnnetta Thompson, Margaret's aide, was their favorite female nursing assistant. The big African-American woman also had a big, warm, and lovable smile. While a child in Alabama, her mother had married a factory worker in Detroit and left her to be raised by her grandmother. She worked on the farm with her grandmother, where she planted and sowed, and picked vegetables and fruit. She learned to can and preserve almost everything. Margaret knew she loved beans and greens and almost every conceivable vegetable boiled mercilessly on the stove. Sweet potato pie and fried chicken were the rewards saved for the winter holidays, or a wedding. Johnnetta didn't make it through the RN program, but she did become an LPN after studying part-time for several years at a local community college. The residents loved her naturalness, her kindness, and her uncanny compassion while still supporting their efforts, however feeble, to cope and survive. She was a model survivor herself, and everyone knew it.

Two youngsters passed by and eyed them. The children's mother was buying them ice-cream. Twin eight-year-old girls, dressed identically in plaid accordion A-line skirts and white turtlenecks. They looked like miniature copies of students at a parochial secondary school. They stopped about ten feet from the table and stared. Margaret listened to their conversation, smiling inwardly.

"What's wrong with them? That's a weird chair, isn't it?" said the first.

"It's for old people who can't walk," answered her sister.

"Those two black women push them. They look like nurses in their uniforms."

"It looks weird. Their faces are all scrunched up. They must be dying."

"No, they're just old. Skin gets like that."

"One of them is blind. Look at her eyes. She can't see. She dropped a piece of pizza, and she can't pick it up."

"They shouldn't bring people like that here. They should keep them in a hospital."

"Where's Mom? I want my ice cream."

"I do, too. I wouldn't want to be old like that, would you?"

"No."

Chapter Five

To Staff:

March 11, 1995. Weather report is for occasional sun with increasing cloudiness in the afternoon and evening. Lo 32, Hi 44. Census is 168. Two expirations. Both administrators at a workshop today on marketing. Director of Nursing in charge.

JA

The strike leaders met in the conference room of the local hotel. All had bundled up in scarves, gloves, and heavy coats to ward off the near-freezing cold. Inside, the room stayed musty and always a little damp, no matter what time of the year. When the rains came heavy, the corners of the floors leaked. The quaint hotel, built in 1892, was small enough for a twenty-five room bed and breakfast, assuming a complete facelift of the aging buff brick exterior and a million-dollar renovation of the interior. Or, it could be torn down and a new, modern Days Inn built on the same land.

Three old card tables pushed together to form an appropriate conference table to seat the nine members of the union steering committee, which represented the nurses aides and maintenance, housekeeping, and dietary staffs, cramped the conference room. The folks who really ran Golden View, cleaned up the place, cleaned up the residents, fed everyone, and kept the place too hot in the winter and too cool in the summer, all stood around. They wanted a thirty-five cent per hour raise for each of the next three years and continued free meals. They also hoped the fully paid health insurance would also continue. No increase in benefits had come for three years. With costs held in check, this public facility could easily become the object of a bidding war between several of the big private companies in long-term care.

Millionaire officers and stockholders proliferated in the health care industry, especially management companies, while they kept wages of the "workers" at levels competitive with *McDonald's*, *Burger King*, and *Pizza Hut*. They were also competitive with front-line staff in hotels and motels, too: those who ran the front desk, performed night audits, and maintained the properties. Many hotel people considered of going into the nursing home business. If one could run one kind of nest, why not another kind, and make more money per room? Oh yes, and help people to boot.

In the dark room the rickety table barely held the overflowing heavy glass ashtrays, large schooners of beer, and big bags of beer nuts. The bluish smoke was heavy, and the airless room held it carefully in place over the table.

The local union steward Tom Smith, a large man bursting from his coveralls like the stuffing in a pork chop, slowly put his huge hand over a beer, lifted it, and drank it down. He wiped his mouth with his sleeve, turned his head, burped slightly, and asked, "What do you guys think? We're getting the shaft. The fucking shaft."

Tom's drinking buddy, Millie Mason, was the head cook, and Tom the chief mechanic. In the kitchen for twenty-three years, Millie had seen the size of the place multiply, and had seen her own staff grow from three to thirteen; ten part-time. Millie said, "We sure are. We most definitely are getting the shaft." She winked at Tom and went on, "And it don't feel good at all."

Tom and Millie both unhappily married, both grandparents, had teased each other with sexual innuendoes for twenty years. Nothing more than the tease ever occurred, which was probably why they were still such good friends.

Tom became more specific. "Could I get another Bud draft please? And maybe a burger and fries? The union consultant told me we were fucked." He hiccuped and explained, "We don't have a strike fund. If we strike, there's no money for any of us for a week or two. We ain't GM or Ford, are we? Hell, let me buy a round for everybody. We may as well have a good time since we're fucked."

Millie winked, the other seven members of the committee nodded in unison, and several gave a strong, "Yeah, right on, Tom." It was not clear if the affirmation was for the insight into being fucked or for the round of drinks, possibly both.

Jeannette Newsome began, "The residents are getting rougher. I don't like it."

"Go ahead," said Tom. "We need to hear it."

Jeannette stood, almost bumping into the waitress carrying a tray of beer. "We get pinched, kicked, and bitten. We get propositioned. Some old guy offered me fifty dollars if I'd . . . you know. I'm tired of it. We all are."

Tom responded, "If we don't get money, maybe they'll do something about it. You girls shouldn't have to put up with this shit." He quickly remembered the male aides and added, "And the boys, I mean the men, shouldn't either." Tom smirked. Real men didn't work as nursing assistants, or even nurses. He pushed his chair back and stood up slowly, walked over to Jeannette at the end of the table, and started to put his arm around her. She darted off to the rest room.

Tom took over again. "Remember, we don't tell them shit. The organizer told me that we still keep them off balance. Tell them we're going to have a strike vote. Tell them we don't give a shit if we close the place. Tell them we don't care if we all lose our jobs. He told me to remember not to swear in the meetings with them and not to drink before the meeting. The next one is tomorrow night. I'll be there with the lawyer and that big-time negotiator from Cleveland."

The head housekeeper stood, a tiny, bird-like woman of about fifty who wore starched uniforms that had the name of a facility she'd worked in fifteen years ago, Great Lakes Nursing Home, emblazoned across the breast pocket. She never threw anything away. Jane O'Shea was a saver.

"I still worry," she lamented. "I still worry about the people. Why, I moved a Kleenex box to dust under it, and one of the ladies screamed and cried last week. Wasn't going to take it, or use a Kleenex, just moved it. She got real upset. Don't want change."

Tom couldn't let such mutinous ideas prevail. "They'll be fine. The union has had experience. Strike won't be for long. So we'll be back with them real quick." He wasn't so sure himself, but the organizer told him to say that. He hoped it was true. If someone died, none of it would be worth it. He'd resign, he told himself. The union people were fucked, but there was no need for the old ladies in the home to be hurt.

The steady whir of the old fan lulled Myra into a light half-sleep after lunch. She drifted back to when John had died. She'd never told Margaret about that period. Her memory was much better then. Although still capable of living independently, the loss stunned her. She had the house and an old Buick sedan. She cried most of the time. Then she became very angry over his medical treatment. She considered a lawsuit.

She would stay up until all hours of the night. Most of the time, she thumbed through photograph albums, the cloudy looks of old Brownie pictures, the strange colors from early Instamatics, and then the clear, specific, more natural snapshots from her newer 35mm. She lived in the past and didn't want to see anyone. She seldom went out, and then only to the local mini-mart where she overpaid for frozen dinners and instant coffee.

She lost weight. Her neighbors worried. "You must go on with life," they all said. Myra pulled the shades, and when she stayed in bed or lay on the couch with the TV on, she pulled the covers over her head. She didn't even notice how hot the house had become since the air conditioner had stopped working properly.

She got a call one morning from the home. They said that they had written to her over a period of several months, with no reply. If she didn't come and pick up John's effects–his watch, several rings, and a wallet with ID and credit cards–they would have to turn them over to the county. Or, she could pick them up in person and sign for them. She agreed, a bit frightened. She had not been with people for any period of time for several months, and wasn't at all sure that she could maintain her composure. She was also embarrassed about her appearance and wished she hadn't totally collapsed physically and mentally. However, she wanted that watch of his very badly.

As she drove out to the home, Myra imagined all sorts of things. She would cry. They would send her to the hospital when they saw her. She would faint. But she steeled herself, determined to get the watch. It was engraved with a message from her on their wedding day, and a special name only John would recognize. She drove very slowly since her eyesight had already begun to fail.

Myra walked haltingly into the home. She wasn't far behind him. How prophetic those feelings. She did, indeed, move into the home a scant few years later as she went completely blind.

A peaceful, calmness came over Myra rather suddenly as she entered the much too ornate waiting room and lobby of the home. The furniture was new and modern; the wool rugs were a dark blue; and the lighting produced interesting shadows in the area. Myra felt better sitting there than she had for a long time. Strange.

It seemed like an hour, but she probably only waited for five or ten minutes. Perhaps John was still alive. Perhaps he worked at the home in the maintenance department. He avoided seeing her because he was so busy, but was alive and well. If she were to come to the home at exactly the right moment, she could hear him, talk to him, and feel him. Relief washed over her; complete relief. The sad, melancholy, mood of the past few months lifted. Forgetting completely about his personal effects, Myra got up, walked quickly to her car, and drove home. If he wasn't dead, no personal effects were left to receive. She felt whole, serenely tranquil, nearly a state of bliss.

Myra ate and slept. At peace, she had no dreams. John couldn't be home because he worked a lot of overtime. He had no time to call her or come home. But, "not to worry."

Myra told her doctor about her discovery and how her depression had suddenly lifted. He viewed things differently, saying that John was dead. He expressed his concern for both Myra and John, and asked Myra to go to the hospital for a few days to rest and get her health back.

In the adult psychiatric ward, things took a turn for the worse. Myra heard a recording in the hallway outside of her room. At three or four a.m. she would hear it. Sometimes she heard it in the afternoon, too. She thought that everyone else heard it and became humiliated, hurt, angry, suspicious, confused, and defensive.

John's high school sweetheart–the young woman who had wanted so badly to marry John and lost–kept saying *very* loudly that John had abandoned her after promising marriage; that he had fathered her daughter, who was born out of wedlock during her senior year; and that he had refused to give her any financial support or help as a parent. She also said that Myra had stolen John away from her and branded her a liar, a drunk, and an adulterer. How could Myra face the doctors and nurses who heard these lies, let alone the other patients? What a mess. She put her head into the pillow and sobbed until she slept.

The doctor came in, and she told him about the voice on the recording.

"I believe you hear it. I doubt if anyone else does."

She breathed easier. No need to worry what the rest of the people thought.

The next day, the doctor came back. "Don't be surprised if that voice disappears soon. Sometimes people grieve after a loved one dies, and all kinds of strange things happen. The medicine will help."

Thinking that her idea about John might be in her imagination, she grew more depressed again.

The doctor replied, "In a week or less, I'll bet you'll realize again that John is really gone. We'll help with the feelings. You'll develop a new life."

The chilly, cloud day had not yet let loose the heavy spring rains. Trudy drove to the home, tears blurring her vision. She wished she could push a button or pull a knob to stop the cascade of sadness. Guilt and shame stabbed her, but she thought she was doing the right thing for herself, for Helmut, and for the children.

Trudy parked her Volkswagen Jetta, which was full of decals marking their international visits. It even sported an old German license plate that she left on the front of the car. She loved it. Their ancestry represented a proud and dominating swath of history. Her crying didn't stop, so she adjusted the rear-view mirror, put on more powder and heavier mascara, and applied lipstick. She got out, put her head down, and tried to muster courage by storming into the meeting with Doc and her mother at full speed.

It didn't work. The receptionist said that Doc was behind schedule, that the meeting would be delayed a few minutes. She couldn't let herself cry in the waiting area.

She still remembered, though, how lovely Myra had looked as a younger woman. How tender she had been. How desperately she had tried to help her two daughters get along better. Her advice and encouragement, yes, her discipline too, had been invaluable aids in later life. Well, Trudy had been a grateful daughter for all of it: the love, college, the help buying their first home, and their first Volkswagen Beetle.

That was then, and this is now. Myra's quality of life was so poor, maybe a two or three on a scale of one to ten, from Trudy's perspective. And they needed and wanted the money. Helmut and Trudy would be old themselves soon enough. Maybe Trudy could some way get this message across to her mother; perhaps Doc could understand.

Her mother's will was unbreakable; the lawyers had told her that. Further, Myra would never reconsider giving her and her sister a substantial part of the estate before her death. What reason could she have for holding onto it? It did her no good, all tied up in a fancy layering of different kinds of trusts. The lawyer had charged fifty thousand, and Trudy suspected he hadn't worked on it for more than a day or two.

Trudy soon looked up into the staring eyes of Doc. She jumped, slightly. She hadn't heard him walk over to her. She hoped he would not be sanctimonious. She hoped they would meet in the lounge, not his tiny office.

"Sorry to keep you waiting, Trudy. Myra and I are ready. Come in. Would you like coffee?"

"No, thanks." She trudged behind him.

In the small interview room, Trudy took her mother's right hand and kissed her. Then she hugged her, twice. Thank God they were not in his office again. This room, painted in mauve and a deeper shade of brown, at least had drapes.

"Mom, you look good. Glad to see you. Helmut and the kids send their love."

Myra simply said, "Glad you're here, Trudy. Doc's got me worried. Even more than I was before."

"What about?"

Doc coughed, but Myra continued, "You were always so attentive to me. You called every day. You came to my apartment or out here once or twice a week. I saw the kids. Helmut came. We went out to dinner. Your sister is so far away. I hardly see her."

Doc simply stated, "You've been lonely for her. You're not trying to manipulate her with guilt. You miss her and her family terribly."

"That's it, Trudy. I do miss you and your family terribly." Then she cried, tears giving way to huge gasps and sobs.

Anger shot through her veins. She'd been blind-sided and ganged-up on. "I wasn't prepared for this onslaught. I didn't know. We've been in Germany and then Argentina–gone for several weeks. The kids are older and need more time. Helmut resented all the time I gave you. I'm just pulled in so many directions at once. I don't know what's happened."

Doc suggested, "Would a plan help?"

Myra asked, "Could you or you and some of the others come visit at least once a week? Maybe call me more often, every few days?"

"Of course. Sure we can. We will definitely do that, Mom. You can count on me."

Doc asked, "Are you sure, Trudy?"

"Yes, of course."

After some chit-chat about Myra's clothes and a pair of earrings she wanted, they said goodbye to Doc. Then Trudy wheeled Myra back to her room and kissed her again several times. "Love you, Mom. See you soon."

The Residents' Council met once a month. "Why was it even necessary?" some asked. Everybody who worked in the nursing home, and all of the friends and family of the residents, supposedly looked out for their welfare and were concerned about their rights and care. Still, the Residents' Council, composed of three elected representatives, met with the head of the board governing the home, along with the chief administrator and his assistant administrator. Three residents, buffered by three nonresidents.

At least the old folks couldn't go too far. A tie vote with a stand-off, hence no clear-cut recommendation to the administrator, could always occur. So the Residents' Council became a useful conduit for the administration, a communication channel and a political mechanism to use. The illusion of democracy fit with the global denouement of arbitrary authority and manipulative dictatorship. So be it.

Flowers in vases sat on the conference table, coffee and tea in silver settings on the side table, and a young aide stood to serve. Cookies (with or without sugar) were served with coffee (caffeinated or decaffeinated), sweetener (sugar or Equal), and milk (half and half or skim). Three well-dressed corporate types, two men and one woman, sat at the conference table across from three residents comfortably settled into their highly polished, clean wheelchairs. The residents sat nodding due to the lateness of the hour, seven p.m. on a Thursday evening.

The head of the board, the totally bald Jack Wheatley, ran the local Ford agency. His round, plump face looked as if a plastic surgeon had created a frozen, toothy grin.

He began, "Good evening, everyone. Here we are again. There are some concerns. The new state survey highlighted several nursing care problems. We'll get on those right away. We have to talk about the strike tonight, and the annual staff-resident-community Bar-B-Que."

Not to be outflanked, the Chief Administrator picked up the strike theme. "We're ready, Jack. If they do it, we're ready."

"No notes on this," commanded Jack through his smile. "No notes. Tell us how we're ready. You folks," he went on, glancing across the table at the residents. "Maybe you shouldn't say too much yet to the others. You know what I mean." He gave them his best used-car salesman grin of appreciation and a cunning wink with his left eye.

"Well, we've contracted with a temporary personnel agency in Cleveland. It had Mafia connections, but not now. They can bus in two hundred nurse's aides for as long as we need them. They get five dollars per hour plus some expenses, and the company will take a twenty percent override. It's the best we can do. So, if the strike went for three or four weeks, we can afford it. Our own aides can't though." The Chief Administrator's chest puffed out.

One of the council members, an early dementia resident named Mabel Waterford, who spoke once per meeting just to let the others know she was there, said, "It scares me. We are all used to the people who help us every day. They aren't just nurses. We love each other. It's like family." Then she added quickly, "It's like *good* family times," before lowering her gaze to the table again.

Susie Wilson, the Assistant Administrator, had finished her BA in business, and almost took a job as an activity director on a Caribbean cruise ship. Reasonably intelligent, a solid B student, personable, she stood five feet eight inches and weighed around one-forty. Attractive. Men noticed her, but seldom approached. If asked, a man might suggest that she probably already had a boyfriend. She didn't. She wasn't sure she wanted one. Maybe she wanted something else . . .

Susie provided a quick summary of her latest discovery. "I recently read a research report on a strike in another facility. They prepared the residents and explained, in detail, what was happening. Then the new aides were introduced by the other aides going on strike the day before the strike began. It went fine, and no one died. There was an increase in anxiety and confusion among some residents, and several got very abusive and used foul language. They used twenty-five percent more psych services. The census went down though; that's a worry. Some doctors and hospitals shied away from using the facility for a year or so. They just didn't refer to it."

"We'd get lonely, wouldn't we, if no one came here?" asked Ann, one of the residents. She had early Alzheimer's, so others had learned to keep answers very short. She wouldn't recall much anyway.

"There would still be plenty of us," answered Mabel. "Don't worry, Ann. It will be good."

Jack Wheatley replied, "It's the American way. They wanted a union. They had that right. Unions can strike. Even if something happens to a resident, the blood is on their hands, not ours."

Administrator John Anderson toyed with his pencil. He had made noise of how well they'd handle a union strike. An exceedingly handsome young man of thirty-eight, he wore expensive suits and shoes and blue button-down shirts with subtly patterned ties. He even wore suspenders. His clothes made him suspect, since most of the aides, even some RN's, lived from paycheck to paycheck. Some didn't even make it that far, and they snitched a free meal or some Kleenex or toilet paper now and then.

Jack said, "Let's take a break and have coffee and cookies. We've got to talk about the Bar-B-Que later. Should we just have chicken and corn, or should we have pork ribs and beans also? Enough about the strike for now. Thanks, everyone."

Margaret's physical therapist, Mary Ann Motler, massaged her arms and legs after engaging her in somewhat painful stretching. Margaret lay flat on a thin mattress.

"It's good for you. You're a doll."

"I don't care if it is. It hurts," Margaret replied. "And don't try to flatter me with that doll stuff."

"Yes, I know. Why not stop a moment. You sit so much since you stopped using the walker that your leg muscles don't get much use. Sorry if I pushed too hard."

"Oh no, no, you're right to do it," Margaret added. "Push me. I need it. I just like to complain a little. I don't breathe too good either, even with this contraption in my mouth and that doggone tank. Don't pay attention to my complaints; just listen."

Mary Ann nodded. "Should I tell you that you inspire me and that I brag to my husband about how courageous you are?"

"You do?"

"Yes, I do. And I mean it. Now let me roll you over so we can work on those lower back muscles. They're in spasm. Maybe I should stand on your back like those Japanese women do." Mary Ann chuckled.

"Ouch. That really feels funny. It tingles. What's your husband say?" asked Margaret.

"Well, he wants to meet you," responded Mary Ann, kneading Margaret's back like bread dough not yet ready for the oven. "He wants to come out here to this facility on a weekend and meet you, and your roommate, too."

"That would be nice. During the week would be better because my sisters and their kids come all weekend. Sometimes they take me out in the car for a ride to get some ice cream or go out to lunch."

"I'll tell my husband. Maybe he could pop in to say hello during the week, right after he gets off of work."

"Do you think I'll ever walk normally again, even without that walker?" asked Margaret. She always slipped this in on Mary Ann. She knew the answer. She always hoped. Maybe a miracle would come.

"If there's any big change, the doctor will tell you. You know that. Put your energy into rehab. with me, okay? By the way, the newest thinking in my field is to add strength training for someone like you. Do whatever we can to make your hands, arms, and legs stronger. Even if you use a chair. When muscles and bones are stronger, you'll be less likely to fall and, if anything happens, you'll heal that much faster. Want to try more of it?"

"Well, this tires me enough, you know. I don't want to look like one of those women who have those bulging muscles."

The two women smiled at one another. "I'll show you another time," said Mary Ann. "Some bars to lift. A few things to push for your arms and your legs. Some exercises to do with big rubber bands, and then we'll try some of those new machines like you see on TV. You'll love it."

Margaret answered, "I'll try. I'd like to get one of those tight designer suits like women wear on TV. Are they made out of rubber or nylon? You know what I mean. You can see how flat their stomachs are."

Mary Ann grinned. "We'll have fun."

Chapter Six

To Staff:

March 20, 1995. Weather report is for a mix of clouds and sun all day. Lo 40, Hi 49. Census is 165. One discharge, two expirations. Director of Social Services is in charge. Other administrators are at a conference on networking with hospitals, physicians, and discharge planners.

JA

The halls in Golden View were very wide, indeed, built to accommodate several wheelchairs abreast, the medication cart, and beds, tables, chairs, and other human detritus wheeled up and down all day long and often into the night. Across the wide expanse, in the room directly across from Margaret and Myra, lived Carl and Norma Schultz. He was eighty-six, and she was seventy-nine. Carl's gruff voice and penetrating, coal black eyes had always scared people. Less now, of course, since he'd gotten old and thin. Norma could still cook, when her arthritis didn't put her back to bed in the morning. She had fourteen bottles of pills in the bathroom and prayed each night that she wouldn't fall and then not be found in time.

He liked it cold; she liked it hot. He favored low humidity, while she favored high. He wanted air conditioning, even into November. She could tolerate a window fan, at best. She still ate meat and would have a beer now and then, while Carl preferred chicken or fish. He walked daily, still unassisted; yet she used a wheelchair to go to the bathroom, to be on the safe side, although she could walk perfectly well herself. She had fallen twice; he hadn't yet. A worry-wart, he liked to charm the nurses and doctors, while she took the medical professions very seriously and still thought they could do something about her myriad of small, non-lethal aches and pains. She took her medicine; he sometimes did and sometimes did not. Their fiftieth approached.

The night of their forty-ninth anniversary, they spent at home in the three-bedroom, two-bath, brick ranch house in a quiet area of town. Two grown sons and their wives had come for a dinner of prime rib, country fries with onions and cheese, and hot rhubarb pie.

Carl had opened a case of cold *Michelob* to celebrate. "Here's to us, Mother. Forty-nine years. It seems like it was yesterday, and you know what kind of a day it was yesterday." Carl had heard the line on a sitcom and liked it, although he wasn't entirely sure what it meant.

"I love you too, you old geezer. Everybody, thanks for coming tonight. Who knows if we'll see our fiftieth or not."

The boys and their wives, all in their early to mid-forties, immediately said the right thing. "Of course, you will," "What a silly thing to say," "You'll both live to be a hundred," followed by "Why don't you take that trip to Egypt and see the pyramids," "Mom, you always wanted to see the Japs," "Now or never, they say, now or never."

Creativity and originality had not been on the boys' report cards in school, nor their wives' either. But they were solid citizens, worked hard in the canning factory, and had extra jobs in the winter cleaning marble floors in homes of the rich.

The evening ended with hugs and kisses, and the boys' wives even did the dishes. They had all chipped in on a beautiful picture album of the five grandchildren to celebrate the anniversary. The forty-nine pages still had some blanks. Forty-nine candles topped the cake and took four people to blow them out. For forty-nine years, Carl and Norma had fought to a draw.

"Dammit," said Carl as the kids drove away. "I wish the boys had finished school."

"Too late now," Norma replied. "I told you at the time to crack down, but oh no, you was too busy with your TV and your beer–that damn beer. Damn near raised them single-handed, I did."

Carl turned on the Late Show with Jay Leno. He'd heard a psychiatrist on Sally Jesse say that if you want to end a fight with someone, take them off-guard and just agree. "You're right. You surely are," said Carl.

Silence from Norma.

When they awoke the next day, Carl had lost his appetite. He didn't, couldn't, or wouldn't eat or drink anything. Not even coffee or beer. He told Norma he wasn't hungry or thirsty. After two days, he told her he couldn't swallow. Nothing would go down. He didn't mind losing a few pounds, but was feeling weak. And when he stood up quickly, he was dizzy.

Finally, Norma said, "I'm driving you to Doc Summers' office. I don't care if you don't care. I do. I don't know why, but I do."

Doc Summers, seventy-five with fluffy white hair, bow-legs, and a huge gut, always wore bow ties. He wasn't in the office, however. A young woman medical resident from the local medical center had replaced Doc for a week while he and his wife visited Hong Kong.

Dr Ruth Schwartz-Goldenberg said, "You need a hospital, Carl. Something's wrong here."

Carl said gruffly, "Nothing's wrong, Doc." He didn't like her big glasses or her big nose. His symptoms frightened him.

Norma said, "You're right, Carl. We'll go to the hospital instead of seeing this young whipper-snapper."

"Miss, please tell Doc Summers we went to the emergency room. Thank you miss . . . doctor." Doc Summers would have talked about his tomato plants, his wife's canned peaches, and so on.

Norma took him to the ER, and they immediately gave Carl the "works," as he called it. They took x-rays, blood tests, and urine tests, and felt him all over, pushed, pulled, tugged, pinched, turned him over, and did the same again.

"We need a full body CAT scan," someone said. "He's dehydrated." So, IV's were set up, and they planned on putting shunts into place later.

Within ninety minutes, Carl was in a room and looked like a patient. "I told you nothing's wrong, didn't I? I'm awful scared. They can't find nothing."

A neurological consult and a psychiatric consult had been ordered and a speech and language therapist would see him, too. If he had bought new batteries for those two hearing aids, he'd be able to understand better. He wasn't sure he wanted to, though. He liked it when a doctor or nurse got within six inches of his head and screamed, "Can you hear me?" so he could say, "What? What's that?" The mob killed people for less than Carl's gruff anger, which he clearly alternated with his passive resistance, strictly on a case-by-case basis.

The next morning, at eight a.m. Ms Sally Airhart walked into Carl's room. "Good morning, Mr Schultz. I'm a speech and language pathologist. I'd like to help."

Carl kept his eyes closed and pretended to still be asleep. "What?" he asked groggily, opening one eye.

Ms Airhart said, "I hear you don't drink or eat lately."

"Yep, not hungry or thirsty. Couldn't get it down anyway. Don't need help," answered Carl, opening his other eye.

"We'll do some x-rays later, but now, we'll open and close your mouth, move your tongue, have you smile, pucker, say 'ah,' see you swallow, watch your palate, and feel your throat. Would that be okay? Would you sit up for me?"

"Yes, but nothing's wrong. I'm not hungry. The next day after our anniversary, I lost my appetite. I don't care. There's not much reason to go on. I'm just scared to death. Nothing's left. I feel weak." Carl closed both eyes and promptly fell back into a deep sleep, snoring loudly.

In the hallway, Ms Airhart and Mrs Schultz crossed paths.

“How do you do, Mrs Schultz. I’m Sally Airhart, and I’m here to help your husband with his swallowing problem, if I can.”

“Call me Norma. How is he?”

“We’re beginning the tests. He’ll see a neurologist and a psychiatrist, as well as me, a speech and language pathologist. Could it be his mind? It started after your forty-ninth anniversary.”

“Oh no, oh no, nothing like that,” Norma explained. “We’ve always been happy. You know, a few squabbles here and there. He worried a lot, but he never cheated. He just drank a little beer like most men. He was hardworking, so I never begrudged him a few pleasures.”

Sally asked, somewhat rhetorically, “I wonder if the onset was caused by some anger or hostility he wasn’t expressing directly to you or someone else.”

Norma eyed her hard. “Not my Carl. He always got real angry. He yelled and swore at us almost every day of our lives, especially when he was frightened about something.”

Tom and Millie had driven to Cleveland after work one Friday evening. They had taken separate cars and stayed in separate but adjoining rooms in a Days Inn near the lawyer’s office. The meeting was scheduled for nine a.m. on Saturday. Tom had two beers during the drive which left ten in his twelve-pack. After they unpacked, Tom wanted to see Millie.

“Come on in and have a cold one when you’re ready,” offered Tom.

"Will you behave?" she asked.

"You know damn well, I will. If you have any chips left from that can you stole from the kitchen, bring them," he suggested.

"No funny stuff. Don't get me drunk and try to get in my pants. I've got those men's type shorts on, and I don't want you to think I'm funny."

Tom got excited hearing this about her shorts, even though he didn't know what she meant. Always on edge with Millie, due to her teasing, hinting, or flirting without fulfillment, he enjoyed it. Maybe, just maybe, she would do it with him once.

They drank five beers each and ate half of a huge can of chips. Tom fell asleep and was snoring loudly when Millie slipped back into her room. She locked the door to his room although Tom had been a perfect gentleman.

The next morning before breakfast Tom pounded on her adjoining door and yelled louder than necessary, "Decent, Millie? Here I come, ready or not."

She yelled back, "Who you kidding? You were too drunk to come. You passed out just when it got interesting."

"How about breakfast then? I'll make it up to you. They've got those huge Belgian waffles next door. They'll fill the gap."

After breakfast, they drove to the lawyer's offices. Tom warned, "We're union people. The union lawyer and the head union guy for Cleveland will meet us. Don't say much. They wanted two of us here. Okay?"

"Yes, master. Jesus Christ, I feel sorry for your wife."

Millie wore a white blouse with a ruffle collar and black and white checked slacks. She had put on a small amount of make-up. She looked good. Tom's wife had polished his brown church shoes, an old pair of oxfords with cracks along the middle of the upper piece. He also wore freshly pressed brown polyester slacks and a turtleneck shirt of tan wool that his wife had bought him for the meeting. He hated ties. Didn't own one. He fidgeted in his car.

They parked and entered the building–four stories of restored red brick, with twenty-foot ceilings, incredibly expensive huge windows, and polished, stained, and thin-stripped, cherry wood floors. The whole place was done in black leather furniture and chrome lamps. Tom and Millie looked at each other wide-eyed.

A receptionist who looked like Bo Derek flashed her teeth at them.

"We're, uh, we're . . ." Tom cleared his throat. "We're here to see Mr Giordano."

"I'll let him know."

Although the firm's name was Kelly, Feinstein, and Wadsworth, the senior partners owning most of it were Lou Giordano and Claudio Fiorelli. They had the stereotypic connections to the union, to Vegas, to Atlantic City, and to the New York, Cleveland, and Detroit families.

Giordano came out of his office and stuck out a huge paw. "Hi, I'm Lou. Glad to see you. Come on in."

Giordano dressed immaculately in a brown pin-striped suit with a vest and a matching tie on a starched white, long-pointed collar. The clothes draped over a big frame–

six foot five inches and three hundred and fifty pounds. "I look like a linebacker, but I'm a lawyer. Coffee?" offered Lou.

"No, thanks. We just ate," said Millie. She shifted her ruffled collar.

"Meet Tony D'Augelli. He's head of most of the big unions. They've got a consortium, they call it, in the Cleveland area," said Lou.

Tony stood up and walked over to Millie and Tom to shake hands. He looked like the lawyer, whereas Lou's puffy, pockmarked face and crooked teeth made him look like a union enforcer.

Tony stood six foot tall and one hundred and seventy-five pounds, dressed in a pair of grey slacks, black loafers, and a rust-colored suede shirt. He looked as though right off the streets of Venice or Florence. A long scar creased under his right eye. Otherwise, he looked like a handsome Italian lawyer from Cleveland, well educated and well spoken. He was the most feared labor racketeer within two hundred and fifty miles of this meeting. Nobody messed for long with Tony Dee.

Tom looked at his own clothes and wanted a cold beer very badly.

Lou began, "We're real pleased you're here. Both of you. My receptionist has an envelope with five hundred dollars in it for your expenses."

Tom said, "Thanks, but the Days Inn was only –"

"That's very kind of you, Mr Giordano," Millie began. "We appreciate it."

Tony offered, "You're both important to us. You're our eyes and ears at the home. We value you. We trust you."

Tom knew he'd better say something. "Everybody's worried shitless. Excuse me. You know what I mean. The old ladies are scared. Aides don't have no money. They'll be picking tomatoes, or they'll have to go on welfare if there's a strike. Our local hasn't got shit for money. Excuse me again."

Lou nodded. "We understand completely. We're with you. We want to help. We don't want to hurt anybody. I'll be with you when all the negotiations about money and benefits take place. Our union wants to get more for all of the people working there. Believe me, we don't want to fuck up anybody's life. Now it's my turn to say excuse me. I apologize Millie."

Millie blushed and said, "What do you want the union folks to do now? We've got a leadership group that meets at night at an old hotel. Any instructions for us?"

"Yes, that's a good idea, Millie, very good idea," replied Tony Dee. "Tell your people to prepare for a strike. To save a few bucks and put off some installment payments on the car, the house, or the clothes dryer. To tighten their belts. We're going to put pressure on for awhile. We know the people who own the temp agency that's supplying the nursing aides if there's a strike. They won't do it, believe me. We're going to fuck up the administrator's plan, fuck it up royally if you don't mind me saying it that way, Miss Millie. Excusa, Excusa." Tony Dee took out his pen knife, and started working on his nails.

Damn, thought Tom but the union did a lot of things. Yes, this union was good. He believed in unions. They worked for the little guy. He did not want to think about the process, whether the ends really justified the means.

Lou stood up and said, "Thank you. Thank you. Thank you. *Ciao*, *grazie*," and ushered Tom and Millie out.

Tony Dee said after them, "We'll be in touch."

Margaret's two sisters from the West Coast came to see her. She had looked forward to the visit for weeks, counting the days. Her sister, Rosalie, was the baby of the clan, only sixty-five years old. Twenty years spread between Margaret and herself. Elsie was seventy-four and widowed for fifteen years, still sprightly and enthusiastic. Rosalie had just retired from her job in Eugene, Oregon, where she had been a teacher of the handicapped for over thirty years. She had never married. Elsie had been a nurse's aide for many years in Seattle, but she had only worked sporadically and intermittently while raising her eight children.

They arrived together, and after the hugs, screams, and tears, they all settled down to talk near Margaret's bed. It was "not a good pain day," as she called it, so Margaret had propped herself up in bed for the early part of the visit. Later, she'd go for the proverbial "walk," and maybe out to dinner. The constant spring drizzle and the unusually chilly nights always made her joints ache more.

Rosalie said, "You know, I always admired you. Mom bragged you were this and that, and you'd always helped her. She'd say 'Do it like Meg did.'"

"I wasn't perfect. You became a helper and had quite a career." Margaret grimaced as she said it. She didn't want to show them how bad it hurt.

"You know," Elsie added, "Mom always told me what a great family you had with your six kids. So I guess I admired you as a mother. Anyway, something happened along the way to get me eight kids." She chuckled.

"Now don't blame her," Rosalie said. "Meg didn't do it." And they all grinned, magically trying to ward off Margaret's obvious discomfort.

Margaret sort of gasped. "Forgive me. In all the excitement, I forgot to introduce you to my roommate, my new sister. Myra, this is Rosalie, and this is Elsie. Myra can't see much, but she's a sweetheart, and I love her to death."

Myra lay strangely silent. Finally, she said, "How do you do, Rosalie? Nice to meet you, Elsie. I'll put the TV earplug in so that I don't overhear your conversation."

Margaret found Myra's reaction strange. Usually, even if she felt great mental or physical anguish, Myra would fake it, at least around family or friends. She'd put on a social veneer, smile, occasionally flash some humor, ask good questions, share a story out of the past, or provide some sentimental reminiscence. But this time, she put in the earplugs and closed her eyes, even added a slight snore to punctuate her withdrawal.

Rosalie asked, "Should we leave and talk to you outside?"

"Oh no," said Margaret smiling. "This is fine, please believe me. You know how much I love you both. I'm so happy you're here with me."

Elsie asked, "How are the kids and all those lovely grandchildren?"

Margaret pointed to the pictures lined up on her wallboard hanging over the side of the bed. "There they are. On a good day, I can get everybody's name right the first time. I'm too excited to try today. My grandson, Donnie, lost his job at the foundry, and I've got a new great granddaughter due next month. They did tests. To tell the truth, it keeps me going. Them and Myra."

"I worry a lot," added Rosalie. "I won't have kids to keep me going. I'll be alone. If I make it at all."

Elsie pshawed. "You're still such a kid. Don't worry about being alone in your old age now. Get there first. Then worry. And besides, when you're eighty-five, I'll be there with you. I'll only be ninety-four. Okay, baby sis, okay. You won't be alone."

The sisters came from a very poor family. Their dad had been a poor dirt farmer who barely put food on the table. Their mother was a rock. She held everything and everyone together. Bible readings came after supper every night, even if rice or potatoes was all that had been served for supper. They were grateful for life and grateful for survival. They had no jealousy. Their mother used to say, "I know that Jones family. They're a bunch of no-good sinners. Don't you worry about them Joneses, not one bit. We'll be fine ourselves."

Rosalie responded, "All right, I feel better. Thanks, big sister. I want some pictures. I'd love a copy of all of those snapshots. Meg, could I get one? I'll pay for it."

"Sure, why not? I never thought of it. One of my kids has the negatives. I'll get you a set for Christmas. And Elsie, you don't have to ask. I'll do it for you, too."

The sisters excused themselves and went to the mall. They returned later with some of the kids and took her to her favorite restaurant. It was her favorite because she had been the head cook there–sometimes the only cook–for more than two decades.

After they left, Margaret's thoughts returned to Myra. She had been acting strangely for a couple of days. Normally she at least would have feigned friendliness to Margaret's relatives and offered candy.

Myra took out her earplugs and explained, "I don't feel right."

"What's wrong?" Margaret asked.

"Don't know. Maybe I should see Dr Ramantha. Maybe I'm just getting old."

"Come on, what is it?" Margaret tried again.

"Well, darn it, I don't have as much company as you do. I'm very lonely. Where's my family? Trudy promised. What's wrong with her? She told me and Doc that she'd call and visit more. She doesn't do it. What do I have to live for? Are they mad? Do they hate me?" No tears fell this time, not even as much apparent hurt or anger, just a sort of benign resignation. That nuance bothered Margaret more than the loneliness and obvious jealousy over Elsie and Rosalie visiting her.

Margaret began to wheel her chair closer to her. But Myra already snored. Her whole body shuddered several times. Myra was probably chilled because she slept with no blanket over her.

Margaret turned down the air conditioning a notch to warm up the room. She also knew about TIA's and TNI's, transient assaults on the brain or heart. She knew that mini-strokes or heart attacks could occur while an individual was awake or even while they slept. Memory could be affected. The ability to concentrate could be diminished, or a person could know what they wanted to say but be unable to say it. Sometimes these effects would show up initially as a shudder throughout the body.

Myra awoke as if startled. "What time is it?" she asked.

"It's twelve."

"Oh, my God. Did I sleep twelve hours? Is it midnight?"

"Oh no, no," explained Margaret. "It's noon. You dozed off for an hour or so."

"I was sort of mixed up for a moment. I don't feel good. Why go on? The headaches are coming back. All I do is eat, sleep, and listen to TV. I've never learned Braille. When I lost my sight, I didn't face it. What good am I?"

Margaret had waited for this opportunity. "What about some more intense therapy with Doc? Maybe more antidepressant pills? There's plenty you can do." She didn't say what was in her heart–what's wrong with your daughter? What about Helmut? Why don't they visit?

Call? Write? Send an audio tape? Candy? Flowers? What's their problem?

Instead, Margaret reassured her. "You know I'm here. My family loves you, too. We all do. The staff thinks you're great. You're not alone."

"Thank you, dear," Myra responded with a slight smile. "Thank you. I know you care. It's just that my own people are special to me. They're my blood. They have their own lives. It's a different world today."

"Come on. Let's go down to the next corridor. There's something I want to show you."

They wheeled with some effort out the door and down the hallway to the next corridor. From fire door, which was all glass, they looked out on a small courtyard. New pine trees had been set in place several years ago, and a lovely garden of small ferns and wildflowers them. In a brown thatched circle, barely visible near the top of a low conifer, sat a nest. Three baby robins were fed alternately by their mother and father, or at least it looked that way to Margaret.

"You know what I see? You hear the birds?" Margaret asked as they "peered" at the nest.

"Yes, yes, I do. I like it," Myra answered. "Are you trying to tell me something?"

"Well, yes, in a way. I guess I am. Life goes on, no matter what. The parents made it through the winter. They had babies. Now they're trying to feed their family. It may sound crazy, but I wonder what these babies will do for their parents. Will they even be together? So, maybe we shouldn't expect so much from our kids. We had them. We raised them. We enjoyed it. We suffered through it. Maybe that's enough."

They sat in silence. Myra seemed peaceful, but Margaret knew she'd feel exactly as Myra did if their roles were reversed. Her kids were loyal and dutiful. She was lucky.

Dr Ramantha's usual monthly rounds were that afternoon. He saw all of the residents for whom he had not been called to evaluate some medical condition or urgent problem during the month. Emergencies automatically went to the hospital. Myra was in the bathroom while Dr Ramantha quickly took Margaret's blood pressure and pulse.

"Not bad, young lady. Not bad at all," he quipped.

"Doctor, Myra's not herself. She's very depressed. She's sick. Her family just doesn't come or call. Something's wrong."

"Thank you for telling me. I'll take care of it. You're a good person, Margaret. A very good person," replied the doctor. "Of course, none of us are getting any younger, are we?" A serious man, Dr Ramantha's occasional attempts at humor usually fell on deaf ears. No one expected it.

He asked that Myra be wheeled to a small examining room between the nurse's station and the beauty shop. The room stunk of disinfectant. "Well, well, how goes it Myra? You've got seven diagnoses, none of them life-threatening. And you're taking eight medications for those problems. None of them are completely doing the job, are they?"

Myra liked him. He never tried the humor with her. "I don't feel good. I'm sick. I can't pin it down. I'm more scared and depressed. My headaches are worse. And my memory . . . well, I don't want to even discuss that. I can't stand it. It's so horrible. One night I almost had them call you. I was hot and chilled, my heart raced, and I thought I would explode."

Dr Ramantha nodded, listening and reading her latest nurse's notes at the same time. "How about a few days in the hospital? I don't think anything is wrong, but we'll see."

Myra grudgingly agreed. "All right, if you think so."

"When you get back, I want you to see the psychologist more often and maybe take more medicine to help you with the blues."

Myra sighed. "All right, if you think so."

Chapter Seven

To Staff:

April 10, 1995. Weather report is for a sunny, pleasant day. Lo 44, Hi 61. Census is 161. Two discharges home and two discharges to hospital. Administrator and Assistant Administrator are in all day.

JA

The rain poured down in heavy dark sheets. Rather than the sweet showers of April, a tornado watch was in effect, and the sharp lightning peals and echoing thunder were disturbing on this early spring evening.

Family members, attorneys, close friends who held Power of Attorney, and assorted others were meeting in the large conference room of a local law firm that represented the nursing home. The offices comprised the entire third floor of the old hotel. No renovations had been done yet. No new furniture replaced the brown Naugahyde that had cracked nearly as much as it could. No sleek lighting. In fact, the old table lamps with their torn shades gaped with missing bulbs. John Anderson had insisted that the meeting be held in town away from the home. He didn't want to add to the panicky fear that had gripped some residents and their protectors.

The nursing staff vacillated between jitters–acting one minute like victims, the next, perpetrators. Most still thought of themselves as defending their own rights to a decent wage and competitive benefits to help their families. After all, they kept the residents alive. Their families couldn't take care of them. Doctors buzzed in and out. Nurses had too much administrative responsibility and spent most of their time filling out endless reports and giving out countless pills or shots.

A nondescript, small-town lawyer husband-and-wife team facilitated this evening's session. Noel and Joanne Crossley. They looked almost exactly alike. Both five feet five inches or so tall, weighing about one hundred and fifty pounds, with brown hair and brown eyes, they presented as far less threatening to the families than the large and powerful Cleveland law firm that made the decisions in this case. The Crossleys' assignment was specific: Find out how many residents and their representatives considered bolting and how severe their discontent and underlying anxiety.

The room overflowed and folks stood on the landing outside the door. Noel and Joanne hadn't seen this many clients in their offices in a year. At least fifty people gathered there. Seven were lawyers who also held Power of Attorney for a resident. They could make legally binding personal, financial and, in many cases, medical decisions for a resident if the resident was incapable and incompetent, or if no family had been identified as medical Power of Attorney. The attorneys strained at the bit, ready with their Socratic questions. At seven p.m. on a Thursday, all had come straight from their offices.

Two residents, members of the Residents' Council, were present, but not Mabel Waterford. She had forgotten the meeting. Parents, brothers, sisters, children, cousins, and close friends of varied residents at the home attended. The unexpected eighty degree humid weather, the overcrowding, and the highly charged emotional atmosphere made the room very stuffy and uncomfortable. The old windows with broad, deep sills swung wide open, but the room felt virtually airless.

The Crossleys presented a brief chronology, taking turns laying out the facts of the case as they knew them–the original contract three years prior, the current wage and benefit demands, the new offer by management, and the possible response by the home to a strike.

"Before we start Q&A," Noel said, "I'd like a show of hands to see how many residents are represented here tonight. If there is more than one person here on behalf of a resident, please raise only one hand. Oh yes, I see," he said as thirty-nine hands rose. "Does anyone know of others? If you happen to know of someone else bothered by the possible strike, or considering a change, please raise your hand." Another ten hands shot up.

Short of a signed petition, or an indication of departure by a resident, this was as accurate as it would get. Nearly one-fourth of the residents were quite unhappy, as the Crossleys gauged it. Noel decided he should call Giordano after the meeting and fax him a full report in the morning.

Noel called on a woman who had been waving her hand during their entire presentation.

"My mother doesn't have to put up with this. Her diarrhea is worse again. She vomits right after breakfast. She loves it there. It's the people."

A muffled applause arose and some murmured agreement.

Joanne said, "Yes, yes, we're very worried, too. Our aunt is at the home, as most of you know. We face the same thing."

A tall, thin man said, "My aunt Mabel is there, and she forgets things. She's always putting her clothes on the bed. Then she packs a big old suitcase. But she don't go nowhere. She just gets packed. I'm a union guy over at the cannery, but this is people. She can't take it. The not knowing. She's worse."

One of Margaret's daughters, Shirley Johnson, spoke up next. "Both of my parents are at Golden View. So I guess I get two votes. We may move them both. It's been hard on them, but at least we'll be done with it, and they can get used to that new fancy private place near the lake. Here, we don't know. Maybe, there will be new staff. Maybe, the old nurses will come back. It's a mess."

"Shirley, you've said it all," replied Noel. "You've hit the nail on the head. It just can't go on, all this uncertainty. And I know what you mean. Maybe a clean, neat move to another facility will do it."

Both Noel and Joanne knew that this was impossible. The Cleveland lawyers had a silent agreement with both private long-term care management companies in the area. They wouldn't accept the attrition from Golden View Rehabilitation Center until such time as the strike became a certainty. These other nursing facilities bought all of their medical, housekeeping, and laundry supplies from H&H Brothers Nursing in Cleveland. Lou Giordano's niece's husband owned H&H on behalf of the Teamsters and Tony Dee. Prices for necessary supplies would go sky high if local facilities tried to profit from a "potential" strike that had not yet been called.

A large man with very dark eyes, dirty work clothes, and a heavy black beard full of grey streaks stood up near the back. He didn't need to yell but did. "Give us a break. With all you charge these little old ladies–hundreds a day–isn't there enough to pay the staff a decent wage? They bust their butts. That Anderson guy in his suits . . . hell, he drives a Lexus to work. And those rich doctors were wrong to give my cousin those crazy pills. She didn't have no delusions. She wasn't imagining things. Her boyfriend really did sneak into her room for the last five years. My cousin is dying. Can't it be in peace?"

An emotional applause followed–no whistles, no yelling, rather applause with true feeling. Noel and Joanne applauded and nodded. They kept nodding in unison long after the applause had stopped. When not even a faint sound remained, they still nodded. They hoped no one from the newspaper was there.

Finally, Noel offered, "Let's stop for now. We'll meet again soon. There's plenty of coffee, cakes, and Krispy Kremes downstairs. It's on us." Noel grabbed his micro cassette recorder and walked into his private office to start dictating.

After Doc left that day, Myra asked Margaret an embarrassing question. "Do you think it's crazy to hold a doll, a little brown furry bear doll to my breast and pretend to nurse it?"

"No, that's okay," replied Margaret. "But why do you want to do that?"

After considerable shifting around of her stumps and moving her hips awkwardly to accommodate them, Myra spoke. "Nursing my kids was one of the best experiences I ever had. It made me feel warm and whole. I was a woman. So I thought, why not do it again? But I'm afraid the nurse will take my doll away and give me some crazy pills. Am I nuts?"

A light rain began to fall from the dark sky as Margaret looked outside. "No, no, not at all. You're not nuts. You're not crazy. You're just bringing some good memories back, and some pleasure into your life. Why not? Who does it hurt?" She continued to peer at the jet black sky.

"Okay, thanks," Myra said voice growing a bit stronger. "Now don't laugh, but here's my new baby." And she pulled out a twelve inch long, curly haired, medium-shade of brown, smiling bear. She squeezed its stomach. It gurgled, "I love you. I'm Barry the Bear."

"He's a doll. How are you, Barry?" asked Margaret.

Both chuckled. Barry squeezed out another "I love you," to which Myra, trying to mimic Barry's voice, lovingly added the word "both."

"Why do you hold Barry over your left breast?" Margaret queried. "Do you move him around?"

Myra glanced over shyly, as if she could see. "Well, you see, I've got a pain in here." She touched the area of her chest near her left breast. "It helps me feel better, and the pain isn't so bad when I hold Barry here and pretend to nurse him. It's like I'm heartsick, isn't it?" She shivered and recoiled slightly, and Margaret knew her suffering and loneliness were somehow eased by Barry's physical nearness.

Margaret changed the subject, not too much, just so Myra could recover her bearings. The rain had let up, replaced by a fine misty light fog. She could see some stars among the black and grey clouds, but no moon was visible.

"Sometimes I wish I had Barry with me, too. I blew my husband a kiss today at lunch. He looked over at me, but that last stroke has nearly got him. His eyes teared up for a second, then he slumped over again and spit out half of his mashed potatoes. If he could only blow me a kiss or give me a slurred, 'I love you, honey.' I guess he can't do it."

"As long as we're going down memory lane today," Myra went on. "For some reason, I just remembered that first night in the john. I fumbled my way into it and sat down. It must have taken me a half hour. I was so afraid I'd wake you. I wanted you to like me. I wanted your eyes to help me see, but I didn't think I had the right to ask too much at the beginning."

Both now sat crying, not loudly, just quiet, constant tears.

Margaret responded, "You should have asked for gosh sakes. What's a roommate for?"

"You're right. I should have. So, I'm finally getting there. The medicine is doing its thing. First good BM in three days, and I'm getting a good feel for the hardware, the sink, the toilet, the toilet paper, and the soap. And then this hand grabs my arm, and I scream to high heaven. Help! Help! Help me! It was you."

Margaret replied, "How could I have known you were sitting there? I didn't turn on the light because my last roommate was bothered by it. I was very quiet. And I got used to going to the john in the dark at night. You didn't see me coming, and I just had my hands out to guide me to my usual spot."

Myra chortled. "What a night. I couldn't sleep. We finally cried and laughed and made up. And I decided to trust you and ask for help."

"And *I* decided to always use the lights because it doesn't bother you any. It takes a while to get used to blind people for roommates. You screamed that night, but it scared the poop out of me, too. Who the hell grabs you in the bathroom but some kook?"

"Where could we have more fun than here?" Myra went on. "You're the perfect person for me. I almost hope I don't get better too soon and have to leave here. We'll have to tell Doc about that bathroom episode, but if you don't mind, please don't mention the stuff about my doll. I don't know what he'd think of Barry the Bear, and I don't want him to think we're a couple of crazies."

"You know I won't, if you don't want me to," replied Margaret.

"We're really lucky, aren't we?" said Myra. "We've got each other. Some roommates here don't know each other, especially if they're not right in the head. I overheard somebody at lunch ask why the other bed in her room was empty. Her roommate had died that morning. She didn't even know it."

"I love you. I shouldn't think it, but it's different from the way it was with James. I love him, but men are different. I didn't know what he felt. It wasn't easy. It wasn't smooth."

Myra was quiet for a moment. "I know what you mean. With John, well, the sex was never what I thought it was supposed to be. He had experience when we married. He knew about it. I didn't. I didn't even know what to expect."

"I felt the same way," Margaret said with a sigh. "I'd heard it was better than it was. The kids came out of it, so that made it worth it. My mother, bless her, told me that's the way marriage was. I loved him more in other ways. I don't even know if James ever understood."

"Having you here is everything to me," said Myra. "It's everything. Not just because I'm blind. It's you."

Margaret nodded. "Alone, I'm nothing. We're lucky. We've got each other."

Doc sat in his cramped office doing his seemingly endless paperwork. He jumped up, startled by his beeper *and* a page for him over the loudspeaker system. Seldom were psychology staff paged. He pressed the beeper button.

"Sorry, Trudy, got to respond," Doc said, and ran out the door. He feared he might write more in a letter to Myra's Trudy and Helmut than he should. Something such as: "How selfish can you be? Have you no human feelings? She needs you." Yet what he knew of their lives complicated his feelings.

Doc ran to the nurse's station, his beeper showing the facility's number, wishing that he had the new interactive beeper with an actual message on it.

The charge nurse soon looked up from her chart and said, "Elizabeth has gone bonkers again." She added, "Doc, the med.s are not doing it. Can you see if you can do anything? We may call 911 and take her to a locked adult psych. See what you think?" These nurses did not panic easily. Elizabeth needed help pronto.

"She still in 312-2?"

"Yes," said the heavy charge nurse. "Please let me know right away. Her doctor will do what we say, sign anything I want him to. Just don't bother him. He's playing golf. This is Saturday morning."

Doc wore shoes by New Balance–running shoes with good arches, yet supple and comfortable. They helped him pad quickly to the room. Ten paces away, he heard her, even through the partly closed door. Two nurse's aides stood listening to the screaming. Several residents leaned against their doorways to listen too, apparently scared by the violent yelling and the language. Past the age of eighty, loud noises, human screams, and foul language often proved quite unsettling.

Doc passed four women posed snugly in their doorways listening and shaking like birds sitting on a telephone line. The double-wide hallways simply provided more space for the harsh yelling to vibrate and disturb the hearing aids, all tuned into Elizabeth. They all knew what to expect from her, but still . . .

Knowing better than to knock and walk in, even after announcing himself, he hesitated. Enter Elizabeth's space, unwanted or uninvited, and your presence mortified her. At her best, she was an iconoclast. At her worst, she was a chronic schizophrenic who parlayed her view into a multi-layered way of controlling her world and keeping people at bay. Yet she was so appealing and needy, so whimsical, so squishy and lovable beneath the volcanic eruptions of craziness.

Elizabeth looked up slyly over the coffee cup, which was raised almost to her mouth, as she spied Doc. "Get out," she said, slowly and with venom. "Get the fuck out of here."

Doc stood his ground in the doorway, but moved one foot back an inch or two so that Elizabeth saw it. "You remember me. I'm Doc."

"I don't need any help. I don't need anybody. *Get the fuck away from me!*"

Doc moved the other foot back a bit, but stayed in the doorway. Elizabeth had thrown food at other residents and staff. She had trashed rooms and furniture. Doc asked gently, "Want more coffee, or some juice?"

"Can't you see? Are you blind? I've got coffee. Get out."

The "fuck" was gone. Perhaps–

"Come on, asshole, get the fuck out of my room, and my life. I want out of this fucking prison. I hate it here. It's for old people who are sick and ready to die. Not me."

Doc decided to try. "You don't fit in. You hate it, and you want to leave."

"I've seen doctors all my life. You want me to suck your dick or lick your ass, don't you? You fucking doctors. Get in bed with me."

"Okay, slow down," said Doc. "Staff called me in to talk to you. Said you were very upset, lost touch with things. What's happening?"

"Oh, you nosy bastard," Elizabeth said. "The nurse stole my Swatch Watch. That's swatch, not snatch. That's all you doctors like is snatch–all you men."

"I'll take care of it, Elizabeth. I'll find the watch, if I can, and get it back to you."

"What about the food? I've had diarrhea all day. They're poisoning me. They're trying to kill me. I'll tear the fucking place down before I let them kill me. I worked in five-dollar whore houses. I used coke. These scars on my fingers are from crack. I've been a street hooker. I know the score, you asshole."

Elizabeth leaned over to her boom-box, pushed a button, and out came Sinatra, way too loud, with "I've Got You Under My Skin."

Doc's fading belief in unconscious motivation was re-confirmed, but he knew enough to stay away from the connection between the song title and IV drug use. "You are like Sinatra. He's got experience and wisdom, too."

"He's a goddamn man, mother fucker. You're a man, you mother fucker. I hate men, hate people. I hate you."

"I'll talk to the dietitian and the cooks. Something may not agree with you. Are you on any special diet?"

"Yeah," she smirked, "a fatal one. They're slowly killing me." She breathed a hair more slowly, and her voice got quieter.

Doc scanned the room. Pillows on the floor. Newspapers scattered. One mattress against a window. Make-up and face powder spilled in one bed. Trashed, but not trashed big-time.

"Can you manage yourself?"

"Yes." She was even quieter now.

"Do you need the hospital?"

"No."

"Can I wheel you to my office to talk this out?"

Sighing heavily with her head falling into her shoulders, Elizabeth said, "Yes, I'll talk. You promise to do what you said."

"Yes," said Doc. "I will."

Trudy made the phone call to her sister late in the morning, after Helmut had left for work. Ursula lived in Phoenix and seldom came back home. She rarely called Trudy. Sometimes she called Myra on the holidays, or sent her a card, never both.

The estrangement developed slowly over the years, but the settlement of the estate proved the capstone, the proverbial straw that broke the camel's back. She got a paltry twenty-five thousand, and her mother made it clear that was it. That Trudy got the same didn't satisfy her. Fairness between sisters was not the same as justice within the family.

Ursula and Trudy had fought and argued over how to divide the estate, how to spend the hundreds of thousands, and how to take care of Myra in her old age. Myra had gotten sick of the bickering and arguing. Even mediation failed to resolve the differences between the sisters. Finally, frustrated and unable to fully grieve the loss of her husband, she gave the girls a settlement and set up the trusts.

Trudy knew Ursula. Knew Ursula's estrangement from their mother was finalized with the signing of the legal documents. Ursula had never liked their mother very much, but surely wouldn't do anything deliberately to harm Myra.

Now their dad was another story. She'd loved him deeply, admired him, wanted to be like him. Probably why she never married. Now, in her late forties, with shimmering green eyes, a five foot seven inch, one hundred twenty pound model's figure, and long highlighted blonde hair, she genuinely didn't care about men or marriage. She could have any man she wanted, singles, widowers, or married, any age, any size, and any occupation, for a night, a week, or a year. She was still a knockout, more beautiful and alluring as the years went on.

The owner of a large Las Vegas hotel kept her in style with twenty-five thousand per month for living expenses, so she had condos in Los Angeles, Vegas, and Phoenix.

"To what do I owe the pleasure, dear sister?" asked Ursula.

"No 'Hi.' No 'How are you?' Just a question," retorted Trudy.

"And you've only got a short time to come up with the answer, too," answered Ursula. "Very short."

"Mom's ailing. She's in the hospital. She'll make it. They don't know what's wrong."

Ursula was silent. Finally, she gave in. “Yes.”

Trudy went on, “Her quality of life stinks. She’s completely blind now. Both her legs are gone. She eats, sleeps, naps, dozes off, and feels sick a lot.”

Ursula said, “Yes, I hear you.”

“Well, I wanted you to know. They’re talking about a strike at the nursing home. She can’t stand change. It could mess her up. She could die.”

“None of us will get out of this thing alive.”

“So, I met with her shrink. He wants me to see her more–and call. Probably would want the same from you. I’ve been the caretaker. What have you done?”

“Just like you to throw it in my face, you little snot. Just what I expected.”

“Mother’s Day is coming up. Do you want to visit? We could make it nice for her.”

“I’ll see.”

“Fine. Good. Thanks. Let me know.”

But Trudy knew Ursula was consistent. She wouldn’t come. Perhaps she’d make a sixty-second phone call this year. Myra would have a Mother’s Day with no calls, no cards, and no visits from anyone. Trudy’s children would be told that Grandma was sick and that she didn’t want to have any family contact for the moment. They could each write a letter, but they wouldn’t be delivered.

Ursula put down the phone and pulled her bellhop’s head from between her thighs with a single violent gesture. She smiled inwardly, more because of an idea that clicked than her lover’s admirable efforts. She walked directly to the shower, humming one of the John Philip Sousa marches. It was like she was back in the band at a high school football game, with the excitement, the noise, the arousal, the after-game show in the back seat of a car, then a very hot shower at home while she planned her next move. Life was a chess game, a series of plays and calculated gambles.

Trudy had mentioned the word “strike.” Anything Ursula could do to help her beloved mother reach her permanent resting place would be appreciated by all concerned–that is Trudy, Helmut, and herself. Her half would amount to a million, give or take. Then she could be truly independent, and the boyfriend could take a flying fuck.

“Thanks, Lee, good job.” She got into the scalding shower. She added, “Your two hundred dollars is on the night stand.”

She decided to fly to Vegas to ask a favor from her lover of the past three years, Carmen Silva, the President, Chairman, and CEO of the new Hilton Heartbreak, an 1800-room hotel, casino, and spa dedicated solely to Elvis. A museum showcased Elvis memorabilia with all of his guitars and cars that weren’t still in Memphis. The bars and restaurants had Elvis impersonators. His music was played twenty-four hours a day in the lobby, the hallways, and the elevators. Some people rode the elevators for hours listening or singing along. Guests were given a CD single of “Heartbreak Hotel” along with one hundred dollars worth of chips when they checked in.

Carmen, the boss there, had grown up on the East Side of Manhattan, gone to VMI, been a lieutenant in Nam, then gone on to get a Harvard "B" School MBA. He served his apprenticeship in Caribbean resort casinos, married a Don's daughter, and was given fifty-one percent of the Heartbreak Hotel when it opened. A year after that, he met Ursula. Within twenty-four hours, they were lovers. They were an exclusive item by the end of that week and, by the first of the month, she was offered twenty-five grand a month, three condos, and a new BMW or Mercedes each year. She picked the color and the model. Carmen said if she ever told anyone about him, he'd kill her. He also stipulated that if she slept with anyone else, he'd kill her, but otherwise, she could do what she wanted and be with whomever she felt comfortable. She had to be available to meet Carmen on a moment's notice, fly to NYC, fly to Paris, be at the LA condo the next day. He'd be there when he said, or he wouldn't. Business always came first. That was fine with her. No strings. No love.

She often said, "He puts business first, and so do I." She had saved almost four hundred thousand in three years. Life was good. She had tapes of Carmen talking about his work that would put him and others in a federal penitentiary, but she wouldn't live long enough to testify, so what good were they?

Carmen sent a car for her, and the driver put her luggage in the trunk. He asked, "To the condo or the hotel, Miss Gronbeck?"

"Take me to the condo. I need to change. Then wait for me and take me to Mr Silva's penthouse at the hotel.

We're having a midnight supper, then take me back to the condo at about one-thirty or so."

"Yes, Miss Gronbeck, got it."

"Thanks, Billy Joe," said Ursula. Momentarily grateful, she added, "I don't know what I'd do without you."

No fool, Billy Joe kept his mouth shut. He dropped her off, and forty minutes later, out she walked. He opened the limo door and stood gaping as she got in–the diamond tiara, the simple black dress, and the skirt six inches above her knee.

"Close the door, Billy Joe, you're staring."

"Sorry ma'am, but you look–"

"Thanks, that's enough."

Billy Joe dropped her off at the private elevator to the penthouse. She had closed her eyes to the bizarre neon world of Vegas during the drive to the hotel. She planned her approach to Carmen and rehearsed the discussion in her mind.

When Carmen walked into the room, Ursula was on her third brandy and water.

"Darling, you look great. So good of you to come."

"You do too." She stood and kissed him for a long time.

Carmen's grey sharkskin suit and black alligator loafers adorned his six foot two inch, one ninety pound frame. His personal trainer wanted him at 180. He had the sleek good looks of Al Pacino, except he'd had his nose broken three times, and he refused plastic surgery. "It's for fairies," he explained. "I got this nose the hard way, and I'm proud of it."

His private waiter served Dom Perignon 1986 and Beluga caviar on a small rye bread imported from London.

"Before we eat, drink, or have fun," Ursula said, "I've got a favor to ask of you, kind sir."

"Have I ever said no to anything reasonable?"

"It's about my mom, Myra Gronbeck. She's old, sick, and dying. She's in a nursing home called Golden View. My sister baby-sits her. Mom's got money that's mine. I want it. She's about had it."

Carmen was pseudo-empathic. "I didn't know these details. Sorry. How can I help?"

"Well, the staff may strike. Old people get screwed up if things like that happen. It messes up their schedule, and sometimes 'scabs' come in. It might hasten her departure. She has no life, anyway."

Carmen tilted his sculpted jawline. "Why don't I have the place burned down?" He winked and gulped champagne.

"You've got connections in Cleveland. Union people. Lawyers. I don't care if there really is a strike. Just scare the shit out of those old fogies, and then dear old mom will sweat bullets."

Carmen unzipped his fly. "A friend of yours has come to see you."

Ursula walked around to Carmen's chair and hiked up her dress so she could kneel in front of him. She asked, "So, do you think I'm a bitch? Do you hate me? Will you do it?"

"Yes to all three," Carmen answered. "Do it slow tonight, and no caviar down there, if you please."

Afterward, Carmen promised to call Lou Giordano. They had been together at a mob meeting in northern Michigan for fishing, drinking, and carving up off-track betting in the middle part of the county. They had struck it off. Lou was hale and hearty, gruff and unpolished, but a savvy lawyer. Carmen was smooth and polished, calm and controlled, and a cunning calculator of profits.

Carmen called Lou while Ursula listened. Sex made Carmen hungry, and he had just ordered a light, early breakfast of tea, scones, and fresh peach jam.

"So, bro, vus machs do?" asked Carmen in a friendly vein. They affected Yiddish, African-American, and Italian dialects, mixing and matching them at will.

Lou responded, "Bene. Bene. Et tu, Brutus?"

"Quick favor, if you please, Mr Barrister."

"Anything, you know that," Lou answered.

"Well, I've got a friend whose aging mother is in an old folks' home near you called Golden View Rehabilitation Center." Carmen gave him the address and location.

"Yeah," said Lou. "Funny thing. My guys run their union. We're stimulating a little strike scare. Trying to get the workers more money. Shake it up a little."

Carmen said, "Small world, isn't it? That's what my friend wants. Shake it up there. If something happened to her mother, God forbid, I think she'd get quite a bundle."

"Oh, sure," Lou said. "Sure, I get it. If you need anything more than that, you let me know."

"Thanks, Bro," said Carmen. "The Gucci store in my joint has a new European designed silk sport shirt with your name written on it. Christ, it's five hundred dollars."

Lou said, "No need, but a dark color in extra, extra large, if you insist. *Ciao*, *grazie*."

Myra felt better than she had in days. The swearing and yelling in the hallway didn't offend her as much. Even so, she was glad that the rattling of the noisy air conditioner combined with CNN made hearing every word difficult.

"There's a crazy lady somewhere near us. She's really got a mouth on her," said Myra. The disinfectant odor from the hallway floor-cleaning machine drifted into their room. She choked and coughed several times. Her side hurt, when she coughed like this.

Margaret said, "God, it stinks. I mean the smell, not the cuss words. Well, those do too, come to think of it. We weren't allowed to cuss at home. Our old man swatted us."

"What's wrong with her? Is she nuts? This isn't a nut house, is it?" asked Myra.

"No, no, of course not," Margaret said. "Unless you think we're all nuts. That's what I think sometimes." Sometimes she teased Myra.

Myra scratched her stumps, so loudly that she knew Margaret heard it. "I itch something terrible. I had a genuine crazy friend at home. We called him Crazy Francis. He was something, he was."

"Tell me," said Margaret.

Myra turned slightly in her chair. A slight smile crossed her thin lips. She readjusted the sunglasses which had become a permanent fixture during the day. "Could you turn CNN down a little for me? I don't have my whatchamacallit handy."

Margaret did it. "That better?"

"Yes, thanks. Well, this guy, Crazy Francis, oh I do miss him. He had thick glasses and grey slicked-back hair, and he wore big black high-top shoes. The front of them flapped a little when he walked, like circus clowns."

"Is that it? What's so crazy?"

"Well, he had some real peculiar habits. He walked along the sidewalks with this silly grin on his face. He spit a lot 'cause he chewed tobacco. He talked to himself, real low, but only cuss words. How he did talk. But, the nutty part was he liked to help women on and off the bus in our neighborhood. He didn't attack them or hurt them."

"He just helped them get on and off of the bus. Helped them with those two short steps up into the bus? That's it?"

"Yes and, if he had a hat on, he'd raise the brim, out of respect. Most of them were strangers he helped."

"Is this true? So, what's nuts? What's so crazy?"

Myra liked to take her sweet time when she told a story. Sometimes she even had a punch line.

"Crazy Francis had gone to high school with me," said Myra. She wished she could walk around the room to create more of a theatrical effect. "He told me his secret.

Are you ready for this? He was a she. He was a *she*." Myra let out a real holler. "He was a woman."

Margaret couldn't stop the laughter. "And he wore men's clothes. Is that it?"

"That's it. He was a woman. Later they put him in a state mental hospital. I mean her. He trusted me. I never told anyone before. You're the first." Myra's face was still contorted with laughter. It wasn't right to laugh at Crazy Francis, but he'd been dead for ten years, so what harm was it?

"Some friends you've got. Some friends. Some memories. Some roommate I've got," Margaret said.

Chapter Eight

To Staff:

May 1, 1995. Weather report is for bright and sunny day. No clouds. Lo 48, Hi 67. Census is 158. Three expirations. Assistant Director of Nursing in charge, all other administrators at a day-long workshop on recruitment, admissions, and retention of long-term care residents.

JA

Margaret, Myra, Elizabeth, and Norma sat at lunch on a bright, sunny day that hinted of summer. Norma had been placed at their table, but Carl sat elsewhere. Margaret's husband also ate at a different table, completely unable to feed himself or converse comfortably with others.

"I still miss him. I don't know who they'll put in his bed. His kids were at the service by the grave, only family. Mr Anderson sent flowers from the home. There was a nice card from you two, Margaret and Myra," confided Norma between bites of meat loaf and mashed potatoes. "He's gone." Norma had befriended a ninety-five-year-old neighbor who had later died in his sleep.

Elizabeth responded, "I'm sick of hearing about it. He's gone for Christ's sake. Dead and buried."

Myra said, "We hear you, Elizabeth. Norma, what did the priest say again? Please tell us once more. It was beautiful."

Margaret said, "I smell something."

The table was in a corner next to a window, and next to the kitchen door, so the servers walked in and out of the doorway constantly.

"It's usually me who smells something first, not you," agreed Myra. "Something's burning, or there's a fire."

The fire alarm rang in the hallway, and the cooks ran out into the dining room, Millie yelling, "Fire, fire in the kitchen." Bluish gray smoke became more visible as it gently poured in long thin wisps into the dining room, matched by a rather pleasant smell of cooked meat or burned fat. Not acrid, but not quite sweet either. The overhead sprinkler system in the kitchen went into effect, and the smoky smell turned bitter fairly quickly. Millie went back into the kitchen for the fire extinguisher and wet soot settled everywhere. The smoke did not trigger the overhead sprinklers in the dining room, but the smoke detectors went off. Not a sound erupted from the residents yet. The doors and windows were opened, and the smoke left the room. Excess water dripped into the dining room.

Elizabeth said, "Oh God," and passed out in her chair. Her head hit the edge of the table, leaving a bloody gash above her left eye.

"She's not dead. She just passed out," diagnosed Myra. "I can hear her breathe."

Norma began to go on, quietly, then louder, "Oh God, oh my God." About half the residents cried and screamed, and about half provided denial or support. "It's out. It's over." The first sound of the fire engines could be heard in the distance.

Millie ran in from the kitchen, her clothes and hair soaked, her face streaked with soot and grime. She held her hands over her mouth. Then she gagged and choked, coughing and spitting as she cried, "Help me, please, the smoke. I can't breathe. I'm choking." She almost collapsed.

Tom raced through the dining room to reach Millie. He grabbed her by the shoulders. "You'll be fine. Breathe slowly. It was just the smoke. You're not burned at all." He took a piece of debris or soot from her hair, and held her tightly. "You're fine. Don't worry. It's me, Tom. I'm here."

Jeremy pushed to the table. "Dear, dear. Oh, my dear. Elizabeth, are you with us?"

She opened her eyes with her head still thrown forward. Jeremy used a napkin to stop the bleeding. Then he pulled a Band-Aid from his pocked and applied it.

"I'm fine. Let me up. God damnit, let me up," she shrieked.

"Please, dearie. I want to stop the bleeding on your forehead," insisted Jeremy.

"I don't give a damn. I'm getting out of here." She pushed her way up and got out of the chair. Then she stood up and surveyed the dining room. A shocked silence remained, interspersed with a growing chorus of agonized crying.

Norma screamed. "Oh, my God, we'll all die here. The fire will get us. We're goners."

Myra had tears in her eyes, though no one could see them. She had not said anything. Her hands trembled. She asked, "Meg, Meg, say we're okay."

"We sure are. I wouldn't let anything happen to you. You know that. There's smoke coming out of the kitchen, but no fire. The smoke detectors have gone off. If it heats up, the sprinkler system will give us a nice cool shower."

Jeremy said, "Don't worry, sweeties. I'm here to tell you that you're safe." He threw both hands and wrists into the air for emphasis.

Some of the more frail residents continued to moan and cry, with an occasional scream of "Help me. Help me. We're dying."

Jeremy stood up and yelled, "It's safe! Don't worry. There's no fire in here. We'll all be back in our rooms soon. I love you."

A traffic jaw ensued, crowding the doorway leading to their rooms with wheelchairs and walkers. Others walked slowly toward the exit sign over the door which led to an outside garden patio. That door had been opened and then held open by a door lock. The residents who could walk went out that door slowly in single file with no delays.

The sobbing and screams had subsided, but many residents were still confused and upset and packing the aisles between tables. Margaret could have quickly pushed her chair out of the exit door, but that would have left Myra behind. She said, "Let's go directly to our room. We'll have to wait a moment. The door is full of chairs. We'll be fine."

"Go ahead. Get out of here," said Myra. "Don't let me slow you down. I can make it. You can only die once, anyway." She chuckled.

"Hush up. We'll be fine. I'll push your chair directly out the doorway into our hall. We'll be fine. Are you scared?" She stood up and moved behind Myra's chair.

"I should be, but I feel more, well, sort of excited. Some obstacle to overcome. You know what I mean?"

Margaret answered, "Yeah, but I was very worried and upset when I first saw the smoke. I thought maybe we'd burn to death. I feel better now. Jeremy settled me down."

The central doorway was finally clear again.

"Here we go," said Margaret. "I'll drive us back to the room. Should we go by the drugstore and get one tiny little piece of candy? You know, for purely medicinal purposes." She pushed Myra's chair toward the door.

"Yes, yes, yes," said Myra. "But I've got to have a chocolate bar. Please don't tell anyone. I'm hungrier than I've been in weeks."

"Good, we'll cheat. And tell no one."

"Thanks," said Myra. "I know you waited to help me. It means a lot to me. You could have been in danger."

"You silly," responded Margaret. "I'm selfish. I just didn't want to go to the drugstore by myself. Besides, we were both sick of it here in the restaurant, weren't we? I hate a restaurant that has kitchen fires. Maybe we should eat somewhere else in the future." They both laughed.

Myra reached up with both hands and readjusted her sunglasses, but Margaret knew she really wiped away the tears from her cheeks.

The local volunteers firemen ranked first in the state in response time to fires. They were fiftieth in fire effectiveness performance, which they attributed primarily to twenty-year-old fire trucks and unrepaired hoses. In full battalion regalia, the local volunteer chief, John Murphy, marched in, ax in one hand, and hose in the other. When he saw only smoldering embers and damage probably under five thousand dollars from an apparent grease trap fire, he took on the role of protector.

"Ladies, it's okay. No sweat. Under control. We'll help the rest of you get back to your rooms. The smell is worse than the fire. You'll have dessert within the hour. I'm Chief Murphy." He flung off his long-tailed hat to reveal himself as John Murphy, forty-nine-year-old real estate broker from town. The crying had slowed down, and the screaming subsided. All of the smoke detectors were turned off and, and the firemen and aides finished clearing the dining room quickly.

Chief Murphy caught up with Margaret in the hallway and seated her in her chair. He asked her, "Scared, I'll bet?"

"You better believe it, John. How the heck could we get out of a fire in these chairs? We wouldn't have had a chance."

"Well, no worry now. It was small, and they put it out right away. The overhead sprinklers worked, and Millie's pretty good with a hand extinguisher. It's a mess, but no one's hurt."

Margaret went on. "It's a big fear in a place like this. We're so vulnerable. I'm glad they don't smoke cigarettes inside. At least the new ones don't."

Myra added, “And I can’t even see. What chance would I have?” Face flushed, breathing rapid and shallow, she trembled and sweated profusely. She asked Margaret, “Am I having a heart attack? It’s weird.”

Margaret called the nurse who was familiar with Myra’s recent diagnosis of Acute Stress Disorder. She reassured her and gave her a Xanax. She would call an ambulance if any other cardiac symptoms developed. They didn’t, and Myra quickly relaxed, felt better, and decided to nap.

Margaret heard Norma sobbing in her room across the hall. Jeremy went quickly to comfort her.

In a bit over the loudspeaker system came the deep, soothing voice of John Anderson, the administrator. “Our problem is over, thank God. As you know, there was a small fire with a lot of smoke in the kitchen at lunch. Millie and her crew did very well. Chief Murphy and his crew were here quickly and helped clean up. It was a concern to us all, and it won’t happen again. That I can assure you. It won’t happen again. So, please don’t worry too much. Dessert today is Eskimo pie and Hazelnut coffee. It will be served to each of you in your room as soon as we can get to everyone. There will be extra baths and shampoos this week, and the clothes you wore at lunch will be washed today. Please let me know if there is anything else that will help. Everyone is safe here at Golden View. Thanks to the Lord for watching over us.”

After the announcement, John Murphy walked into John Anderson’s office without knocking. His boots and coat were wet, and he dripped smoky, dirty water onto the rugs. Anderson frowned at the mess and the intrusion.

"There's something rotten in Denmark. There wasn't enough grease to do it. Something's fishy here."

"What the hell do you mean? Couldn't you have left your fireman's costume outside? Weren't you an actor in the senior class play? Christ, my office is a mess," replied Anderson.

"Sorry, wanted you to be the first to hear it, and directly from me. Something doesn't add up."

John Anderson thought out loud, "Are you thinking what I'm thinking? Would the union people do this? Scare the shit out of us? Intimidate us with violence? Oh Jesus."

"Your problem, buddy. As the fire chief and chief fire investigator, I smell arson. I'll take samples and send them to Columbus. I'm about ninety-five percent sure."

"Oh shit. That's all I can think to say."

Chief Murphy walked out, as unceremoniously as he had walked in.

John Anderson called his attorney. He told Noel Crossley the story as he knew it, and let the attorney take over. Bad publicity for the home could be devastating. It would erode public support. Families would pull their loved ones out. A strike. A fire. He had to ask his assistant administrator to draft a statement for the newspaper, maybe the TV, and a letter to send to all family members, POA's, guardians, and lawyers. Not to worry.

Jeannette and Johnnetta were too much alike to be really good friends. Each had aspired to more in life, yet made the best of their personal disappointments. They had failed careers, broken marriages, and children with all of the problems so endemic in current ghetto life. God was very important to both. Their faith kept life going and made it meaningful.

In the nursing staff lounge before their shift started, Johnnetta said as she changed into her blue scrub uniform. "The fire worries are awful."

"Worries me too," agreed Jeannette. "Never had one before. You know what I'm saying? Rumor has it that the union did it."

"You think so? I heard that, too."

"Yeah, somebody told Tom, the mechanic guy, that there was a car here in back with two guys in it before first shift. I'm on the strike committee. Would the union do that?" asked Jeannette.

Johnnetta, fully dressed, closed her locker. "It ain't worth it. It would be more money and stuff, but it would hurt these old ladies. No way."

Jeannette agreed. "Sure not. This place worries me too. Everybody's scared. May lose their job. Women worry about moving or new nurses. It's stressville. I might just quit and go back to working in a hospital at night. You know what I'm saying."

"Well, Jeannette, you know there aren't as many residents, either. The home is in trouble. That's for sure."

"Ham, green beans, and yams for lunch. That can handle a lot of trouble, can't it?" joked Jeannette.

"See you, sister. I'm hungry for lunch already," said Johnnetta.

Doc sat with Elizabeth and Jeremy in the Arts & Crafts room. She had been more composed since his last visit. The small room contained a series of different size tables filled with games, clay, paints, paper, yarn, strips of colored plastic, knives, scissors, and glue. Hammer, nails, and wood were all available nearby. Built-in cupboards filled the walls, where the staff and residents stored their artistic materials, as well as radios, cassette recorders, and TV's.

Jeremy had taken a particular interest in Elizabeth and wanted to improve his capacity to understand her and assist her. Most of the female nurses and aides simply did the least that could be done for Elizabeth. Her erratic behavior, her occasional screaming and swearing, her rigidity and intensity, and her ingenious efforts to draw people to her and then wall them off had the intended effects on staff. But Jeremy didn't give up that easily.

"I don't give a rat's ass about any strike. My family had a car in the late thirties, strike or no strike," Elizabeth said.

"Well, this is different," said Jeremy. "This is more personal. You can't stand it when things change here."

"You're full of shit."

Doc said, "You're feisty, Elizabeth. What do you think will happen if you have different nurses and aides? That's what Jeremy's talking about."

"I won't like it. I don't like it now. I won't like it then," Elizabeth snapped.

"Right, you've got a special feeling for Jeremy, don't you? You trust him," suggested Doc as he moved uncomfortably in the hard-backed chair.

"I'm special. He's special. So what?" she countered.

"Is there any way to express it? Show it in some project here?" Doc asked. "Maybe make a tangible expression of your thoughts and feelings."

Jeremy brightened. "You know, Rehab says you're ready to use your cane more often. You don't have to be in your chair so much, or even use a walker if you don't want to."

"Canes look like shit, aluminum with rubber handles and three prongs on the floor. Look at this piece of shit. Looks like I'm an invalid in a hospital. I like pretty things. I won't use one." Composed, Elizabeth sat calmly at the table, her fingers toying with some wet clay.

Doc walked to a cabinet. "What could we use on a cane?" He paused. "Paint?"

"Yes."

"Colored paper?"

"Yes."

"Stones from costume jewelry?"

"Yes."

They quickly gathered material, glue, paint, velvet, pieces of antique lace, fragments of jewelry, synthetic decorative stones, and pieces of plastic. Jeremy bounced around, saying, "Yes, girlfriend, we could decorate you the only cane in the place."

Elizabeth actually smiled. "Well, it would be something worth talking about. People would notice. But they couldn't touch it. No sirree."

And from this chance decision, out of this search for a way for Elizabeth to express herself, came the most famous piece of equipment in the history of the home: Elizabeth's cane. American decorative and folk art sought new heights.

Elizabeth put out her cigarette, grinding it mercilessly into an old ash tray. She grabbed her cane, brought it up to table height, and eyed it closely. "It's dirty." She got up unassisted, walked to a small sink, and carefully washed the cane in soapy water and dried it. "Now it's clean."

"Girlfriend. Cleanliness is next to godliness. Love a clean cane." Jeremy's eyes flashed with his smile.

Both men sat quietly in their chairs while Elizabeth sprang into action. If she asked, they would answer. Any reasonable requests would be met. Praise and encouragement proliferated. For the moment, she was in her own world, but not one of delusion or demons. Her face opened. Her skin was tighter and smoother. Her eyes shone. Her teeth looked whiter.

Jeremy and Doc stared at each other, speechless. Elizabeth was at full speed. Her body, mind, and soul combined; motive and goal connected. She was bright-eyed, bushy-tailed, transformed, transfixed, and transcending.

She cut the black velvet into six two-inch wide, foot-long lengths. Then she pasted or glued a group of shining, glittery stones onto the velvet. At a distance it looked like diamonds on a velvet neck scarf. Next, she took water soluble paint and, simulating the Hippie era of the sixties, made colorful interlocking swirls on the handle and the three-pronged feet of the cane–blues, purples, reds, green, and yellows. Doc hummed some Beatles music. Jeremy added a bit of Led Zeppelin.

Elizabeth said nothing. Focused and goal-directed she did not swear, light a cigarette, or complain for twenty minutes. As the paint quick-dried, she bathed the cane in super-glue designed for metal. She then wrapped the velvet in conical movements around the cane and pressed it slightly into the glue. It stuck perfectly. It was a gilded cane with a painted top and bottom, wrapped in jewel-encrusted black velvet. She made a wrist thong out of plastic strips, a quick job with only three loose strands. This fitted to the handle so that she could carry or drag the cane without having to hold tightly onto the handle. She could also hang the cane on a hook behind the door in her room. She appeared to simultaneously think of everything: Its purpose, its aesthetics, its storage, and the anticipated reaction of the other residents.

"I may have started a revolution," she said softly.

Jeremy sat, wide-eyed, open-mouthed.

Doc hadn't known what he wanted to say exactly, and didn't have a solution to the issues. He knew it would be tough going with Mr Anderson. Individuals, companies, allied health staff, marketing reps, and salespeople were after the administrator of the long-term care and sub-acute facility from eight a.m. to six p.m. Doc unfortunately fell into the category of those chasing Anderson. It was always better to be chased than to do the chasing. They were in the middle of a conversation that Doc had wanted to have for some weeks.

"You know I agreed to see you ten minutes ago because you said it was urgent. So far, you're worried about the strike and one of your patients. One of our residents isn't getting much quality family time. So what else is new, Doc? Gimme a break," John said, shaking his head.

"Gimme a break, too. I know I'm being vague, but this union stuff is on people's minds. They worry. They sweat. They're afraid of losing their own nurses, their friends who are here and may leave. This kind of change can be devastating. Look at the flip-side. There's a lot of evidence that family and social support, if they're decent enough, help people survive and thrive emotionally. You chat with your barber, get a kind word from the mailman, and the guy at Midas tells you your brakes and struts are fine, and that you've got a nice 1993 Accord. So, you don't worry."

"Nice spiel, Doc, but they'll have support, new aides, and maybe better nurses. If we have to replace everybody on the staff, I guarantee we'll do it. Few will leave. Where are they going to go? We have agreements. We have contracts. The residents will be helped and supported to the best of my ability. You know there are only a few studies of nursing homes that have faced disasters like fires or earthquakes. There are even fewer studies on the effects of a strike or walkout. Life is change, even for the elderly. Some of them can take it better than we can. Who in the hell knows?"

Doc leaned forward. "If people have someone they feel close to, another person with whom they share deep personal feelings, a so-called confidant, they live longer and they live better, richer lives. Take the confidante away and disrupt the support system, and it'd be like pulling apart the wooden scaffolding that holds an old-fashioned roller-coaster in the air. Boom." He hit the desk. Then he put his hand to his mouth.

"Do you want ice or something to put on it? This is a nursing home. Got plenty of medicine around here."

Doc said, "Thanks, it's all right." Both men chuckled before Doc continued, "Do you know what's happening to Carl Schultz? Norma thinks the stress here will kill him."

"Come off it, for God's sake. There's stress everywhere. Who can tell? People die of old age in their sleep after a very full life. Get off my back." Anderson hurriedly stacked some papers on his desk.

Little discussion time remained. "Well, what about Myra Gronbeck? It's her family, her daughters, who are doing her in. She and her roommate are unsettled by the strike possibility. Myra's daughters have apparently withdrawn even further. She's been in the hospital. Dr Ramantha can't find anything other than 'acute stress,' even after all the cardiac tests, an upper GI, and a full body MRI. Just acute stress."

John Anderson's movements became more clipped, and his face darkened. "Sure, Myra's daughters have pulled away. Ursula did years ago, but Trudy, I don't get it. *That*'s what put Myra in the hospital for acute stress? Doc, you better get more continuing education this year. Your diploma's getting old and brittle itself."

Doc couldn't help laughing. "That's not all that is getting old and brittle, by a long shot. I'm glad we chatted. Thanks. I wanted to plant a seed. I've got some ideas about how to help reassure the residents as we get closer to a strike deadline, to let them know we're aware of the problem and how important it is–and they are."

John smiled as he led Doc to the door. "That's what I like, Doc, solutions, answers, a strategy. You know I'll listen. My door is always open to you."

Doc walked out and heard John's door close quickly, a little too quickly.

Five minutes later, Doc's cell phone buzzed. John said, "So what should I do? Call Trudy or Ursula? Tell them to get their fannies in here to see mom? That they're killing her? Elder abuse? You can't ignore children, leave them alone in a car or apartment. They can't be abandoned by parents, so why should family be permitted to withdraw from their ailing, old loved ones? Is the analogy any good?" asked John.

"No, the problem is real," answered Doc, "The issue is valid, but the analogy stinks. They've put Myra in Golden View, a facility devoted to her care, quality care in her declining years with all manner of speech, rehab, OT, medical, social, and psychological services. You feed, clothe, and house her here. You provide activities, cater to her interests, suggest options, plan events, introduce her to people, show movies, and take her places. You don't ostracize her because she's old, blind, and has no legs. So, the analogy stinks. The family can say it's doing everything for her by placing her here."

"Right," answered John. "There's no law, no legal duty to visit, call, or support your mother."

Doc replied, "What about God's law to honor your mother and father? Did that go out with the nineties too?"

Myra returned to the home after a two-week hospital stay. Her eyes were sunken into even darker cavities, giving her a slightly ghoulish look. She had developed bed sores on her bottom, one quite large and oozing reddish mucous. Nothing to show for it either. The tests continued to be negative. She had been incredibly lonely in the hospital, and felt estranged from the nursing staff. She didn't know a soul, and she chose to say little, complain a lot, and sleep hours on end, only to wake up exhausted.

The staff had her sitting in a chair two hours a day. The rest of the time was divided between CNN and sleep. The food was awful and so bland compared to the home. At least the nursing home served spice, grease, and sugar, in measured doses of course, for someone in an advanced stage of diabetes mellitus. The driver and his assistant from the ambulance company wheeled her into the room and shifted her onto the bed. Her spirits lifted instantaneously.

"Thank you so much. A nice smooth ride. If I weren't blind and poor, I'd give you guys a big tip."

"No need, ma'am. Nice to see you, and I hope you're comfortable," said the driver with encouragement.

"See you. Take care." Myra had been up since five a.m. getting ready to return.

In the middle of her brief nap after breakfast, Margaret said groggily, "Hi stranger. Welcome home. Missed you a lot. Glad you're back."

Myra responded, "Me, too. Been awful. Bad food. Lonely. No results. All those tests. I've been pricked, poked, and punched. Nothing but my nerves, they say. Big help they are. Am I glad to see you."

Margaret nodded. "When they don't know what's wrong, they call it stress."

In walked Jeremy and Doc after knocking and asking permission.

"It's the dynamic duo," Jeremy said, "here to welcome you to home sweet home, girlfriend. Love you to death." He leaned over, took Myra's hand, and kissed her lightly on the lips. He was supposed to use her cheek for hygienic purposes, but Jeremy didn't always follow the rules.

"Glad you're back, Myra. We've all missed you. Glad you're okay, too," said Doc. "Wasn't so great at the hospital, was it?"

"Well," Myra began, "if I tell you I'm very happy, extremely happy, to be back in my cozy bed in a long-term nursing facility, does that tell you something?

"It's stress, is that it?" asked Doc. He had already read her chart.

"That's what Doctor Ramantha says," answered Myra.

"Talk about stressed-out sweeties. I'm at the end of my rope. My significant other, you get my drift, *cheated* on me. This job is good. I love it, but a strike. How can I do it? I should have become an auto mechanic. I come from a long line of mechanics. And look at me, bedpans and bed sheets." Jeremy sucked in his cheeks, threw back his head, swirled degrees and strutted out with a "Later, girlfriends. Later, you too, Doc."

Everyone smiled. Margaret laughed. "I couldn't live without Jeremy. I just couldn't."

"It's serious time," Doc said. "Let's talk stress.

Myra hiccuped twice, then explained, "I wish it had been cancer. I wish they said I had two months, even one. Don't care at all. No one else cares about me, so why should I? Can't do anything, a blind invalid living a life without my kids. Now neither daughter calls or sees me. I should have just given them the money. Then they'd take care of me." The tears poured out of Myra's eyes onto her cheeks, nose, and mouth like a cascade of balm over a face full of hurt. The tears stopped. She smiled

Neither Doc nor Margaret said a thing. Both were on the verge of tears.

Myra spoke again. "So, yeah, my nerves. I can never count on anything here. Margaret could move. The nurses could leave. We could move. It's too much for me. Then there's the not knowing. At this point in my miserable life, I want things the same. Do you hear me? The same, the same, the same . . ."

Margaret added, "Me too. I want things the same. Same place. Same toothbrush. Same Jeremy. Same Doc. I agree."

"What about your daughters, Myra? What's doing with them?"

"Ursula hasn't had much to do with me after my husband died. She doesn't forgive. But Trudy just changed completely. Helmut doesn't come. The grandkids finally sent me a card. It said, 'Sorry you've been sick. We'll see you, Grandma, as soon as you want visitors again.' What's that supposed to mean?"

Doc asked, "Do you ever get angry at Trudy or Helmut? Maybe they deserve it."

"No, that's hard for me. I figure I'm what's wrong. It's me somehow." Myra wiped several huge glistening drops from her cheeks and then blew her nose. Then she hiccuped twice more. "Anything you can do about it, Doc?"

"What would help, Myra? What would you like?"

"Could you call Trudy? Tell her I'm sick and need her. Please? I'm dying without her. Would you ask her to come here? We'll have a meeting again. Bring Helmut, too."

Doc nodded. "Yes, I'll call, but I don't know if it will help. She promised at the other meeting. It's beyond my understanding. Your children are highly intelligent and educated. It just doesn't figure, but I'll try again. I promise. I'll try again." He paused, then said, "This will sound a little unusual to you, but you must leave room in your mind for Ursula and Trudy, even Helmut, to behave in strange ways. None of us like their behavior now. People often have difficulty accepting illness, disability, and death, especially when it concerns their parents."

Chapter Nine

To Staff:

May 24, 1995. Weather report is for clouds in the morning, then mixed sun in the afternoon. Lo 54, Hi 72. Census is 156. Two discharges. Assistant Director of Nursing in charge, all other administrators attending a two-day workshop and panel discussion on crime prevention and security procedures in nursing facilities. Crime report is as follows: One car broken into last night and suspicious car observed several times in the rear parking lot.

JA

Tony Dee wanted to please Carmen with results, just as Lou wanted to please Tony. Lou had told Tony about the kitchen fire at the home, and Tony complimented him. Lou had some balls, yet Tony cautioned him–they needed him for the negotiations. For Christ sakes, he was a lawyer and more valuable to the unions and the mob as a legal mouthpiece.

Tony's mind wandered quickly, too quickly. He really couldn't hold any thought for very long, so he didn't say much. And when he did, he made the sentences or phrases very short. People didn't know how often he covered up.

"Keep the fuck out of doing shit, unless I tell you," commanded Tony Dee.

Lou looked up from his desk at Tony, who stood by the window peering out at the dark Cleveland skyline.

Lou looked like he needed a drink after that mild rebuke. "Hey now, be nice. I got you off that assault charge. Be nice to Lou. I am an officer of the court, God help us."

"Just keep the fuck out of the action," said Tony.

"Okay, yeah," replied Lou.

"I think I want to talk to the contractor at that home. Take his time. Fuck it up. Mess it all up at once. Do wiring. It'll fuck 'em up royally."

Lou laughed. "You've got a real concern for the elderly, Tony. You really do."

"We'll fix the place. It'll be beautiful, but it'll take awhile. Stressville."

Lou asked quietly, to show obeisance and loyalty, "Anything else?"

Tony smiled. He liked it when Lou licked his boots. "Well, I was giving some thought to union violence and intimidation. Carmen wouldn't mind that, either. He wants there to be trouble, but nothing too horrible. No killing. No deaths. Just trouble, Okay?"

"Could I do it, Tony, please? I'd like a piece of this."

"What do you want to do, Mr Barrister?" asked Tony.

"I can get those two assholes who lit the grease trap fire. They're back from Florida, and they're both broke. The ponies didn't run right for them this time. They lost big time," answered Lou.

"So, what would they do?" Tony asked a second time.

"Just some general shit. Hang around the parking lot. Stare at the nurses. A few flat-tires. Steal a car. Shoot out the lights in the parking lot. Worry 'em. Piss 'em off. Make 'em hire more security. That kind of shit."

"If you'd flunked out of law school," mused Tony, "you'd have made a good street guy. You have my blessing. Do it. You get credit for it with Carmen. Remember, if shit happens, we cause it to happen."

Tony Dee walked out briskly to a small office that he occasionally used at the law firm. He kept some records and notes in the safe, and had a computer, modem, fax, and telephone. He put in a call to Carmen immediately. The "project" was mutual, shared to some extent, since anything they did for Carmen helped the union's cause too. It put more pressure on the board and the administrators. Any pressure kept the mood unsettled, and left staff or residents to draw their own conclusions.

"Hi Carmen, it's Tony Dee in Cleveland. How's by you?"

"Real good. I'm beat. Just resting a little. This hotel work is exhausting," answered Carmen.

Tony knew that meant his boss was in bed with some dancer. "Well, wanted to keep you posted on that project here. We're keeping the heat on. Nothing real big. No need for a hospital or anything like that. Real nuisance. And can you believe it? Renovations are taking weeks, not days. Good carpenters are hard to find. The union may have a strike."

"Thanks, Tony. Thanks a lot. One of those damn old folks' joints, maybe yours, is getting some of our used slots we give to charity. We're opening up a whole new market for gambling. People in nursing homes. *Ciao, grazie*. Stay in touch."

The architect's rendering of the renovation project for Golden View was neat, tidy and color-coded. It had been placed on a heavy cardboard sheet approximately four by six feet long, and on an easel to bring it to eye-level. It had a place of honor in the main lobby of the home. The first group of rooms to be cleaned and painted were coded bright red. The first two large resident bathrooms to be brought up to safety code and made more attractive were identified by a mustard yellow. When Doc looked at it, he thought it had to be a sick joke. Of course, they could have used dark brown.

The windows to be replaced were color-coded green on one side of the building, while the opposite side, the first to be replaced, were coded blue. Usually, renovations would proceed with two or three rooms at a time to minimize the inconvenience and to maximize safety and security needs, while still allowing construction workers, electricians, carpenters, and painters to work effectively.

A planned meeting, chaired by John Anderson to present the plan to the staff and construction workers was delayed. A memo describing the events and placing them in a tentative timetable circulated instead.

Nursing staff questioned whether the rights of residents would be protected and what steps would be taken to address the stress and strain. The administrator listened, but stated no massive infusion of resources would occur to address the anxiety and tension, the feelings of being displaced, or possible anger and resentment. Everyone would have to deal with it, keeping the eventual goal in mind.

Ursula used her contacts again with Carmen to manipulate the situation. Lou Giordano and Tony Dee got the contractor in charge of the project to deviate from the plan, especially when they were working near Myra and Margaret's room. Specific orders were given that they would work on far too many rooms at a time, creating much more sustained disruption. They would use non-toxic paint that had a stronger odor than was customary. And they would stall on the project and keep the residents at loose ends and unsettled for several weeks or months instead of days.

Furniture, carts, and all of the supplies and equipment needed for the renovations crowded the long hallways. Paint buckets and wallpaper rolls leaned against the walls to make room for the wheelchairs and the residents with their walkers or canes. Occasionally, a traffic jam resulted. Two or three wheelchairs would be lined up back to front, much like cars at the start of an auto race. The rare resident who used a walker tried to maneuver in and out, like a motorcycle driver through rows of stalled racing cars.

Some beds angled in the hallway opposite a room while the floors were cleaned and polished after the paint and new wallpaper had been applied. The colors were light blue, pale green, and a soft grayish-white–calm, tranquil, comforting for the elderly. Even the fresh paint smell, annoying and discomforting as it was to most residents and staff, proved preferable to the human stench. People sneezed, sniffled, and used inhalers, but few complained about the paint odor. A strangely welcomed change.

Several residents roaming the halls appeared to be aimless. Not the typical wandering dementia residents, they were either temporarily removed from their rooms, or the psychological sense of upheaval had affected them, maybe both. Though not Alzheimer's patients, they searched. They had lost their homes. Talk and explanation helped somewhat, but they didn't know how long it would last. Doc had proposed a series of support groups for the residents before, during, and after the renovation to focus on the feelings of uprootedness, annoyance, and resentment. John said no. The administrator had, instead, written this memo to the staff, and they had passed on the basic information to the residents and their families.

To: All Staff
From: John Anderson, LNHA
Re: Renovation

"I would like to share with everyone the time-line for our renovations. The main work has been approved and is set to begin. The project will begin in the long-term areas and move from around room thirty-six towards room seventeen. The first focus will be the resident bathrooms, along with the painting of the resident rooms. The windows along the front of the building and the halls will be the next major projects.

"This process is going to take abut eight to ten weeks to complete and will undoubtedly be a major inconvenience for all. However, remember, no pain, no gain. If we want this center to look good, we will all have to endure inconveniences and additional problems over the next few months. We must allow the construction workers to do their jobs as free from resident interference as possible and not allow ourselves to harass them when they get in the way of doing our jobs, which they will. In short, we all need to practice patience and control during this process.

"This place will be a bit of a mess at times. However, we must still practice good safety and use common sense. If the handrails are being replaced on one side of the hall, be certain all of your carts and equipment are parked on that side of the hall. This will ensure that the residents and patients still have a handrail to use on the other side of the hall. The construction workers can move items out of their way as needed. Also, don't assume that every construction worker understands the safety issues of our center. Watch for unattended tools or open doors and politely tell the worker the need to correct these habits.

"The bottom line during this process is that all of us–residents, families, and staff–are going to be faced with major inconveniences and frustrations. There will be temporary room changes. The water will be shut off at times. The parking lot will lose spaces to a work trailer, and many other issues will come up. All I can ask is that everyone tries to keep their cool and be patient."

The construction foreman had received the message early on the job. He had trouble comprehending it, but knew it came from the union goons in Cleveland. He was told to make the renovations more upsetting than usual to the residents, especially the two old women at the end of the hall. His orders were to take longer with their room and to delay finishing their wing of the building, so as to create more of a sense of disruption. Instead of working on several rooms at once, the crew stripped the wallpaper and disabled all of the bathrooms in the whole wing at the same time.

The effect would appear to be efficient working on an entire wing, but the crew could keep Margaret and Myra's room under repair for many days. Quite an issue with their electrical wiring would occur. All the wiring had to be torn out and replaced. Next, the termites had supposedly eaten away part of the wooden window molding, so the windows had to be replaced as well.

Myra was strapped into her chair as she sat near the nurses' station. Margaret had been placed in the lounge to watch TV.

"Johnnetta, I feel weak. Could you please push me over near Margaret?" asked Myra. After she did, Myra thanked her several times.

"So, here you are," Margaret observed. "I don't like it one bit, do you?"

"How long do you think? I thought it'd be a week or so, maybe two. Now they say they don't know. I feel worse. I hate the noise. I don't know where anything is. Can't find my toothbrush. Who needs this?" Myra complained.

"Couldn't agree more. The colors are nice, and the wallpaper makes the hall pretty and seem brighter, but I'll have to be on portable oxygen tanks all the time now because they say our wiring is broken. Seems like it all happens at once. Just plain makes me nervous and cranky. I had everything in a certain place. I've been in that room for several years. I hope someone will help you with the bathroom. Two of the residents can't be in the main bathroom at once, so an aide will help you. You'll be fine."

Myra's lids drooped. "I feel dopey. I sleep too much. Tell me more about what you see, not that I'm very interested. I know my sugar's up, but the tests don't show it. I've had funny feelings, like electric shocks, throughout my body. And everything hurts. I wish the doctors knew what was wrong with me. Should I go back to the hospital?"

"Well, now, as I look at the hall, it's crowded with everything and everybody. Elizabeth is trying to force herself ahead, but she's stuck. She'll probably pour out a tirade at someone. Jeannette has the med.s cart, but she can't seem to find the people she needs. Rooms are being painted, and residents are scattered all over the place. Lucky us; we got our med.s on time. The wallpaper is great. It's textured and looks like it's easy to wash and keep clean. There are little drops of pale yellow, blue, and green scattered in the gray-white background. Looks like colored raindrops on a grayish snow background. Very cool, as the kids say. By the way, is the AC broken too? It's so hot for me. I'm sweating. How'd I do? Can you see it? I know you can smell the paint, the glue, and the burned out wires." Margaret looked over at Myra, who was snoring lightly with one eye partially open. Margaret pretended to be more relaxed and accepting of the chaos around her whenever she described it to Myra. Her friend was very sick.

For some reason, an old memory of wallpaper kept popping into her mind. She had searched for months for the right pattern for her bedroom at home. James had liked it, too. Angels and harps in a white and gold print filled their bedroom. How many nights she had stared at those angels while James was on top of her. Those angels were her angels. They kept her spirits alive while he pleasured himself.

Margaret looked closely Myra sleeping. It wasn't polite to stare. It wasn't a pretty sight either. She had been told more blood filled Myra's stool and that she had vomited blood lately. Myra's eyes had sunken further into their sockets, and the black rims that etched them were wider and darker. Her cheekbones protruded. Her mouth had more slack, and her lips looked rubbery and flaccid. Thinner, she looked frail and bony. Since they'd lost the use of their bathroom, Myra only had one bath a week. Her white blouse was stained. Her light blue cotton slacks needed to be laundered now.

Margaret decided to help arrange a change of clothes and undergarments for her. No reason why Myra shouldn't look as clean and neat as the sighted residents, though her friend didn't really care very much about her appearance. The home being a mess upset them.. Margaret trembled, helpless in the face of Myra's decline. A sob formed in her throat, and tears of hopelessness appeared at the edge of her eyes. She would do anything to help Myra–anything.

She couldn't stand the idea of losing her, not like this. Myra did not have cancer or anything like that. Yet her intuition, and years of experience with the dying process, told Margaret a painful truth–Myra was dying before her eyes. And she couldn't do anything about it. Maybe the new paint was making Margaret cry, or else that horrible-smelling wallpaper glue. The memories of her own wallpaper prolonged the sense of loss and sadness.

Casanova wheeled himself in, directly between the two women, but facing toward them. Everyone knew Cas's story. He was not shy. In his prime, he'd told everyone who would listen, he'd been six foot two inches tall and weighed two hundred and ten pounds. He boasted that he looked like the Charles Atlas whose picture had been part of a full-page ad on the inside of the back page of comic books and movie star magazines. Of course, at age seventy-three, he was not mistaken for Charles Atlas, although he was still Raymond Casonorkiewicz of Hamtrammack, Michigan.

Cas had been brought into the sub-acute unit after being found by neighbors. Virtually comatose in his somewhat remote cabin, he was lying in blood, feces, and vomit. The cabin stunk of urine and decaying food. Rats and other critters used it for food, warmth, and home base. Cas had seen better days before drinking a fifth of vodka every day for two years and adding in a six-pack or a twelve-pack of Stroh's as his Social Security pension allowed. He'd been surrounded by thousands of paperback books, westerns, mysteries, romance, whatever he could pick up for a few pennies at garage sales or bookstore specials. In descending order of importance, he loved alcohol, reading, and women. In ascending order of importance, he hated discipline, effort, and jobs.

He was still sure that he was god's gift to women. He had fathered five kids by three women, but he never married. He didn't know where the kids were. He hadn't seen the women in years, and he just a "kept on rollin," as he told folks. Curiously enough, the women didn't hate him, and the kids had done all right. People enjoyed him while they had him, and during those periods of involvement, he was loving and devoted. It just didn't last, a fact that he made clear to anyone near him. Forewarned, others did not expect genuine intimacy, and had no illusions about the relationship lasting, or about him being overwhelmed by a compelling sense of responsibility, guilt, or despair. Much to his surprise, though, Cas had gotten himself into a very deep depression, which the booze and lack of friends made even more severe. The DT's had returned. The blackouts were worse. He coughed up blood all of the time.

Then he woke up one night in the ER of a small-town hospital. The next thing he knew, he was in a sub-acute ward, then into long-term care, "temporarily," his case manager had said. Pumped with vitamins, fed three meals a day, and given cans of Ensure, he gained twenty pounds in three weeks. His smile came back, as did his need for women and sex. He told the young social worker who'd helped him enormously on a daily basis for several weeks while he was suicidal, "Go fuck yourself, Honey. Don't need you. Cas is back."

"Hey, Margaret. How are you? Good to see you," Cas began.

"Hi, you're sure looking better," she answered.

"I could kiss you for that, Margaret, I surely could, and I would if you weren't a married lady. I'd get out of this contraption, stand up, lean over, and give you a quick kiss that even your husband wouldn't mind. Just like a cousin kissing a cousin. Nothing more. Nothing less. Why are all the good ones taken?"

Margaret blushed. "Cas, I hate to admit it, but you've got a way about you, don't you? Is that why you're called Casanova, your way with women?"

"Well, yes, but my problem is my love life. I'm smitten with Elizabeth even though she's an oddball. We smoke cigarettes together, and we talk a lot about books and music. She's plenty smart. And she knows about life and the streets, too, but I can't get her to go on a date. I want to take her for drinks and a smooch or two on Friday at five, but she's playing hard to get, said she doesn't know about Room 212-A. I'm frustrated. Heartbroken. What should I do? I think I'm falling for her." Cas's skin was clearing up. The brownish blotches and red welts becoming less noticeable. His nose seemed smaller, the skin on it less prominent and cleaned of its blackheads. With his pencil-thin mustache and the glow of Vitamin B-12 shots, Cas was becoming somewhat of a looker once again.

Margaret asked, "Cas, are you asking me how you should treat Elizabeth?"

"Yes," said Cas, "I am." "Women know how to treat women. Help me. I'm lost."

Such boyish appeal, such genuine need, and such bald loneliness got to Margaret. "If you love her, just tell her. Tell her what you feel. Feelings get to women."

"Thank you. That's it," replied Cas. He knew how to flatter, how to console, how to persuade, and how to manipulate–but not how to give honest, open expression to his feelings. He needed a reminder of that one. "Thank you so much. I appreciate your help, Margaret," as he flew off in a cloud of dust, doing his best Clark Gable raised eyebrow, a white towel around his neck to simulate the white silk scarf of the early fly-boys as they took off in rickety two-seaters from bumpy dirt runways.

If anyone could get Elizabeth to quiet down, to pay attention to someone else's needs, Cas would have a chance. She was crazy and unpredictable, but Cas had the smooth raconteur's knowing ways. He even stood a pretty good chance of some hanky-panky after a drink or two, several cigarettes, and mood music with the lights down low.

If only her own husband had something left for her, Margaret groused, but then she was probably too sick herself most of the time to do anything with it if he did. But a guy like Cas made one wonder . . .

She looked over at Myra, snoring more deeply, but wearing a placid, carefree look. She'd slept through the whole encounter with Cas, and she would undoubtedly want to know the story in painful detail–what he said, what she said, and how he looked. Margaret decided to tease Myra and tell her that Cas had asked about her.

Myra snored more loudly, then gasped suddenly awake. She said nothing. Had she been dreaming? had some kind of motivational burst? Or had a new and different medicine taken hold? Her mind seemed clear. She focused. She had made a decision, an irrevocable one. Margaret would argue. She hated to leave her. Dr Ramantha might try to talk her out of it. Trudy and Helmut might even encourage her to think it over and reconsider. She would *not* reconsider.

She wanted to die. The how's, when's, and wherefore's would have to be worked out. She didn't know if hospice was the right source of assistance yet, or whether she should ask for certain medicine. She would even consider asking Dr Ramantha to help her to die.

Myra's fantasies took over. She had directly felt the effects of all of the incidents and activities inflicted on them by the renovators. Her headaches continued; she experienced more pain in her stomach and chest; a large bleeding ulcer on her right thigh refused to heal properly; her blood sugar level was out of control; and she was more depressed and anxious. She slept a lot, enjoyed nothing, and had no pleasure in life. She complained bitterly to Margaret, if and when she even talked. She swore at her sisters on their rare visits and put up an angry wall with others. She was "ready."

As her condition deteriorated, the doctors grew more befuddled. She uttered only two or three word sentences at most, and occasionally muttered " The Lord's Prayer." She asked the aides to read it to her several times a day. Margaret stayed very worried and very depressed about Myra's condition. Dr Ramantha had consulted with specialists and gotten nowhere. Doc continued the psychological angle, but couldn't get through. Sometimes she would see him; sometimes she wouldn't.

Her lungs began to get plugged up due to inactivity, so they decided to use a vent to assist her with her breathing. Not strong enough to fight it off, she went to the hospital to have the surgical intervention that would allow for a feeding tube. Her negativity finally built up and exploded, and she used a fork to pull out a trach tube to stop her breathing, ripping out the G-tube so she'd starve, tipping over the IV's next to her bed, and in a final dramatic act, saying no to the technology of her "full code."

She had originally stated that all reasonable efforts were to be made to save her life, that all medical technology and medication should be utilized if she neared death's door. She would alter that arrangement now. She made a second decision–this one somewhat impulsively. She decided, contrary to her earlier thinking, to tell no one of her first decision. They would all find out soon enough. She did not want to defend it, not even to Margaret. Especially not to Margaret, whom she hated to lose and hated to leave. She knew that her death would hurt Margaret terribly. She would be so alone in their room, bereft once again in the home to await her next roommate.

Myra imagined her complete demise. She went further than usual in the fantasy. She pictured the funeral itself, her friends and family gathered in their grief at a traditional church service. The plentiful flowers, more than she recalled at funerals, stood in large arrangements, typically seen at cemeteries surrounded by varieties of green garden plants, which relatives could take home to plant and remember her by. A myriad of glorious mums, all in vivid colors, bright shades of yellow, white, pink, and purple. The small blue cornflowers crowded potted plants with purple or red geraniums. Roses in almost every bouquet, large, full, long-stemmed, red, and yellow. But the small pink tea roses provided the most unusual, delicate, and fragrant.

Flowers almost hid the minister, a small, frail man she'd never met. He headed a local Baptist church that Trudy and Helmut had attended and found compatible with their beliefs. He had a goatee and large, black-framed glasses. He hummed to himself as he prepared to read "The Lord's Prayer."

As she saw herself in the casket, her legs were full and complete again. She had knees, ankles, and feet. How good they looked, even though hidden. Only her hips to her head was visible. Her beautiful greenish-blue flecked eyes were hidden by the softly falling lids. Those eyes could see as she lay dead in the open casket of light mahogany, the interior with white ruffles and white velvet. Her grey hair shone so beautifully against this background. The organ music started. She couldn't discern the music, but the soprano voice was elegant and inviting. Yes, one of her favorites, "Amazing Grace," reflected her sense of humility and love of the Lord. The melody always had been moving, the refrain almost haunting in its feeling of mystery.

The minister stood again, dwarfed by all of the plants and floral arrangements, his dark, baggy suit and white shirt in stark contrast to the radiant beauty of the flowers. When he spoke, she focused on his voice. Unexpectedly deep, resonant, and powerful, yet it so tantalizing in its feeling of closeness and purity. He spoke with eloquence and sureness. Her daughters had told him just enough about her so that he had personal and private material to blend in with spirituality and the concise but relevant biblical references. He spoke of First Thessalonians 4, verses 14-16, of no need for undue worry, that family should not be unnecessarily distressed by Myra's death. "I would not have you be ignorant–about those asleep." He was affirming and celebratory, convinced that Myra was going to be with the Lord. She was already on her way to heaven's gate. Her good deeds were to be continued, her kindness, concern, and love for others. "Pass it on," said the minister, citing the "Great Commission." That's the best way to remember her, give to others as Myra has given of herself to you.

All was forgiven. Peace had been forged with Trudy and Helmut. Peace with Ursula, too, who looked so ravishing as she cried and sobbed in her lightweight, black wool pantsuit. Her grandchildren looked uninvolved; too young to grieve. Myra was pleased that they were there, but not too sad. She'd miss them terribly, not seeing them grow up, no longer sharing in their lives. The minister repeated the word "celebrate" as he described several Myra stories, in the most famous of which she won an appliance at a church raffle. A new Frigidaire. Instead of keeping it, she immediately gave it back to the church.

Myra awoke slowly this time. Had she been consciously imagining the funeral? Having a fantasy? A dream? Whatever, it was peaceful and serene for her. The others would find their way without her. But oh! Margaret had not been at the funeral in the dream. She wanted Margaret to be healthy enough to attend. It would help her. Maybe Jeremy, too, and Jeannette and Johnnetta.

Several aides now wheeled her bed back into their room for the evening. The paint odor was different. Were they using an oil-based paint by mistake? All of the moving back and forth, never knowing where her personal toiletry articles were located, continued to bother her. A blind person in a nursing home needed the sameness and security of places, objects, and possessions. She felt more lost than many of the others. Why couldn't Trudy come visit, and take her home for lunch?

Tom called a meeting of the strike committee for that night. Instead of meeting at the hotel, he asked the group to come to his house. He bought three cases of Budweiser and a box of cheap cigars. He asked Millie to come early to help set up. Tom's small house had two bedrooms and one bath. His two sons had shared the second bedroom when they were young, and his daughter used the pull-out couch in the living room.

After Millie arrived, his wife left to shop for several hours. Tom and Millie chilled the beer and opened the cigar box, and Millie ordered in four large pizzas with everything. They took dining room and kitchen chairs and spread them around the living room for each of the eleven members coming that night.

"It's nice, real nice," said Millie. "I'm glad I finally met her. God, how any woman could live with you."

"You're right, Millie. I don't tell her much, but it's great. I'd of been nothing without her. Hell, I couldn't raise kids."

Millie popped open a Bud, lit a cigarette, and decided she couldn't wait. "What's going on? Why here?"

Tom responded as he often did. "You like it. My wife is very creative. She buys antiques. She makes all these little flower and basket dealies. She picks all the crosses and pictures of Christ, too. There's stuff on every wall and corner. Like it? Isn't it nice?"

"Tom, why here at the house? Yes, it's nice. Tell me before the others come. What's going on? Don't be an asshole. Well, you *are* an asshole, but don't be a bigger one that you usually are. Please, pretty please." She wheezed and coughed. "Please."

"I'm scared shitless. This thing's out of control. Tony Dee told me to keep the pressure on, to set a strike vote and then a strike date, and to go right up to the wire with Anderson, or with Miss Susie what's-her-ass name. He wants them worried to death."

"Well, that's the way unions get what they want. A strike is all they've got when all is said and done. Don't be such a chickenshit. You want me to take over?"

Tom walked around in circles. He put a napkin and a small bag of chips on each chair. He checked the fridge to make sure the beer was cold. He looked in the driveway to see if the pizza delivery car was there yet. He scratched his head repeatedly.

Millie shook her head repeatedly. "What the hell's wrong? I need a beer. You're nervous as a cat. Tell me."

Tom couldn't stand still. "I think the union guys are doing other stuff."

"What other stuff?"

"Maybe that kitchen fire."

"Are you sure?"

"No."

"What else?" she asked.

"Maybe the shit in the parking lot–all the pranks. The flat tires and graffiti."

"Sure?"

He shook his head glumly.

"Anything else?" she asked again.

"Maybe."

"What?"

Tom sat on the old royal blue velveteen sofa, worn out in spots. He rubbed his hand over the back of it lovingly. "I think they fucked up the renovations. The head contractor was drinking with a friend of mine, and he told him and my cousin that the union big shot in Cleveland told him to fuck it up, to do more rooms at once than they should, and to pretty much keep the facility messed up for months instead of weeks. Why would they do that?"

"I guess it shows the administration and the board how much clout the unions have. You know, our union is part of a bigger group of unions. You know that, dummy. Give me another beer, for Christ's sake."

Tom went to the fridge and got Millie a cold one. He tossed it to her, and she caught it perfectly. "They play hardball, Tom. They really do."

"Yeah, I know, but I'm not a violent person. I don't want nobody hurt. I don't want any blood on these two ugly hands." Tom crushed his beer can in his right hand as he said it.

Millie agreed with him, but sought clarification. "I don't hurt people either, deliberately that is. What proof do you have?"

"I called the contractor guy, and he told me it was true, but he said I should keep my mouth shut. He said that Tony Dee plays rough, but that nobody was going to be hurt or killed–deliberately. What does he know about old folks. Shit, he's only forty."

Millie frowned. She got up, walked over to the couch, sat down, and took his hand.

In all those years of flirtation and kidding around, they had never touched each other, never hugged or held hands, or even brushed up against each other. She had finally violated the unwritten rule. He did not move his hand. He was a damned wonderful guy, and she was very scared of those "feelings." Much more scared of them than of Tony Dee or any of the union goons that worked for him. More scared of the "feelings" than of Lou Giordano, attorney at law, whom she knew in her heart was a union crook, too.

Millie looked directly into Tom's eyes. She asked, "What should we do about it?"

The pizza delivery man showed up at the front door, and two members of the group arrived.

Tom dropped Millie's hand and jumped up. So did she. "I don't know what we do about it. I don't want to hurt anyone."

Millie nodded. "Me either."

Chapter Ten

To Staff:

June 15, 1995. Weather report is for a hot, cloudy day cooling off quickly in the early evening. Lo 58, Hi 78. Census is 153. Two expirations and one discharge. All administrators are in the facility today. Crime report is graffiti painted on one car and the driveway of the main parking lot.

JA

The early evening had quickly turned colder. Black-blue swirling clouds filled the cloudy skies, much more like winter than mid-June. The board meeting was called without public notice, and no residents would attend. State administrative laws governing public facilities backed up the county's interpretation of its own human resources guidelines–private meetings concerned with high-level personnel matters allowed no visitors, could hold resident members out, and owed the press nothing. They had decided to invite both Doc and Dr Ramantha, although neither could be there on such short notice.

A heavy and somber mood descended upon the board members of Golden View. A top-flight consultant had been called in by the board to help provide a more objective viewpoint, but not to take away the board's autonomy in decision making. He had recommended that John Anderson be terminated.

Jack Wheatley vacillated. John Anderson had been in his job several years and had stood up to the union, unwilling to cave in to their more unreasonable demands. He'd closed down free meals, reduced health care benefits, and given very small raises. He was currently very unpopular with all of the union people.

His Director of Nursing, Donna Ashley, R.N., had been on maternity or sick leave for five months. She had many complications from childbirth and nearly died. She tried to run things from her computer at home, but it hadn't worked out very well. As a result, Maria Rodriguez had been "running things" at the home, but without the authority or the pay of the Director of Nursing. She threatened to quit in the face of all of this uncertainty if not given the job of Acting Director of Nursing, at least for the foreseeable future. She played by the rules and had written a memo to John Anderson expressing her feelings to him and the board. He passed it on without a recommendation.

The typical long-term care administrative response to problems–union, fires, renovations, a declining census, a threatened strike, and increased security needs–was to blame staff and fire them, then hire others into their jobs, or create new jobs to fill needs. Problems sought a scapegoat in facilities such as Golden View.

John saw that the head of the board, Jack Wheatley, was energized. He knew that Jack liked conflict and confrontation, especially when he could control it or mediate it; command some sort of damage control. John wore a new shirt and tie and his double-breasted Italian suit. His wife had bought him the new French blue shirt with a contrasting white collar. He wanted to look particularly sharp to hide the underlying fear. He was on the bubble, and he knew it.

Susie, his assistant, attended for reasons he didn't understand. Typically, she met with the board only at the administrator's direction. And John had not invited her. The three other members sat silently, looking at their hands on the table; one still shuffled some papers.

Jack's eyes glistened, and he was freshly shaven. He looked up from some three by five cards and said, "Let's start. No minutes tonight unless someone insists. Noting none, this meeting is commenced in private for a discussion of personnel matters. Susie, you'll become the Acting Administrator as of the end of this meeting."

Susie's jaw dropped. Unable to speak, she swirled forty-five degrees in her swivel chair and began to perspire.

John's chair did not swivel. He didn't move a muscle. Nothing twitched. His heart beat with loud throbs, and his pulse raced, but he didn't show it. He knew he had to respond. "Is there any discussion? Who decided? Why? There has been no warning," he stated in a dull monotone.

Jack began, "We're very appreciative of the job you've done for us. There's a severance package of six months' salary. We'll help you relocate. The reasons are simple and obvious. First, the census has declined steadily for months. Second, the union can't stand you and won't settle with you. Third, the renovations are an absolute mess. Fourth, security has been awful. Sorry, John, but heads roll when things are like this. Remember, President Harry Truman said, 'The buck stops here.' You are ultimately responsible as the administrator. Nothing personal, just good solid business practice. Just like selling cars to the public."

Susie gasped. "I don't know whether–"

"We can talk later about your role, Susie," John said. "The future is where it's at for us now, not in the past."

John walked to the door. "I guess that's that. I've enjoyed it folks. I did my best." The tears came as soon as he was out the door in the hallway. The white collar of his new shirt was drenched.

As the new day began, Susie Wilson picked at her fingernails, bit the cuticle, and was annoyed at herself for not having her nails done when she had her hair highlighted the day before. She wanted to look good for the meeting. She wore her one double-breasted, navy blue, wool-poly suit with medium-heeled, black pumps and black designer lacy hose. Trying to hide her fear, she did look good. The meeting was her first about a serious issue with a resident since she'd become acting administrator. The nursing staff was still in shock, although not overly disappointed about the unexpected and merciless demise of John Anderson. "Here today, gone today," was the staff motto. The forty-year employee who loved job and company, the good benefits and retirement, and was eventually rewarded with a gold watch, was missing in the long-term care business of the nineties.

How long would pass before the board decided to get rid of her? She wanted to stay. She had to do well. She wanted to succeed in the worst way. A meeting with doctors, psychologists, nurses, and relatives of a resident over a serious issue scared her, and rightfully so. She wanted to help, but knew she'd gotten herself into a miserable business, driven relentlessly by costs. Maybe being an activity director on a Caribbean cruise ship wouldn't have been such a bad choice.

John's office fit her though. She'd use the oval conference table for the meeting. Dr Ramantha would attend, so would Doc and Maria, now the acting Director of Nursing, as well as Trudy and Helmut, Myra's daughter and son-in-law. Susie was very fond of Myra and Margaret, and had to be careful not to take sides in the discussion. Susie had trained the secretary to announce visitors over the phone first, then wait for her to request that they be shown into the office. The secretary did it just right, avoiding the confusion of John's open-door style with people roaming in and out of his office.

All participants were shown into her office at once.

"Good morning. Please take seats around this table. We'll be comfortable here, and we'll be able to see each other," suggested Susie. So far, so good. She picked at her nails.

Doc walked in with the small group. No one mentioned the weather, or the time, or what they'd seen on TV the previous night. People sat down, put their hands in front of them, and looked at each other until, finally, Trudy spoke.

"Thank you for seeing us. Mom is worse. We don't know what to do. Can you tell us? What should happen now?" asked Trudy. Her narrowed eyes hinted of anger, but she feigned cooperation and understanding.

Helmut said, "Yes, we are appreciative. But my mother-in-law is fading. She's not the same person she used to be." He drummed his fingers on the table, then quickly brushed his hand through his buzz cut, which bristled under the attention.

"Perhaps the professionals could update us."

Susie began, "Dr Ramantha, perhaps you should give us a brief report."

He stared evenly at Trudy. "As Myra's family, you have my heartfelt concern, just as Myra does. She has more diffuse pain, her breathing is worse, and it seems as if many of her systems–cardiac and pulmonary, especially–are in chronic distress. Hospital observations, various MRI scans, x-rays, and imaging studies tell us little else. Her diabetes is under control. She's taking antidepressant medication, and she's seeing Doc for depression and apathy. Acute Stress Disorder is her most recent diagnosis, in addition to her hypertension, pulmonary disease, arthritis, ulcers, hypothyroidism, and diabetes. She's taking a lot of medicine, such as Cipro, Catapress, Synthroid, Betopic, TTS, and Ativan and Zoloft for anxiety and depression, if my memory serves me correctly. I wish we could do more. In my home country, the women in my village would call her heartbroken."

Before the others could respond, Doc added, "Yes, the depression is deeper. It's as if she's given up. I think the pain is worse, but she doesn't complain much and hasn't requested painkillers such as morphine yet. It's a medical puzzle, although as I've mentioned on several occasions to family members, there has been an abrupt change in family visitation and family attentiveness, and Myra's heart and soul have responded directly to such changes–responded very poorly, indeed."

Helmut glared at Doc and snarled. "What about this place, those fixing-up people. It's been weeks. That upsets the patients, upsets them a lot, I'll bet. And you had a fire in your kitchen."

"And you still may have a strike. What kind of a place is this?" asked Trudy. "How can Mom get any rest here? How can she get better with all of this going on? Maybe we should move her? Maybe we should have moved her weeks ago."

Maria, the new acting Director of Nursing, coughed, and Doc looked closely at her. She wore a new, form-fitting, white uniform complete with a nurse's cap and medallion. Her hair was up in a chignon, and her lips were painted a very bright red as were her nails. A beautiful gold antique watch and several chains that held religious charms adorned her wrists. She looked extraordinary with her dark olive skin highlighting the white uniform.

Doc asked, "Maria, what do you think? The nursing staff knows Myra quite well, and her roommate, too."

Maria cleared her throat. "Yes, Doc. Myra is well-known and loved by us. Despite her declining health, she's not difficult to care for. She takes her meds and still makes an effort to eat, although she's lost weight steadily in the last four or five weeks. Jeremy tells me that her sense of humor is nearly gone. That bothers me as much as anything else. Our question is whether she's given up. Of course, she has the right to do that. But she's not medically terminal. It's not time for hospice yet."

"Really, are you really so sure of that, Miss Rodriguez?" asked Trudy. "Maybe hospice should be called in now. Don't they help people who seem to stop fighting evaluate whether to keep up the struggle or not, so they can more easily cross over into heaven at the right moment?"

"Eventually, she'll be at peace with no pain," Helmut said.

Doc guessed at the contradictory directions in which the discussion would go, but couldn't avoid them. Logically, bad care for Myra at Golden View met the family's true needs. Yet, the family viciously blamed the facility and its staff for numerous shortcomings, would still refuse to give more TLC, and felt that since Myra's productive, useful, and enjoyable life stage was over, a way should be found to end it. The denial of the family's role as a catalyst, or the role they could play in a positive way during Myra's final phase of life–sharing memories, making sure Myra had seen or talked to those whom she wanted to see or converse with, making sure she spent time with her grandchildren, and visiting often–was unyielding.

Susie reddened, and then took a series of deep breaths.

Doc jumped in, “I agree with Maria. It’s too soon for hospice care. But, Helmut, you’re right. The pain can be controlled quite well by hospice and our doctors when that time, when the terminal time, comes.”

“Don’t some medicines hurry that time along?” asked Helmut. He looked directly at Trudy.

“Yes, but Myra is not currently on such medicine,” replied Dr Ramantha. “And in my judgment, it’s too soon, and she has not made such a request. Such medicines leave people comatose or delirious much of the time.”

“But you’re not in her shoes, Dr Ramantha. You may be wrong,” argued Trudy.

Dr Ramantha nodded. “Yes, and you may want additional medical opinions on that issue. I may be wrong.”

“We don’t question your medical opinion so much as we want to do what’s right for Mom. If she were able to stop the pain after a moment, be more realistic, perhaps she’d request the Dr Kevorkian thing. She’d want to end it, but not slash her wrist or connive to get pills somehow and do it. She could legally have an abortion, take a potential life.” Trudy’s voice and face relaxed. “Can’t she have a doctor help her end her pain and die? Could you help her, Dr Ramantha? Could you help her do that?”

“No, it’s illegal in our state. There’s no constitutional right to die, at least not yet,” replied Dr Ramantha.

Maria added, “And she has not requested doctor-assisted suicide.”

"Have you asked her point-blank?" Helmut said. "Why not ask her?"

Trudy said, "If she said 'no,' that she didn't want it, it still wouldn't mean that she shouldn't want it. She's so sick. She's not in her right mind. She can't make a good, solid, informed decision like we can. She's just too sick to really decide, but if she could, she'd want to end it. I know she would."

"Do you mean she's unable to decide important matters for herself, that the family should have a legal guardian appointed?" asked Doc.

Susie added, "But if you had a judge declare her legally incompetent, she couldn't decide for herself. She couldn't ask for physician-assisted suicide. If family requested it, wouldn't it be more like homicide? You can't legally act on her behalf and take active and intentional steps to end her life, can you? After all, she's not even on life-support systems or brain dead?"

"That is tricky," agreed Helmut. "We don't want to try to declare her incompetent, even though we don't think she knows what's best for her. It could be costly, and our lawyer is not certain of the outcome. She's not really crazy, you know."

Doc said, "From a psychologist's standpoint, we must consider that Myra does know what's best for her. She's sane and competent in my personal opinion, but she's very sick and in a prolonged depressive state. Control over her life, the ability to influence what happens, is critical to her maintaining herself in this place. It's all she's got, immobile and blind as she is. She desperately needs some feeling of control, for us to listen carefully and sensitively to her, although we may disagree, even disagree violently, with her wishes. It's her life."

Dr Ramantha added, "As Myra's pain worsens, I can change medicines for the pain. Several will help with the pain, but they may well shorten her life."

Trudy exploded, "Why wait? You people are *wimps*! You can't do what's right. Do you just keep these old people alive, no matter what, so you can keep these damn beds full, make money, and keep your stinking jobs?" She gasped, and her head sagged.

"Trudy is upset. It's her mother," soothed Helmut. He rubbed his wife's back. "She's right, you know. Myra's life is over, so why can't you understand that and work with us? We gave up months ago. We decided to do nothing to delay her death. We felt it was not morally or spiritually right and honorable to keep her alive like this."

"Who in the hell are *you* to decide that for her?" Doc asked. "Who gave you the right to play God?"

"If you cared so much, you'd run this place better," countered Helmut. He looked directly at Susie. "This place stinks. There are fewer patients. You've had so many problems. The place is a mess; there's paint, ladders, and plumbing fixtures everywhere. You're not helping her, as you say, quality of life. I wouldn't live in this dump for five minutes. She's not at peace, or even comfortable, in her room."

Glancing at his watch, Dr Ramantha stood and slipped on his sport coat. "You have my sincere concern. I'm glad Myra's family is nearby and thinking so seriously of her condition. Please keep in touch."

"We want a different doctor. You aren't right for her," said Trudy.

Dr Ramantha looked over his shoulder as he left, but he did not respond.

"If you want a new shrink, too, I'll understand. I hold you both responsible, to some extent, for Myra's demise. You have deliberately pulled back your attention and love."

Susie jolted. "Doc, perhaps you've said enough."

Trudy and Helmut got up and walked out.

Maria said, "They want her dead. They want her money. They are assholes. Can we call the police?"

Doc said, "We've got to try to understand their feelings and their reasoning. They're all that Myra has."

Susie's eyes teared up. "Let's think about it. We'll talk later. This was truly horrible."

Doc returned to Margaret and Myra's room nearly two weeks later. He strode in quickly.

"You know," Margaret said, as she looked up from her game of solitaire, "my firstborn was an accident."

"I didn't know that," said Myra. She came awake quickly and began to scratch.

Doc agreed. "I didn't either. Do you want to tell us both about it?" Margaret's style often surprised him. She'd blurt out an uncomfortable feeling or conflicting memory, then back up and tell the story slowly at her own pace. She liked to get things into some kind of order, then try to make some sense of the pieces. Doc readied his note pad and pen.

She stood for a moment, then changed her mind and sat down. "Well, I was about sixteen or seventeen. I don't remember which. I was working part-time as a maid and cook for a rich family in town. They had a big white clapboard house and a huge kitchen with black iron stoves and ovens. It was big enough for a restaurant. Everyday after school, I'd walk about a mile to their house, change into a white smock and a little white cap, and do whatever needed doing. I'd cut beans, shuck corn, help with the little kids, and wash the pots and pans. Kind of an all around helper. I even helped chop wood for the stoves in the wintertime."

"Got you ready to be a wife," said Myra. She giggled. Then she rubbed her hands together in a nervous gesture.

"Yes, and they even paid me a dime each day. I sometimes worked extra and made a dollar a week. We had plenty of mouths to feed at home, so a dollar helped plenty, and sometimes they let me take home some of the extra food. Even some of the hard cheeses that Mr Kohut didn't much like." Beads of perspiration dotted Margaret's upper lip.

Margaret finally stood up and rearranged her blouse and slacks. "That was their name, Mr and Mrs Oscar Kohut, and they had three little daughters, none of them older than five. The Mrs wore a big corset, the old-fashioned kind that you had to lace up in back. She had a good shape. She was very beautiful, but one leg was shorter than the other. She wore shoes with a very, very thick sole on one foot to balance her walking. It didn't help much. She still walked with a big limp. It bothered her a lot. She talked about it all the time. When she was pregnant, it really caused her a lot of pain."

Doc scribbled furiously. "Tell us more."

"The mister was a huge man. He ate and drank a lot, but he was very gentle, too. He hugged the girls. He kissed his wife all the time. He was scared of things like snakes, lizards, and roaches. He hated bugs. There were stories at school that he had other women, but I didn't pay any attention. He was nice to me. He called me Miss Meg. He was always very polite and very punctual. He paid me after dinner every Friday night without fail. He wore a huge gold chain and pocket watch. It hung over his Santa Claus belly that was draped in a grey pinstriped vest."

Myra said, "What about your firstborn? Did you forget what you're talking about?" She took off her sunglasses, an unusual gesture for her.

"I'm getting there, Myra. One fall night he called me out onto the large porch. It was just turning dark. He said he had something to give me besides my money. I felt safe. I'd worked for the Kohuts for over two years. Believe it or not, he said, 'I love you, Miss Meg. I love you very much.' No man had ever said that to me. I didn't think I was much to look at then, although my breasts were pretty good. He said, 'I have something else to give you.' He took my hand and put it on his gold watch. Then he took the watch, the fob, and the chain and put it into the pocket of the sweater I had around my shoulders. I was shocked and overwhelmed. It felt like a dream. Then he took my right hand and put it on something warm and hard. I closed my eyes. It was his 'you know what.' He had it out of his pants. His breathing was shallow. He didn't say a word. He pulled up my smock and pushed me against the wall. Before I knew what had happened, he stuck it in me and lunged against me four or five times. Then he sighed contentedly, wiped it off on my smock, and kissed me on the forehead. He said, 'I love you, Miss Meg. Thank you,' and walked away."

Doc said, "That must have taken you completely by surprise. What a shock."

Margaret turned her back on Myra and Doc. She spoke to the wall next to her bed, on which hung a large wooden cross. "I never went back. I never told anybody. I hid the watch until I sold it to a pawn broker ten years later. Eventually, I told my parents that my boyfriend, Tim, and I wanted to get married because we were going to have a baby. I hoped the baby was Tim's, although I didn't do it with Tim until after Mr Kohut. Tim and I got married, and I had a son and named him Ralph. My marriage to Tim only lasted a year. Then I met James. My life really began with James. He meant everything to me. I usually blank out the whole incident with the Kohut family."

Doc said, "That's natural. You never understood it. It scared you. It repulsed you. Did you feel ashamed and guilty?"

Margaret said, "Yes. I just let him, even though he did force himself on me." She began to sob quietly, almost with contentment. "I just let him. I just let him."

Doc's voice broke as he talked. "I know it's painful to recall, and there are guilty feelings, but you did the honorable thing, Margaret. You had your son, and you gave him a name. He had a father. Many people are afraid to speak out when they are attacked like that. It wasn't your fault. Mr Kohut raped you, if you don't mind me saying that."

Myra nodded. Her stumps shook. Her eyes brimmed over with tears. "He surely did, Meg. You did the right thing. The watch would be worth a fortune today." She clearly tried to lighten things up a bit. "Too bad you didn't keep it and sell it later. Gold got more valuable, you silly. We'll never tell anybody any of this. I promise."

Doc took off his sport coat and loosened his tie. He stood behind Margaret's chair. After she seated herself, he gently rubbed her shoulders. She liked that contact with Doc. "You're a brave woman, Margaret, very brave," he said. She was nearly asleep in her chair, and her head hung down as she slumped over.

The gambling idea had started in an offhand, accidental way. Doc was talking to Susie over his cell phone later that day about the lack of fun in the life of the ordinary resident. With close friends and family often dead, illnesses left residents unable to pursue many previous leisure activities or sports. Chronic illness brought squabbles and irritability among friends, which only made things worse. But so little pleasure existed, such infrequent novelty or genuine enjoyment to counterbalance the pain and loneliness.

"We need to fill the gap," said Doc. "More fun for those who can stand it."

Susie agreed. "I've had a really wild idea ever since I went to that gambling place run by the Native Americans in upper Michigan. Bus loads of seniors flocked to it, many in chairs, some with canes or walkers. They played cheap slot machines by the hour. Kind of got into a zone with the background noise, the constant hum of the machines, the smoke, the drink, and the laughter, with the occasional screams of joy at a jackpot."

"So what's the wild idea? Take our folks to a casino?" asked Doc. "That would be a scene. The county people would be all over us for promoting gambling and all of its related vices and sins. 'Golden View Rehabilitation Center Supports Crime' would be a nice headline for the local papers."

Susie laughed. "I agree. But what if we brought gambling here? Not real gambling, just the slots. Used slugs or tokens so no one lost money. Excuse me a moment. I've got to make the nine a.m. announcement."

"Good morning, everyone. Hope you had a good sleep and enjoyed the blueberry pancakes and Bob Evans sausages for breakfast. I want you to offer a silent prayer for two residents who have expired this week: Harold Cline and Betty Lou Hinson. We'll miss them. They've gone on to a better place. Also, please save some good wishes for Linda Larson, who went home to her son's farm to live there. Have a good day, and be patient with us. The facility will be much more beautiful and enjoyable once it's all fixed up. This is Susie Wilson, your acting administrator, signing off for now."

"Good job, Susie. Now tell me the rest. What's your plan for the gambling?"

"Well, it's like this," she began again. "I called a hotel in Vegas, the one that is exclusively devoted to Elvis the Pelvis." She chuckled. "Well, I asked what they did with used slot machines when they wear out. Guess what? They repair them and give them to churches and hospitals for charity events. If they're still not working perfectly and can't be totally repaired, they sell them to other countries, especially to resorts in the Caribbean. Unless they were pulling my leg."

"So, how does our facility fit in?"

"Well, they can arrange for the machines to use coins that look like money, but aren't. We can have our folks play slot machines to their heart's content without spending a penny of their own money."

Doc almost jumped up. "Will they sell us some or loan them to us?"

"Better yet, Doc, they'll give us five fully functioning machines, and H&H Distributors in Cleveland will set them up in the spare storage room where we used to keep extra wheelchairs and walkers. It'll only be a week or ten days. How's that?"

"I'm sure someone will object, on the premise that it might promote gambling, tie us to Las Vegas mobsters, or something like that. But what fun it would be."

"Yeah, you're probably right. I've got to get approval. I can't wait to tell the residents. I know at least twenty or thirty who'll want to move their beds into the gambling room. The storage room is next to the smoking lounge, 212-A, so I guess it will be Room 214-A. Smoke a cigarette, have a beer, and go next door to win a jackpot of 'three bars' on an Elvis slot machine direct from the strip in Las Vegas."

"By the way, Susie, anything else about the Casanova and Elizabeth story?"

Susie put down some papers, took off her glasses, and looked straight at Doc. "You know, I don't really care for either of them that much. But it's sort of a moral dilemma. Neither has ever married. Elizabeth has been everywhere and done it all. She's even been a prostitute. Cas has been a derelict, an alcoholic, a well . . . a real bum. Nearly dead when we got him."

Doc nodded.

"Well, they got drunk in 212-A. The nursing aide was called, and he threw them out. They were having sex with such wild abandon that it upset the others. I told them to stay away for a week, then go back and behave more appropriately. They thought I was a snotty little virgin."

"Other residents have their rights, too. Cas and Elizabeth often forget that there are other people in the world."

"Get this. They want to room together. They say they are in love and might marry some day. They say married folks live together here. They say some of the ladies are lesbians and that several of them live in the same room."

Doc swallowed a laugh. "How'd you handle it?"

"I told them I'd see about it. Talk to the board. Check our policy. See if there's precedent anywhere, maybe check out the Internet."

"It's a hot one, Susie, very hot. The slots will get the green light. But two unmarried residents of different genders living together and cohabiting, even with consensual sex, will never make it here. San Francisco, maybe, well yes. Here, not in our lifetime."

Susie smiled. "I'm hoping one of them will be discharged or transferred, and the problem will fade away. Why can't they just make love quietly and soberly on Friday afternoon in 212-A?"

Doc shook his head and smiled, leaving to go make his rounds.

Elizabeth came unglued again. In her bathroom she pounded on the mirror with her house slippers. They were green velvet with a soft, lightweight rubber sole, which combined with her weakened state to render the mirror safe. The language provided more danger, however. The nurses didn't know what to do. No doctors would arrive until morning rounds at about ten a.m. If they gave her an injection of Ativan, she would not be evaluated properly by the physicians. If not, she'd upset everyone else on the station and take valuable time away from treating the other residents.

Doc walked in and said, "Good morning."

The nurses were about to strap her into her chair and wheel her to the nurse's station, pending a decision.

"Doc's here, may I come in?" But he didn't wait for an answer. He still didn't care for someone to say, "Get the fuck away from me," when he arrived specifically to help. He committed himself to continue to work on that problem. Then he gave a second knock, this time on the bathroom door.

"Hi, Elizabeth, it's Doc. Please come out so we can talk it over."

She shrieked, "Get the fuck out of here, *you asshole*!"

"My, my," Doc replied. "You sound upset. Let's talk it out. I don't want to call the nurses. I don't want them to use restraints, do you?"

She was crazy, but smart. "Okay, fuck brains. You coerced me, and I'm filing a complaint. You forced me out of my own bathroom, you sneaky son of a bitch. I hate your fucking ass. I'm reporting you for Medicare fraud. You tried to get in my pants, you piece of shit." She opened the door and hobbled out slowly.

Doc said soothingly, "Thanks, you made that easy for both of us. Appreciate it. What's on your mind?"

She sat on her bed, her legs spread, so Doc simply put a spare blanket on them. "Don't you like to look at pussy, Doc? Afraid you'll like what you see? Want some?"

Doc considered requesting that a nurse join him. This woman was fully capable of making false accusations about him later.

"What's wrong, Elizabeth. I know you're upset. Cut the garbage."

"My daughter, Georgia, just called me. She said she hates me. I need her bad. I want her. Send for her. She's my only friend. I can't live without her. She's my lifeline, damnit to hell. I'll kill myself without her. Fuck. Shit. Christ on a crutch. That bitch."

The tears welled up in her eyes. She began to sob and gasp. The hot tears steamed down her cheeks and onto her nightgown.

Afraid she'd grab him, he stepped back one pace. Better not to touch Elizabeth. "Why the hell do you need the 'bitch' so much, to use your word?"

Screams and shrieks followed. Loud moans, sighs, and hiccups came out of her as she tried to speak. " Hold me. Please hold me."

Doc did. Without thought, without any consideration of what would help, he held her lightly and began to rock her, as one might a sobbing, hysterical three-year-old. He began to sing softly to her, "No gal made has got a shade on Sweet Georgia Brown . . ." Please let him be doing the right thing . . .

He hummed the melody, and Elizabeth joined in. They rocked and sang, and hummed together for the next five or ten minutes. Doc repeated "Georgia" and "Sweet Georgia," and Elizabeth settled down, apparently soothing her need for Georgia. Doc had not done anything like this since rocking his own daughter, Frannie, to sleep in the middle of the night. God knew what Elizabeth would say or do next, but for the moment, she rocked, comforted and reassured. Georgia was still with her. Doc craned his neck and looked into her eyes. They were closed. She snored rhythmically. She had soiled herself as she relaxed.

When Susie awoke at six a.m. and showered, she could think only about having several glasses of cold Chardonnay when she returned home from her office. She prayed for no emergency calls–no more fires, no more robberies. Painters and electricians be gone. John

Anderson had left her a real mess, and she half-hoped that the board would remove her, too. The other half wanted to show good-old-boy Anderson how to effectively manage a nursing facility. Long-term care needed a woman's touch. Nurturance, support, and affection, with a solid foundation for the residents and their families.

Susie called a police detective, Lieutenant Grocchi. Sloppy, with hygiene a C+, at least he didn't smoke in her office. His brownish-yellow teeth suggested snuff or chewing tobacco. Above the mismatched and clownish polyester pants and a suit coat, he had the dough-like look of a clay model used to make a bronze casting: rounded, puffy features with small, dull eyes. Standing maybe six foot three inches and two hundred and eighty pounds, under his Birkenstock sandals he wore black socks.

He had taken two days to return Susie's phone call, but only an hour to come visit once he'd heard her story. Susie knew the public conventional wisdom about her staff. That they weren't too bright, just nice martyred folks trying to deal with their own deep fears of death, that infinite abyss nearer than we think. As they had limited ability and not much training, paranoia might run wild when they became fearful and anxious. Too easily, they might see criminal intent and evil lurking everywhere. So, police didn't always respond quickly to their calls.

Susie shifted in her seat as Grocchi stared at her too long, with almost a leer. Then he took out his note pad and an old yellow pencil with teeth marks on it.

"Sure you don't want coffee, Lieutenant? It's hot," asked Susie.

"No, ma'am, thanks anyway. I drink *Kool-Aid*, with real sugar. You mentioned some suspicions here at Golden View?" Grocchi tilted that round face.

"Well, things have gone wrong here, especially since the renovations began. Well, we really have had union troubles way before that, now that I think of it."

"Yes, miss, just tell me everything. I've heard there could be a strike."

She took a deep breath and began, "They've been holding a strike over our heads for months. The contract isn't settled yet. My boss was let go. He couldn't deal with them. We had a fire in the kitchen. Fire department found nothing. We've had two cars broken into. One car had spray paint on it. An elderly resident saw a man with binoculars looking in her window from the parking lot. One resident had her window broken."

"Yes, ma'am, anything else going on that's unusual?" asked the Lieutenant.

"Two residents escaped out of the side exit doors, despite the fact that they wore wander-guard ankle bracelets for security that were supposed to ring alarms as they went through the doorway and also set off a buzzer at the nurses' station. Neither alarm nor buzzer worked on either of these occasions. There was the rumor of two men in a car at the back of the home on the night of the kitchen fire. On one occasion, there was a disruptive individual singing and drinking in the outside parking lot who awakened residents, yet quickly disappeared before the police got there. These incidents add to the level of tension and concern among staff, too. I have arranged for a security guard to be available on evening duty now. I wrote this memo to staff and visitors to describe the new security program." Susie handed a copy of this memo to the Lieutenant.

Attention: all staff and visitors.

Beginning today, we will have security services for the exterior of the building.

Initially, we will only have coverage on nights, but we are planning on coverage during the afternoon as well. The primary responsibilities of the guard will be as follows:

1.Patrol the exterior of the building and parking lots.

2.Provide security for staff and visitors to and from their vehicles.

3.Assure that the rear parking lot is utilized by visitors only and not staff. The only exception will be those staff members who come and go from the building, such as marketing.

4.Provide a deterrence to crime, not function as the police. Any lost or stolen vehicles or articles will still be your responsibility. The guard is not empowered to apprehend criminals, only deter and report to the police.

5.De-fuse the situation or escort a disruptive individual from the building.

Lieutenant Grocchi's beady eyes scanned the page. He looked up at her. "You're really worried aren't you? Concerned for the old ladies, and all the old men, too. I can see that, how much you care."

"What do you think? Could it be planned? Would the union do it? Our business is way down, too. Last year at this time, our census was one hundred ninety-two. Today it's one hundred fifty-three. We're losing money."

"You did the right thing to call me. It should be looked into. Yes, miss, I'll investigate. I'll get to the bottom of it. What's Jack Wheatley think? He and I go way back, you know."

She shrugged. "The board is confused, too. They'd like to think it's just coincidence. There's more crime all around us, so maybe we're just getting our share. It was Jack's idea to hire the security guard, so I've done that. But you know all these things happening are very hard on the residents. They are very fearful. Some of their illnesses have gotten worse. It's hard to recover when the home is so unsettled by the renovation, too. Nothing's working right."

The Lieutenant nodded. "Murphy's Law. Be patient. Don't you worry. I'll look into it." The Lieutenant pushed his bulky frame, with some effort, up from the armchair. "I'll nose around a bit, ask a few questions, talk to Jack, maybe see the union steward, too. Here's my card. Why don't you go ahead and hire an afternoon guard, as well. Can't be too careful, can you?" Grocchi added as Susie rose to show him out. He scanned her white hose and heels as well.

"Thank you, Lieutenant," she said. "Thanks for coming over so soon. I hope you don't think I'm crazy, but maybe there's a pattern to this. The union's the only thing I can think of. Please call me anytime." As he walked out, Susie realized that Lieutenant Grocchi had not written any notes on his pad, and had only chewed on the pencil.

Chapter Eleven

To Staff:

July 3, 1995. Weather report is for a very hot, humid day with a bright sun and occasional clouds. Lo 64, Hi 87. Census is 151. Two expirations. All administrators are in the facility today, although the Director of Nursing will leave early afternoon to attend a discharge planning seminar. Crime report: suspicious male was observed several times last night in the main parking lot. Have a Happy Fourth of July.

SW

Somewhere deep inside Ursula a tiny spot of guilt grew. She had been a selfish, unloving daughter to Myra for too long, getting even in any way that she could. When Carmen told her about the slot machines going to Golden View, Myra's facility, a pang of daughterly shame got to her. She decided on a quick surprise visit. A quick call to Trudy told her that Myra was ailing, so Carmen's efforts were evidently working. God, why didn't the old bitch do the honorable thing and simply die.

While overcome with this less than burning desire to see dear old Mom, Ursula was ending a four-day visit to her Beverly Hills condo. A female director friend had sent a fresh, young Brad Pitt wannabe to her for polish and experience. She had done her best, sweating fearfully the whole time that Carmen would catch her. This thing with him was too good to lose until the right time.

She might even see Trudy and Helmut, possibly reunite with Mom, and screw the brains out of her old high school boyfriend if he could slip out on his wife and five kids one night. So, she prepared to leave the opulence of her southern California condo–done in all white damask, with white goat-skin furniture and African tiger and lion rugs scattered over the bleached oak plank floor–for the sounds, sights, and odors of long-term care. She dialed her travel agent, who could get her on a plane that night. She could be at Myra's bedside by late morning the next day.

The candles had burned down. The kid was actually posing on one of the tiger-skin rugs.

"Once more, Mrs Gronstein?

Ursula looked down. "No, no that's fine, Raoul. That's enough. You were great. It's Gronbeck, by the way, not Gronstein. And I'm not married. I'm not a Mrs ."

"Oh, I'm sorry. My English is not so good. You're not mad. You'll still put in a good word for me with the director, won't you? I'll do anything you want," he pleaded.

Ursula wanted him out of there. "Everything is fine. Here's the money I promised. Call me next week. I'll do whatever I promised you. Just call me. Bye." She leaned over and gave him a quick peck on the forehead, then padded to the combination whirlpool-sauna-shower.

During the ride to the airport, she called Carmen to tell him where she'd be for a day or two. Preparing for a European business trip, he gave her clearance.

Ursula wanted to make sure nothing got in the way of her half, a cool million, give or take some change. Yes, her own million, and she could kiss Carmen good-bye, too. She'd saved almost half a million with him, had all these clothes and jewelry, and now a new Rolls–not bad at all. She had a new life ahead of her, and one and half million to bankroll it.

The plane landed with an abrupt bounce, and Ursula woke with a start. She had packed only one carry-on bag, wore no make-up, and had slept soundly for three and one-half hours on the plane. It was mid-morning, so she'd be able to see Myra and talk to her. At some point, she had to ask about the money.

As she walked into the nursing home, the chaos and disruption hit her hard. Residents were scattered about hallways in beds or in wheelchairs. IV's, monitor equipment, and even ventilators accompanied the beds. Painters hung from ladders; electricians strung wire into holes; and wallpaper was being unrolled and glued onto bedroom walls. How could old people live in this confusion? Ursula always moved out of her condo when she made repairs, returning only when all of the improvements were completed. The receptionist greeted her with a helpful smile.

Ursula asked, "May I see my mother, Myra Gronbeck? I'm her daughter, Ursula."

"Yes, of course," replied the receptionist. "I don't recall meeting you before. I'm Cathy."

Ursula returned the smile. "Hi, I've never been here. I live a long way away."

In the doorway of her mother's room she paused. For a moment, she wasn't sure which of the two old women in the room was her mother. Both slept, bent over in wheelchairs. Myra had lost both legs at the knees, so Ursula walked over to the nearest woman, checked her legs, and tapped her mother lightly on the shoulder. She wasn't sure what to say. She probably should have alerted the facility and Myra that she was arriving, but what the hell.

"Hi, Mom. It's me, Ursula." She gently shook her shoulder. The shawl fell away, revealing the bony, skeletal upper body. Ursula jolted. Someone should have prepared her for this. She shook her again. This time, she leaned over and kissed her gently on the cheek. "Mom, Ursula is here. It's been a long time."

Myra opened one eye gingerly, then the other, momentarily confused. "Who? What did you say? Who are you?"

"Mom, it's me, it's your daughter, Ursula. I'm here from the west coast to see you. Wake up, please. I'd like to talk."

Myra stared blindly into space. "Let me feel your face. My hands, hold my hands. Is it really you? I'm completely blind now, you know. I can't see a thing. Yes, I remember that ring. Your nails are so long."

Ursula let Myra feel her face and touch her skin. They held hands, for an instant the past put aside; the bitterness left behind; without need, fear, or disappointment. The moment wouldn't last long, and they both knew better than to waste it.

Margaret awoke and stared at Urusla, rubbing her face and readjusted the breathing apparatus. She buzzed a nursing aide to check the tank. "I'm Margaret," she said in too loud of a voice. "I'm Margaret, Myra's roommate and friend. Do we know each other?" Her face contorted momentarily with pain, but she continued to gaze with narrowed eyes.

"Nice to meet you, Margaret. I'm the black sheep of the family. I'm Myra's daughter, Ursula."

"She came to see me from the west coast. How do you like that?" Myra added with pride. "And she's no black sheep. It's just been a long time. Isn't she beautiful?"

Margaret agreed. "Yes, very beautiful, and she has beautiful clothes too. Nice to meet you, Ursula. Glad you're here. Do you want privacy with your mother, because I can wheel myself to the lounge if you want to visit in private."

"Oh no," Ursula said. "Thanks, but this is fine. I was in California, and I got homesick and wanted to see Mom. So I just did it. Flew all night, and here I am. What do we do for fun?"

"Well, well, a chip off the old block. Myra and I were talking about fun just this morning at breakfast. Fun isn't a word you hear a lot around here. Since Myra's been feeling better the past few days, we were talking about playing the slots after lunch. Do you ever play slot machines?"

Ursula answered, “Yes, in gambling clubs in Vegas and Reno, but you only have river-boat gambling here, don’t you?

“No,” Margaret corrected her. “We do it right here.”

Carmen had told her about the slot machines going to the nursing home, but she simply replied, “Well, I’d love to see it. I’m going to go get a room nearby and clean up. I’ll come back after lunch, and we can gamble the afternoon away.”

“It’s not for real money,” explained Myra. “They use tokens that look like coins. That way, we have all the excitement, but we don’t lose any money. Tell the nurse, Meg. Tell her we want to be on the list for this afternoon and that there will be *three* of us. Tell her that my daughter, Ursula, will be with us, and that she may stay for dinner, too. It’s three dollars for a guest. Tonight we’re having meat loaf.”

Ursula leaned over and gave Myra a quick hug and a kiss on the cheek. So frail. In her dirty and stained dress, she needed a bath. The room needed to be aired out and deodorized. The hallways were too full of people and things. So many confusing sounds erupted, a cacophony of electronic music, and the creaks of ancient wheelchairs–old bones trying to walk or roll, going nowhere fast, as they say. Who in their right mind could live in this? She felt about to either pass out or go crazy, maybe just explode.

“Bye, honey, take care. Remember how I called you ‘Ursie,’ and you didn’t like it? You thought it sounded too much like horsy. I always liked it, though. Can I call you Ursie?”

"Yes, Mom, it's okay. See you both after lunch."

Ursula took a cab to a nearby motel. She ordered a steak sandwich and a bottle of Heineken's dark beer, and then she luxuriated in the tiny shower stall with its weak water flow. She missed the decadent luxury and the calm predictability of her own life.

Myra and a nursing home were not part of the definition of her own life. As she laid-out fresh clothes, a black linen skort, a simple white silk Polo t-shirt, and gold sandals, she realized how different from Myra she had become. If she were old and frail, she'd want round-the-clock nurses, and she'd want to be closeted alone in a plush condo with a view of the sea. Young sybaritic men could do as they wanted with her body.

Later, she walked back into their room without knocking. Jeremy sat talking to Myra and Margaret.

"Well, girlfriends, toodleloo. Good luck gambling. Well, this must be Ursula. Give me your autograph, Miss Movie Star. I'm Jeremy. Myra, you've got some good looker. Sweetie, trust a man's eye. She's a total knockout. Nice to see you, Ursula." Like a whirlwind, he breezed out of the room before Ursula could answer.

Ursula stood there. She decided to be positive. "I've eaten and cleaned up, and I feel lucky. Let's go win enough to cover our expenses, as we say in Vegas."

The charge nurse had informed her that Myra was better today than in weeks. A cloud had lifted momentarily. Apparently, the nausea was gone, and she almost seemed like herself.

"Okay, Ursula, you push me, and Margaret can wheel herself into the hall until we find Johnnetta or Jeannette, okay?"

"Yes, Mother." At least Myra had shown a little spunk. Maybe some hope existed. She half-wished for some.

"You haven't asked about your sister and her family yet," chided Myra.

"I talked to them not long ago, Mom. They keep me posted on your situation. Last Christmas, I bought you the new wheelchair. Trudy made all of the arrangements for it. Remember?"

"No, she didn't tell me. What about your life? You haven't told me anything yet. You're not married, are you? No children?"

Neither of them had said much, intimate details missing. As she deteriorated under the stressful physical and psychological conditions, Myra understood virtually nothing concerning Ursula's life.

They walked very slowly. Ursula offered, "Nothing new. No marriage. No kids. No husband. I date a nice guy who's in the hotel business, got a good job as a consultant, so I travel a bit. I live in a nice condo, just like you always liked, and I've done it in white and leather, in California. You got my postcards, didn't you? Let's go gamble. I'm getting itchy to make a killing," Ursula said with a smile. "Let's get an aide to help Margaret."

"What kind of a consultant are you, Ursula?" asked Margaret. Ursula tilted, slightly off balance for a moment. She suspected that Margaret was well aware of the truth of the family situation. The negligible contact with Myra these past few months. They had fought with each other. The daughters seldom talked, angry over the settlement of their father's will. Myra's old and sick, Margaret would reason, so they'll have their money soon enough.

"On various business matters. Hiring women and minorities. How to open management up to new ideas and practices. I do some training of high level staff on these issues of diversity and affirmative action."

Margaret began, "Must be fascinating–"

Jeannette grabbed the chair's handles. Margaret's smile kept broadening as she stared at Ursula.

The charge nurse had said that Myra almost always said "no" to everything–to food, to movies, to TV, to books on tape, to the music and exercise program, to church services, and to life itself. Today, the feisty tomboy in Myra shone through un-dulled by the years of suffering and disappointment.

As they approached Room 214-A, the crowded hallway echoed with laughter, the low screams of joy, the "Oh no" of the close calls, the near jackpot. Urusula's heartbeat quickened until she realized that the casino had sent along an audio tape that ran for hours–an actual recording of the interior of a small gaming room from Reno, Nevada– the long, low hum of the machines, the clicking sounds of dice rolling, roulette wheels whirring, highball glasses clinking in toasts of hope, and the high-pitched, electronic music of the slot jackpot. The tape provided a very real, actually surreal, atmosphere to the gambling experience.

Ursula smiled at the machines and the sights and sounds of the little old gray-haired ladies sitting hunched up in wheelchairs at odd angles to the pull levers on the slots. She wanted to bolt. The sooner she got out of there, the better. She'd have to tell her mother what each pull produced. She could fake the fun. Hell, he'd never see Myra alive again anyway.

The room, approximately the size of an ordinary living room, had been quickly painted all white with simple white linoleum tiles on the floor. One or two slot machines leaned against each of three walls for a total of five. All walls held machines except the one near the door that contained a homemade wooden bar holding coffee, tea, and orange juice. The machines were Bally. Two had been dollar slots; two quarter slots; and the other was originally set for dimes. Three types of tokens were available, one unique for each type of machine. Each resident received ten dollars worth of each type of token for their assigned hour of play. If one lost, more money was available.

"Three bars. I got three bars. That's worth one hundred bucks, Cas. How do you like that?" screamed a made-up woman.

"That's Elizabeth," Margaret whispered as they entered slowly. "She beats the machines with her shoes."

Elizabeth screamed at Jeannette as she walked by, "Bring me a Beefeater martini and a pack of Dunhill cigarettes, right away. Hurry, and there will be a five dollar tip in it for you. Goddammit, I said get off your butt and get me a drink, or I'll tell the pit boss you're a lazy bitch. He's a friend of mine, and he'll fire your sorry ass out of this hotel."

Cas whispered something to Elizabeth and pointed to the three newcomers.

Three machines sat vacant, so after obtaining their tokens, each of them went to a machine. Margaret wheeled herself to a machine that used playing card figures as a theme, while Ursula's had Elvis Presley memorabilia and Myra's had a sports theme.

Myra almost bounced, feeling more alive than the first time she had gone gambling. Ursula could help if she had a problem, and she could get additional tokens.

"I can't reach it. I'm too weak and small. Don't forget, I'm blind," she said, wanting Ursula to help her, although she could play by simply pushing one of the buttons. She wanted to win a big jackpot. Susie had set up a competition so that the individual who hit the most jackpots, regardless of size, got a prize at the end of the month, probably a paperback book or a set of playing cards. If she won, the gift could go to Margaret.

Ursula was there! And she'd kissed her earlier. Her daughter had *come to see her*. What could be better? At least a year or two had passed since she'd been with Ursula, maybe longer. Time slipped away from her now and again. Bittersweet tears rimmed the edges of her eyes, but no one could see them with her oversized dark glasses.

Ursula said into her ear, "We shouldn't have fought like we did. I don't blame you for getting sick of it. We should have been more patient."

"Yes, dear," replied Myra. "I'm sorry, too, that it happened the way it did. There will be plenty for you and Trudy when the time comes." She wanted to make sure that Ursula felt reassured. Ursula had apologized in her way, and now knew that the millions were still there. Trudy had surely told her they were in trust earning interest–Medicare and Medicaid and her private indemnity insurance took good care of Myra's financial needs.

"I'm not worried about money. I'm here to see you. We're together."

A jackpot lit up in the corner on the card machine. Reds and blacks were striking as Margaret hit two hundred and fifty quarters with three "spades." Everyone cheered, however weak their voices. Then Margaret pulled off another one hundred quarters on the machine with three cherries, but she had bet three quarters instead of one, and the payoff was magnificent. Myra loved the music–kind of like an old time nickelodeon–when a jackpot hit. She, herself, just hit fifty quarters.

"Mom, you got fifty. Want to put it down on winnings, or play it off?"

Myra said, "Let's play it. Let it ride."

"Fine, you got three orange baseballs, with two of three black baseball bats on the next line. If that had hit, you would have won five hundred dollars. You'd have to report that much to Uncle Sam and pay taxes."

How surprising that Ursula shared the pleasure! Her daughter had actually laughed. So did Myra. Myra was in the zone. Relaxed and calm, her feelings were suspended in a kind of self-hypnosis brought on by the music, the background noise, her daughter, an incredible desire to win more than the others, and a deliberate, almost unbelievable degree of concentration. She focused on Ursula's description of the rolling visual numbers and symbols before her, her mind's eye on the three objects as they lined up. She wanted three gold baseballs, a twenty-five hundred dollar jackpot. She'd win the prize for the month. She knew it. If she could only get three gold balls. Come on balls.

Myra sat almost upright in her chair. Mind over matter. She recalled the great baseball pitcher Satchel Paige's motto: "If you don't mind, it don't matter." At the moment, it didn't matter. She was high; excited but controlled; that tomboy again, trapped in a tree with three guys trying to get her. King of the sand mountain at the beach, keeping the other kids off her hill. Riveted on the slot, she felt positive, joyous, and exuberant. Was it a miracle? What happened to the constant nagging worry? Where was the sadness? Blues turned to green. Could she trust it? Should she tell Ursula? Did Margaret feel it, too?

Now that Ursula returned, the next step was to see Trudy. She envisioned daughters reunited, at peace with their mother. After the bonds of love and need reattached, then she could truly leave this world at peace. The family would be together.

Myra stopped playing for a moment, motioning Ursula closer to her left ear. "Can you hear me?"

"Yes, of course I can. Glad you're enjoying yourself. What is it?" Ursula asked.

"There's something I need to say, now that you're here. It's been a secret."

"Yes?"

"I've never told Trudy or Helmut either," confided Myra. "You won't get angry at me again and stay away? I need you."

"No, no, Mom, I'm here. I'm right here."

"I gave half to Margaret and her husband," whispered Myra.

"You did what?"

"I gave half to Margaret. I changed my will. There will still be plenty for you girls."

Ursula's body shuddered. Ursula let go of the wheelchair, turned to walk out, leaned over, shrieked at her mother, "Goodbye, forever!" and ran out of the gambling den.

In a room full of tokens and refurbished Bally slots, Myra began to cry.

Tom talked on a pay phone in the basement of the home near the utility room to Lou Giordano. "So, we should go ahead and do it?"

"Yeah," Lou confirmed.

"Okay, they voted one seventy-nine to eleven to do it whenever you guys say so."

"Yeah, Tony Dee wants it now. No rough stuff. Burn wood in some barrels. Looks good. Stand by the front and walk back and forth with the signs."

"Do we try to block the driveways to either the rear lot or the other parking lot?"

"No."

"Will the security guy give us any heat?"

"No, he's been talked to."

"Should we yell or cuss at the RN's or the administrators? Or the food company when they drive through?"

"No, well maybe a little bit. What the hell. You gotta have some fun, don't you?"

"Just for one day."

"Yeah."

"We should tell the administrator that. Just for one day. No rough stuff. Just to show 'em what we can do."

"Yeah, fine. Do that."

"Maybe this Susie-puss will cave in. The other guy was a dick, wasn't he?"

"Yeah, he wouldn't budge on money. Thought he was a big time hard-ass, that Anderson did."

"Do my union staff get anything?"

"Get what?"

"Money. They'll lose a day's pay, maybe more. Their clothes will get dirty. Gas money. You know."

"Yeah. Tell 'em they'll get the same money as their job for that day. And all they can eat. We'll have donuts, sandwiches, coffee, Cokes–maybe beer–all day long. Got to enjoy it, have a little fun."

"Only for one day?"

"Yeah. Just one. What are you worried about?"

"Well, we care about the old ladies. We know them. We don't want them any more scared or upset than they have to be. They've been through enough out here."

"What have they been through?"

"Well, the place has been a fucking mess, like a hurricane was here."

"Too bad. Hey now, you don't think the union . . . You don't think we had anything to do with that shit, do you?"

"Hell no, I know that."

"We play by the book. We're ready for a strike. Or a mediator. Tony and me want you guys to get what's coming to you. We're for you. We'll be there when we have the final sit-down, the negotiations. When this is over, you and Millie can go to Vegas. It'll be comped, won't cost you a thing. You two have done good. You deserve a long weekend to relax."

"Thanks, Lou. Thanks a lot."

"It's okay, Tom. Don't mention it. *Ciao*. Keep me posted. Give my best to Millie, and your wife, too.

Doc walked through the hallway, dodging med. carts and IV stands, touching a shoulder here and there with a supportive pat. "How are you this morning, Mary Lou?"

"Doc, Doc, a moment please?" requested Jeremy.

Doc headed straight for him. "Morning, what's up?"

"Well, I'm worried. M&M's are not doing too well. Margaret's awful depressed about Myra. Yesterday, she just sat there. No humor. No jokes. No smiles from either."

Doc nodded. "Thanks for the update. I'm on my way there." He paused and scanned Jeremy's frowning dark eyes. "Something bothering you?"

Even with residents and other nurses within earshot, Jeremy said, "I made a mistake."

"So? Mistakes happen."

"I gave Elizabeth Zantac, not Zyprexa. No problem, I gave her an antidote. I told Dr Ramantha, and he told me what to do."

"Good, then no harm was done. She's okay, isn't she? I don't prescribe, but it doesn't sound fatal. Shouldn't have any side effects or adverse reactions, except nausea."

"I didn't write it down. I didn't put it in her chart."

"Why not?" asked Doc.

"I'd be disciplined by the Director of Nursing. Maybe lose some money. Can't afford it. What should I do?"

"You're an honest guy, and a good caretaker. You have to look in the mirror when you shave every morning. You know what to do."

"Thanks, Doc. I've been feeling lousy. I could grow a beard, but I'll do the chart." They did a high-five. Jeremy's smile was back. "You're all right, Doc, for somebody over forty. And you're straight. Oh, my God. You *are* a hoot." They both laughed.

Doc wanted to introduce himself to his new patient, Virginia Barrett, so he stopped briefly at her room on the way to see Margaret. He knocked, announced himself, and then peeked into the darkened room. The blinds had been pulled on both windows, so only a thin sliver of light cut the room in half from the floor to the ceiling.

Disheveled bed clothes adorned the empty bed on the right. A woman lay under a heavy wool blanket in the other bed. She turned over suddenly to glare at Doc.

"Who are you?"

He'd startled her. "Sorry. I'm Doc, a psychologist to see Virginia Barrett. Is that you?"

"Yes," she squeaked, "I like carrots. Love carrots."

"No, sorry, I'm here to visit Virginia Barrett. Are you Virginia?"

The squeak turned into a high-pitched whine. "I like carrots."

Doc backed out and looked again at the nameplate near the door. Yes, Virginia Barrett lived in that room. But this woman was her roommate, Dawn Kowalski.

Doc hurried to Margaret's room, regretting scaring Dawn. He'd rarely gone to meet a new resident without asking for a description or examining the individual photo near the front of every medical chart. Perhaps Dawn wouldn't remember what had happened–and would forgive him if she did.

Doc knocked more loudly than usual, then asked, again with more than customary volume, "Morning, it's Doc. May I come in?"

After a moment of silence, Margaret looked up from her crossword puzzle and said weakly, "Yes." Myra appeared to be asleep, still in bed. Margaret was dressed and sitting in her wheelchair, trying to do the *New York Times* crossword puzzle from Sunday's paper. She never could do more than half of it, a fact she blamed on those fancy people in New York City.

"I did win the spelling bee in eighth grade," she told Doc. She looked up at him. Then, she glanced away quickly. "I know I look worn out. I don't want any sympathy. I'm sick of it. I just want to be left alone. Sometimes I wish I was blind like Myra."

"Feeling real blue today. Tune out the world. Shall we hook up the portable tank and do some traveling?" asked Doc, wanting to provide her with a moment of cheer and support and unwilling to give in completely to her need for privacy. "It won't be a long trip, I promise. Guess you're not much in the mood to see me."

Margaret continued to look down. "If you want to, but not for too long. I'm tired. My stomach hurts terribly."

Doc took the handles of her chair and wheeled her to the lounge. "Let's go visit Billy the bird."

Billy, a very fat parakeet with green outer feathers, a yellow bulging belly, had a long curved beak that often got in his way. It needed trimming to allow him to eat and drink more easily, but possibly provided a natural barrier to obesity. Billy jumped and hopped from his swing to the stand in front of his mirror, then rubbed his beak on several white chalky chunks attached to his cage. The bottom of the cage provided supporting evidence for the overeating habits suggested by his protruding belly.

"Billy looks good, Doc," said Margaret. "Please push me closer to him." The resident and family lounge was probably too cold for Margaret, but she didn't complain. She simply pulled her lap robe closer to her body and tried to button the top buttons on her sleeper. She couldn't do it, so Doc helped. "Do you think he knows he's alone, locked up in a cage like he is?"

"You're really worried and sad today, aren't you? Even Billy doesn't make you smile."

"It's kind of crazy. I want to be alone like Billy, but some things keep going around and around in my mind. Can't seem to stop them."

"What are they?"

"Well, you've heard this before. You know about my first child and my first marriage. You know all that stuff. I told you already."

"Yes, go ahead."

"Well, you know, I feel bad about it. I never told my husband, or my parents, the complete truth. We got married, but in my heart, I was never sure it was his baby."

Doc nodded. "You protected them. And him."

"No, I kidded myself. I protected myself from the truth. From their wrath. From his mistrust." Margaret shook with tremors and sobs, but no tears.

"You felt the shame and guilt long enough," offered Doc. "Can you forgive yourself?"

"I've tried. Can't seem to." The tears began to pour out. She'd doubtlessly cried over these events many times. "I tried to make it up to James, and my parents, too. I did in ways, but I never told them everything. I guess I'll take that sin to my grave."

"Forgive yourself. There's nothing to be done about it now. It's over and done with. Don't you agree, Billy? Margaret's okay, and she should let it go." Doc badly imitated a parakeet's voice. He squeaked, "Yes, Doc, yes. Margaret's a very good person. A good friend. A great mother. A good wife. Tweet, tweet."

Margaret relaxed for a moment. She smiled wanly and looked down. "I'm ashamed of something else. I get sick of being brave. Sometimes I just wish it would all be over with. I love to see the kids and their kids, but they've got their own lives. They could use our life insurance money. They don't need us anymore."

"It's a long road, isn't it?"

"Sometimes I don't want to have a meaningful death. Just fall asleep, and that's it. All these goodbyes and thank you's. It's a lot of work for me. Birds don't have this pressure to die with so much hooply-doo."

Again, Doc tweaked, "It's easier for me, but it's so lonely in this cage. I overeat. No friends. No family. Just hop around. Can't fly. Haven't ever seen my children again. I'm just a bird in a cage." They both laughed this time. Billy tried to bite Doc's finger and rubbed his beak furiously on the cage's wire wall.

One of the aides walked in and offered to clean the cage and trim Billy's beak. Three votes yes, no nays.

"And I'm so worried about Myra. She doesn't say anything. Sometimes she's delirious. Ursula got mad and left because Myra told her she'd given me half of everything in her will. I didn't know it either. I'm ashamed of myself. I can't take it."

Billy nipped the finger of the attendant as she held him, and tried to use a fingernail cutter to trim the edges of his beak. She gave up, cleaned his cage, and left.

"I've almost been ready to ask for a new roommate. She drags me down. She doesn't talk. She looks like she's given up. She's given me wealth I don't need, or deserve. What can I say to her? I'm shocked. I don't want to hurt her feelings. I love her too much for that."

"Margaret, that's quite a statement, so many different passionate feelings in it–love, frustration, and shame. You're really quite a person," said Doc. "You're in long-term care, and Billy's in a cage. Both of you have lost your natural homes, where you wanted to be, but Billy couldn't, and doesn't, have what you have. You understand so much. You know what's happening in your life. You have the feelings and knowledge that make you a very wonderful, honest, and lovely human being." Billy almost seemed to understand as he sang furiously and hopped to his swing, much like a happy and exuberant child on a playground.

"Here's the worst, Doc. If she's going to die, I almost hope it's soon. I don't have time to grieve for months or years. I just want someone to care for. I'll miss Myra, but I'm too old to let it ruin what's left. You sure made me talk today, Doc. I don't know whether to thank you or not. Billy's nice, isn't he?"

Chapter Twelve

To Staff:

July 10, 1995. Weather report is for continued hot and humid weather, with a slight chance of rain. Lo 61, Hi 88. Census is 150. One discharge to the hospital. Administration is in today, but all other department heads are attending a mandatory seminar on "Death and Dying." Crime report: one staff car broken into in the rear lot–CD player stolen.

SW

The dawn, grey and overcast, provided unseasonable ground fog hiding the adjacent fields in full mid-summer bloom. Neatly arranged layers of pale blue and pink-white clouds whispered at the horizon, with swirling foamy white ones closer to the home. The sun would come up soon and quickly dismiss the fog and clouds.

Six strikers, four women and one man, trudged in front of the home, not yet blocking the driveways or the walkways.

Tom and Millie led the way, holding placards on thick wooden sticks. Phrases, clearly visible even at early dawn, included "Unfair To Labor," "We Want Our Rights," and "Honor Its Agreements," the latter pointed directly at the administration and the board. Johnnetta, Jeannette, and Jane walked as well. The women either wore green and yellow paisley smocks from the kitchen or French Blue hospital-type blouse and slacks uniforms used by the nurses' aides. Tom was smoking; so was Millie. He felt slightly chilled although the temperature topped seventy this early morning. The chill came largely from excitement and fear. The excitement could be traced to the long-awaited one-day strike, the fear to the anxiety over the strike failing to get the union what it wanted, added to the potential backfire if it unsettled or disturbed residents beyond its intent.

The union people praised Tom for telling the administration the facts: one day only, no intimidation, and no one would be hurt or threatened. Scabs were acceptable, or else the regular RN's and administrators could manage and operate the home for a day. See how they liked bathing and cleaning the residents and their rooms. In an emergency, a real emergency that threatened a resident's life, a few strikers would come back to work.

Modern unionism, thought Tom. Millie had smiled seductively at him throughout, obviously proud of him as well.

An old police cruiser, probably a 1988 or 1989 Plymouth, dark blue with white trim, drove up slowly with flashing lights, but no siren. It parked on the side of the road, and out-squeezed Lieutenant Grocchi who hiked up his low riding, brown polyester slacks and began to stroll over to the strikers, with a slight smile on his beefy face.

"Morning, folks. I'll have ham and four eggs, over easy. Corn muffins, if you got 'em fresh."

Tom and Millie had known him since the second grade at St. Joseph's. He was still an anachronism, and Tom found accepting that he had become a detective difficult.

Millie feigned a petulant frown. "You know I didn't cook this morning, you big tub of lard. We're on strike."

Tom offered, "We'll have donuts and coffee in a few minutes. Come on over, have a smoke, and protect us from this cruel world."

"This place has me worried," Grocchi began. "All the troubles they've had. Not just the union–the fire and the car break-ins. What do you folks think?"

"Yeah, it's something," Tom said. "But the fixing up is better. The painting and wallpapering are almost done."

Millie added, "I've wondered about it, too, Lieutenant, to be honest with you. I've wondered myself. It could look like us union people, but it's not so."

"No, no I wouldn't believe it of any of you. I've known you and Tom most of my life. I wouldn't believe it for a minute." Grocchi took out his Marlboros and offered them to everyone. "You're my friends."

Jeannette said, "I heard there was a car with two guys in it in the parking lot on the morning of the fire."

"Yes, your administrator mentioned that. Can't find them guys or the car. I've written to the FBI to see if they could let their bomb squad investigate. We couldn't find anything." Grocchi shifted slightly from one foot to the other. When he stood still for a few minutes, his weight was difficult to balance. He reminded Tom of Orson Welles in his full maturity. Grocchi turned toward his car and almost nonchalantly asked, "Would your union bosses in Cleveland do all this stuff, worry people to death? You know."

Tom sighed. "We wondered too. But they said no, absolutely no. So it's kids, coincidence, and accidents, I guess. Shit happens, you know. What can go wrong has gone wrong. Maybe it's not over yet. Our strike is only one day, though, and there will be absolutely no rough stuff here."

As he opened the door of the cruiser, Grocchi looked back and said, "Thought so. Thanks Tom, Millie, and everyone. Knew I could count on you all. Don't be too jealous, but I'm going downtown to the diner for corned beef hash, six eggs, and fresh cornbread. And ketchup. You know how I love ketchup on everything." He drove away slowly.

"He'll add sausage and gravy when he gets to the diner. He thinks we're up to something, doesn't he?" asked Millie frowning.

"Yeah, I suppose it looks that way to him," agreed Tom. "The barrels need more wood. Keep up the fires."

Margaret wheeled herself to the window. She liked the new pale pink and white striped drapes. The mechanism to open and shut them worked perfectly.

"They're burning wood in barrels. They've got signs. It looks like a real strike."

Myra tried to turn over in her chair. "How many of them?"

"Maybe six or seven. I see our two aides. They're there. So is Millie. I'm trying to wave to her, but she doesn't see me. I can't get my arm high enough."

"They won't hurt us?"

"Oh no, and the RN's will change our beds and clean us up. We'll get food and medicine, just for the day."

"I don't care anyway, not enough to be scared," concluded Myra. "I really don't." She coughed slightly and fell back to sleep. It was more of a coma these days than a waking-sleeping cycle.

Margaret felt increasingly helpless in her attempt to cheer Myra up or make useful suggestions. As for the strike, she still believed in it, but now it angered her. She felt exploited and used by both sides. She was paying good money (or at least government insurance was paying good money), to the home for proper care. Why should she be inconvenienced or have her routine disrupted?

She wanted Jeremy to nurse her and either Jeannette or Johnnetta to help her ambulate. She didn't need or want one of the other RN's or nurse aides. Let them do paperwork and hunt for better-paying jobs. At least that's what she'd been told they usually did.

She figured they got blamed for a lot of things going wrong. The administrators and the union could fight it out. Of course, she favored the working union people, but didn't want to be caught in the crossfire. She was just plenty disgusted. Plenty. She tried to wave to Millie again. Millie had been standing near the fat cop earlier, but now she was facing the home and still didn't see her.

A local TV station truck with a small round antenna attached to the top pulled up near the placard-carrying strikers. The pretty-faced news reporter stepped out of the passenger side, while the driver, a slender, bearded man, carried a portable TV camera on his right shoulder with several black bags strapped to his left shoulder.

"You ought to see this," Margaret said. "You won't believe it."

"Well, what is it? I'm awake now. Don't tease me. I don't feel so hot, and you darn well know it."

"It's a TV crew," said Margaret. "They're here because of the strike. I'll bet they interview some of the staff. My gosh, they'll be on TV."

"Who's there?" asked Myra.

"It's a woman and a man," answered Margaret. "I've seen her do the news sometimes. She's good, and she's real cute." Margaret shifted her position and sat down in her wheelchair. She could just barely see out over the window sill.

"I know, it's WNHA Channel Seven. I've seen it. Shift my gizmo for me, and turn off CNN so we can see her if it's live."

"What do you mean, *live*?" asked Margaret.

"If they put her on TV right now, then it's called live," explained Myra. She had been moved to the Barcalounger type chair, in which the stumps of her legs barely reached the front edge.

Margaret watched as the newswoman fluffed her blonde hair and smoothed the wrinkles on the collar of her white blouse. She patted her cheeks slightly and wet her full, ruby lips.

Myra listened attentively to the television.

"Good morning. This is Mary Anton with a live Channel Seven special report from the Golden View Rehabilitation Center on County Road Fourteen. An unusual event is taking place here as a one-day strike gets into swing at Golden View. Many staff such as nurse aides, maintenance workers, dietary staff, and others are involved. Their local union is flexing its muscles in the ongoing battle with the local board and management at Golden View."

Mary then walked directly to the striking group. She approached Millie and asked, "Can you tell us your name and what you feel is going on here today?"

Millie put her placard down. She smoothed her hair and hiked her jeans. The camera man captured her actions. Now presentable, Millie said, "Well, Ms Anton, we're having a non-violent one-day only strike to make our point. We want more wages and more benefits. We deserve it. We only want what's coming to us." She kept putting her hand to her face, turning her head for the microphone and moving her shoulders rhythmically. The TV screen was not kind to that image.

Myra yelled, "Hey, it's Millie on TV. How's she look?"

Margaret stared out and watched, but couldn't be sure of the details. She'd have to look at their TV screen for the minutia that Myra liked to know.

"What do you see? Tell me. I can't stand it!"

"All right, I'll look at the TV for you." Margaret wheeled herself around the chair to the front of the wall-mounted television. "Millie looks beautiful. Her eyes are bright and shiny. Her hair is real curly and you can almost see the highlights. Her figure looks good."

"She spoke beautifully. She really did." said Myra.

"I know. I heard it, too. They're interviewing Tom now. He looks good, but his shirt has got some big spot on it. Too bad he didn't clean up, but he didn't know the TV people would come out here."

Tom answered, "Hell, you know, we wouldn't hurt a soul. I know every one of those sweet little ladies. We love them all."

Mary asked, "So, it's only a one-day strike to make your point."

Tom finally looked down and brushed at the large discoloration furiously with the back of his right hand. He answered, "Yes, definitely just one day. We plan to end by four-thirty today, so that staff can be back on duty by five o'clock for dinner and bedtime pills. If anything breaks today, toilets or showers, I'll go fix them, strike or no strike. I've been the head of maintenance here for many, many years."

Mary's pretty face filled the TV screen. "Thanks, Tom. It's obvious that the staff members on strike today want to make their point, but not frighten or upset any of the residents unnecessarily. It's been widely known in the community for years that staff at Golden View are overworked and under paid. Mary Anton signing off from Golden View Rehabilitation Center for Channel Seven news direct. More later from this strike scene."

Margaret looked out the window again. The camera operator turned off the camera and the additional artificial light. Then he panned the sparkling flames in the barrel, and the other strikers who now marched more vigorously with their placards. Finally, he took a full shot of Golden View from the front, where the circular driveway curved into the main entryway that fronted the facility's lobby and admissions office.

Mary unbundled the wires from the hand-held microphone and freed herself from several other small pieces of equipment. Margaret watched Tom give the others their coffee or donuts.

The driver and Mary rushed to the TV truck and opened the doors quickly, enveloping them.

Margaret said, "Tom looked nervous, but what he said was good. They do care about us. It's only for today. I'm still for them. I hope they get it."

Myra said, "My, my, our own place on TV, and we heard it, and it was right out in front. Maybe they should get what they want. I just don't want a whole lot of strangers coming in here. It's bad enough to be here."

Margaret laughed. "You change your mind often enough. If you hadn't come here, we wouldn't have met. Do you ever think of it that way?"

Myra chuckled reluctantly. "Please put CNN back on. I have to make the best of this place."

Residents seldom visited each other's rooms, but the strike had later stimulated a congregation in Myra and Margaret's room. Margaret had mentioned the idea of meeting to discuss the strike to Norma at breakfast. That brief conversation led to Cas, Elizabeth, Norma, and Carl crowding onto Margaret's bed, while Myra snored peacefully in her chair with CNN on low volume. They awaited Mabel's arrival. Margaret sat in her wheelchair, breathing more comfortably than usual. She was the titular chairperson, if such were needed, even though Mabel was their official representative on the Resident's Council.

"I'm busy as a cockroach, everybody, but I'll try to answer any questions you have," said Jeremy. The strike kept him so busy, however, that he couldn't promise to stay for the entire meeting. Jeremy stood with his back to the partially ajar door.

"So, where is she?" asked Norma.

Margaret answered, "You knew she'd forget. Mabel can't remember what she had for breakfast. I did ask her charge nurse to remind her, but they're so busy now."

Jeremy suggested, "Let's go ahead. You folks can have a paragraph typed for her to bring to the Council meeting, when you decide what your position is on the strike."

"Position, my ass," said Elizabeth.

Cas said, "What he means is what we want to say. Our position is our viewpoint, as residents here, on the strike. What it means to us. Okay, Elizabeth?"

"Yes, but who gives a shit. I want food, a shower, a cigarette, and some medication to sleep better. Who gives a shit about the strike? Besides, that new aide today is a real cute young guy. He turns me on." She glanced at Cas. "Just kidding, honeybuns, just kidding." She reached for his hand, but he pulled it back.

"So what are your questions, all you sweet things. And you, too, Cas," Jeremy said, winking at Cas.

Cas replied, "What do you think of what Elizabeth said? She said what she wants from this place."

"Yes, she did," answered Jeremy. "She wants good personal care. She deserves it, and she expects it. She'll get it, too. All RN's are here today. Other staff are helping out. She'll get good care from all of them, I promise."

"What if the strike lasts?" asked Margaret. "Or, another strike comes up soon."

"Yes, Margaret, good questions," said Jeremy. "You're a sweetie, and you should know it's only one day–just today. The union voted on it and made it clear. Just a one-day show of union feeling and support."

"If it lasted, it'd be shit. Real shit. We wouldn't know the people. They wouldn't know us. I'd feel horrible. There could be spies, too." Elizabeth said.

"Christ, Elizabeth, let's just get it over with. It's just a big worry to us all. We never expected anything like this." Carl's brow crinkled and tense lines surrounded his pursed lips.

"Carl, you shouldn't worry so much," said Norma. "You always worry about everything, and then it doesn't happen."

"I don't care. I'm against it. Hell, they've all got jobs. Let them work hard and get raises that way. I'm against a strike where us old-timers are concerned. Dead set against it."

"Carl, please relax," said Norma.

Margaret said, "Jeremy can't stay forever. What do we need to know from him?" The pain on her left side came sharp and constant, yet she didn't want to complain or be too irritable.

Myra awoke suddenly, face contorted.

Margaret explained to her quickly, "It's sort of a committee. We're meeting about the strike. Jeremy's here, too."

"Oh, yes, I remember. Jeremy. CNN says unions can be bad."

"Well, I'm no expert," replied Jeremy. "This union has been good for staff. They've gotten higher wages and more vacations. They have a pension plan, so it's been good."

Margaret knew that Myra looked awful to the others. Dark rings around her eyes, and she'd lost more weight. But her feistiness still arose at times.

Myra asked, "What about people who want to work here, but don't want to have anything to do with a union? Don't they have rights, too?"

"Yes, they do, Myra. They sure do. Once staff members see that the union helps them, they all seem to join it."

Mabel wandered in, her hair disheveled, and the middle button on her purple silk blouse missing. She wore one red sock, the other foot bare. "Is there going to be a strike?" she asked. "Why are you all here in Margaret's room? What's going on anyway?"

"Christ, she's crazier than I am," muttered Elizabeth to Cas. "What did you have for breakfast, Mabel?"

"Enough," said Margaret. "We invited you to a meeting of residents to discuss the strike. Glad you're here, Mabel."

Mabel wordlessly walked out as Margaret finished her greeting.

Cas flexed his right bicep so that his shirt fluttered slightly. "I have friends in the union. They're good people. They won't do anything to hurt us. Let's give Mabel a note saying we support them, so she can take it to the Council meeting."

"Let's vote. Who's for it?" asked Margaret. Everyone raised their hand except Carl.

Myra said, "I'm only for it here, but some places there are gangsters in the union."

Carl said, "Let's just get on to the next thing. End the strike. Get back to normal."

"Yes, dear, we'll do just that," cooed Norma. "You worry enough for an army."

When Mabel reached the hallway door, she mumbled to herself, "Why didn't they invite me to the meeting? I'm on the Council, aren't I?"

Maria passed by in the hall. "Hi, Mabel. How are you?"

"Fine," said Mabel. Did she know that woman? Must be a nurse in a white uniform. Was this a hospital?

Mabel kept walking directly to a door with a red neon sign marked "exit." She liked red. She'd had a read corduroy dress in the third grade. It had been her favorite. Red was her lucky color. She reached down to scratch her ankle, lifting up the red booty sock worn with her brown oxfords. Something was missing. A bracelet? The gold chain with an "M" on it that her husband gave her? She'd forgotten something. She didn't recall, but the temporary nurse aide forgot to put the wander guard back on her leg after her bath this morning. Mabel forgot that she even wore the wander guard. She forgot a lot of things. Sometimes she realized that she forgot and sometimes she didn't.

She opened the door and walked out.

The screaming sirens of three police cruisers approached the strikers who still carried placards in front of Golden View. Having behaved according to union guidelines, so they stood puzzled by the police arrival.

The first cruiser stopped near them. Lieutenant Grocchi squeezed a small section of his upper body out of the passenger side window as he spoke. "Don't worry. Mabel has run away. Probably hasn't gone far. Do you want to help us search? They say she walked out of a door without her wander guard on, so we'll have to track her down."

Tom replied, "You can count on all six of us here, and there'll be another group of six aides here in an hour or so."

Grocchi said, "Good, let's fan out in the fields on either side of the home. We put out a bulletin just in case some driver picked her up on the highway. They said she's probably out in somebody's garden eating vegetables and talking to her dead husband. They told me her memory is shot."

Millie offered, "She's a character, that she is. Every now and then she's really with it. Not as much anymore."

The police parked the three cars in the rear lot. Five officers got out in addition to Lieutenant Grocchi who said, "Spread out guys. Go through the fields on either side of the home. She's probably out there. Be patient when you find her. She may be confused or upset."

Surprisingly, they didn't find Mabel until the next dawn. A farmer moving his irrigation equipment saw her body and called out to the police. They had searched all afternoon and several hours into the night using search lights and flashlights. Mabel's body had somehow become hidden in natural cover, shielding her from easy view, somehow entangled face down in a bent corn stalk. Grocchi figured she had died from exhaustion and exposure, and had worn herself out by running through the fields with no sense of direction. She had simply run until her body had given out, and then collapsed and died where she fell.

"There's dirt under her fingernails, Lieutenant," said a tall red-haired policeman. "She must have clawed the ground after she fell. She's face down. She was probably only partly conscious."

Grocchi's partner, a squatty weight lifter, asked, "Then why is she wrapped in the corn stalk? Why would she do that as her final act on earth? Maybe she knew she'd be there overnight, and did it to protect herself and try to stay warm."

Red top restlessly circled the death scene several times and stroked his chin. "That's possible. I wonder if there is anything in her mouth." He bent down and examined her lips and jaws carefully. He did not try to open her clenched jaws. "There's little pieces of corn around the edge of her lips. She may have been crazy, but she wasn't stupid. She tried to eat."

Grocchi bent down and peered at Mabel's remains. "I'll be damned if you're not right. She couldn't recall things people said, and got confused, but she tried to have some dinner out here. That was her farewell number. She tried to feed herself."

The raw corn dinner resulted in an ugly scene. Maggots already feasted on Mabel's nose, mouth, and eyes. She'd been dead at least twelve hours. Her rigid body looked as though it had been frozen in a meat locker. A very faint greenish-red tint hinted from her head. The body felt cool to his touch. Under Mabel's half-eaten face, her head and neck showed a ghastly purplish color. Since she'd been more-or-less face down, her facial and neck skin were horribly discolored.

The coroner's office staff wore masks to fight off the stench of the putrefying remains. Some rodent had been there first, nibbling on the body and pulling away the entrails.

A car drove up, nearly hitting Jeannette as she rearranged her hands on the sign. Tom stared at the two men sat in the front seat of this late-model black sedan.

"Hey, you guys, here's the chow Lou promised." Several big scars marked the cheek of the man in the passenger seat, his face framed by stringy, greasy, dull-brown hair.

The trunk popped open, and the driver, younger, more clean cut with almost a collegiate look to him got out and removed three large boxes of food and drink. "There's sandwiches and fried chicken, some pie, coffee, Cokes, and a case of Bud. You've got Lou and Tony to thank. They said to tell you that you're in their prayers. Got it." He smiled and put a toothpick in between his front upper teeth.

"Thanks," said Tom. They drove away. He added, "You guys are in our prayers, too. You need them more than we do."

Tom walked over to Millie and gave her a very slight wink. "Their car matches the description of the car that was here at three or four a.m. the morning of the fire in the kitchen. Think they did it?"

Millie looked at Tom and winked back. "Think it's too early for a Bud and some fried chicken? What flavor are the pies?"

"Make that two," said Tom. "It's not too early at all." He turned to the others and said, "A few eat and a few walk with the signs. Got to keep up the picket line. This is a strike; remember that. We're on a one-day walk-out. This ain't no picnic."

The fog was lifting. The sun shone through, drying out the ground and the trees. A slight warm breeze brushed over the strikers. They fidgeted, getting bored, and complained of their feet hurting after two hours on the picket line. The food and coffee heartened them, as did the arriving cars carrying the Board of Commissioners. An emergency meeting was called, no doubt, hope of a settlement reigned. Their demands might be met at long last.

Inside Golden View, the RN's performed yeoman's duty, carrying breakfast trays, handling all the med. carts, feverishly writing notes for the medical charts, reassuring each other and the residents that the inconvenience was only for a day, and repeatedly saying, “Yes, Johnnetta will be back tomorrow,” or “No, Jeannette has not been fired,” and “Oh, I’m sorry, Mrs Radley. I’m sorry. I didn’t know you had your nails done on Tuesday morning only. Please forgive me.”

There would be no slot machine winners today. Insufficient staff remained to monitor that activity.

The RN’s prayed for no emergencies, no urgent matters that could distract them from the day-by-day management that was theirs for the strike day. After all, Susie and Maria really couldn’t be expected to give a bath, clean a bedpan, or sweep up dried vomit. They were dressed in street clothes and thought to be ensconced in their office hideouts performing administrative duties.

Actually, Susie and Maria were with the board. Neither Doc nor Dr Ramantha had been invited.

“Well, here we are again folks,” began Jack, “sitting around the table with union picketers outside and used lumber burning in barrels. Looks like a small-time movie production out there. What’s your pleasure? The Residents Council wants us to negotiate seriously with the union people. They want us to get the Cleveland reps down here to talk.”

Susie’s secretary burst into the conference room, flushed and gasping as she said, “It’s the union lawyer, line two.”

“Put him through on the speaker phone, please,” said Susie very calmly.

"Good morning, this is Lou Giordano. We represent your union. How are you doing, young lady?"

Jack put his finger to his lips and looked at Susie. "Good morning, Lou," Jack said. "How are you this fine day? This is Mr Wheatley, head of the Board of Commissioners. Not so young and no lady."

"Oh, yeah. Hi, Jack. It is Jack, isn't it?" responded Lou. "Sorry about the lady thing."

"Yes, it is Lou."

"Well, I just wanted to touch base. There'll be a one-day strike, only the one day. No rough stuff." Lou belly laughed. "We're businessmen and lawyers, not hooligans. So, there's nothing to fear. It's part of our need to show you that we're serious about the contract. Our people got the short end of the stick. It's got to change, and soon. It's got to. More money. Better benefits. You help us. We help you."

The group listened in hushed silence, and Jack's perpetual smile contracted.

"Is there something specific you want us to do at this point?" asked Jack. "We're meeting to discuss the situation."

"No, nothing specific now. You know what we want. If it's okay, Tony and I would like to come meet you and your guys in a few weeks or so. Let the dust from the strike settle. Then we'll want to get real specific. Glad that guy John won't be there. We like those cute young ones you got now. Talk to you later."

Jack smiled, but regretted the speaker phone. Maria and Susie both blushed. Even Jack flinched at Lou's sexism, though not surprised. Lou was what he was.

"We've got some time then, don't we?" Susie asked, exhaling. "No emergency today."

Susie's secretary knocked, entered again, handed her a note, and left. She unraveled it and read aloud: "Cas and Elizabeth need to see you. They say they plan to leave together today. The idea of a strike is the straw that broke the camel's back, states Cas."

She paused and added, "Yes, please excuse me. Maria, I'll need you, too."

After the commissioners left, Maria found Doc and they joined Susie in the conference room. Fresh coffee, tea, doughnuts, and sandwiches sat on the table. The dietary staff was on strike, but a couple of cooks from the local cafeteria were helping out with the meals.

Doc asked, "What's up? Why the rush-rush and hush-hush?"

Maria explained that Cas and Elizabeth wanted to leave AMA, and they wanted to leave together.

"I guess it's no surprise. They're quite a team, aren't they? What's the game plan?" asked Doc.

Susie began, "Responsibility, Doc. Don't we have a responsibility to help them evaluate their choices and decisions. They have the right to do what they want. Nobody here thinks that they should live together or leave here."

"I completely agree. Let's try to talk some sense into their heads. Let's try to understand them, but be prepared for the worst, for anything. We should see them together, or they'll get even more suspicious than they already are."

Cas and Elizabeth were shown into the room. His face was beet red, and his hands trembled. Elizabeth put on her deepest pout, her eyes steely dark slits. They had never been in the administrator's office before, but in no way acted intimidated. Each had a small handbag, ostensibly with personal toilet articles in them, as if on their way out.

Doc and Maria sat on one side of the conference table, Cas and Elizabeth opposite them, while Susie positioned herself at the head of the table. More fresh coffee and pastries came. Doc knew two voluntary discharges just wouldn't do, so if something to eat or drink smoothed the way, Susie wanted to pull out all the stops.

Maria said, "Both Elizabeth and Cas have expressed their desire–"

"We want out," Cas stated. "That's it. You can't keep us."

Elizabeth added, "I shouldn't be here at all. I don't have any idea why I was put here. It's a prison."

Susie asked, "Do we have anything to talk about then, if your plans are definite?"

"Well, well, young lady," said Cas, "now you're making some sense. We came because Maria asked us to. She said that when people left without the blessing of the home it was good to talk to the administrator."

Elizabeth said, "This place is a shithole. They steal money. My good watch is gone. I know you think I'm paranoid, but my stuff is missing." Her voice rose with, "This place is a prison."

"There are several reasons for you to be unhappy here," began Doc. "You aren't able to live together.

Things are stolen. It feels like a prison. Anything else? We want to correct those things that are possible to correct."

"Correct my ass," said Elizabeth. She waved her hands wildly. Then she pointed her right thumb at Maria. "You just want to give me medicine so I don't know which end is up. So I behave. So I don't bother those damn nurses while they sit and write whatever it is they write. I've been talking directly to God about all this shit."

Doc noted her psychosis in the middle phase of the dementia process.

"The nurses work hard. They take good care of the residents here. I'm proud of them," Maria said. Her eyes narrowed. She began to perspire, and her make-up was becoming damp. Her cheeks glowed red.

"What else is wrong here?" asked Doc. "Is there any way we can discuss you both staying here? Your doctors and nurses think you should be here. They don't think either of you will be safe away from here, or that you should go together. You know their reasons better than I do." Doc squirmed in his chair and then added, "And you have some fun together here. You have a few drinks and play the slots once or twice a week. And you can smoke together in the lounge."

"Fuck you, Doc, and the rest of you, too. Excuse me ladies, but I don't like to be talked down to. I'm free, white, and twenty-one. I can do as I please," Cas snapped. "Come on, Liz honey. Let's go."

Elizabeth did not move. Her head tilted to the left and slumped onto her chest. She sometimes did that. All eyes darted to Maria.

Cas got up and stood behind Elizabeth's chair, shook her gently, and repeated, "Liz, Liz honey. Liz wake up. Let's go."

Maria went to Elizabeth, bent over, and lifted her eyelids. The pupils were already taking on a slightly dull and lifeless appearance. Then she felt for a pulse in her neck and wrist. She blanched. She said, " Code. Call 911 to get her to a hospital emergency room. I think she's dying. She's nearly dead."

Maria immediately lay Elizabeth on the floor with Cas's help and cleared her airway. Then she pumped and pressed her chest and blew air into her mouth rhythmically.

"You people will pay for this. Goddamn it. You'll pay for this if you've killed her with all your carrying on–a strike, a fire, and the months it took to get her room fixed. The goddamn nurses and . . ." Cas sat down on the floor, put his head in one hand, and sobbed, never letting go of Elizabeth's arm with his other. "You'll pay . . ."

Doc called 911 on his cell phone. Then he went to the secretary's phone to call in a code to the nursing staff, who started bringing life-saving equipment and medicine to the administrator's office. Maria sat back on her knees, palms helplessly up. Elizabeth had simply died sometime during the discussion about leaving the home with Cas. Dr Ramantha was gone, and Golden View did not have the "proverbial" paddles to shock the heart. It was not equipped like an emergency room or paramedic vehicle.

Maria said. "There's no pulse now. There is some very faint breathing, but it's going, too. She must have had a massive heart attack."

Susie had not yet moved from her chair at the head of the table. Finally, she said, "Thanks, Maria. Thanks, Doc. Cas, we'll do everything we can. I'm very sorry."

"You'll pay," Cas promised. "Don't hand me this sorry shit. You'll pay. What's that gurgling sound anyway? She can't be dead."

Ursula lay stretched out with Carmen in his sixth-floor corner pied-a-terre in the St. Germain area of Paris. They had finished a late lunch after a long morning of lovemaking and intermittent naps. A huge green satin sheet more than covered Carmen's antique king-size bed. He liked to quip that it wasn't just king-size but that some king probably owned it or slept in it given what the antique dealer had charged him for it. The ornate French phone rang, and he grabbed it, though not at all sure he was ready for a business call.

"Hi, sorry to bother you, Carmen. It's Tony Dee in Cleveland. Wanted you to know that the one-day strike is on for that nursing home."

"Good, Tony. You've done good there."

"You still want it clean, right? No rough stuff, nobody hurt, nothing like that?" asked Tony.

"Yeah, I guess so. Just make all those patients worry a little more than usual. Nervous, you know. Let me check with somebody here. Hold on just a moment." Carmen put his hand over the mouthpiece. "Anything you need, Ursula? You know, where your mother is. We'll keep up the pressure on the joint. Is that enough?"

Ursula didn't respond immediately. On her back, she yawned, stroked her lustrous hair, yawned again, stroked her long thighs, rolled over onto her stomach, and smiled at Carmen, who was then sitting on the bed. "Take the slots out. They don't need so much fun."

"You sure? You get the slots. You enjoy them and get used to it. Then to have them yanked out. You sure?"

Ursula began to delicately run her long nails across Carmen's inner thigh. His breathing got heavier. He said huskily to Tony, "Yank out the slots next week." Then he hung up.

Chapter Thirteen

To Staff:

July 12, 1995. Weather report is for mixed clouds and bright sun in the morning with possible afternoon showers. Lo 65, Hi 85. Census at 148, with two expirations. All administrative staff will be in today. No crimes reported. Remember that the Bar-B-Que is in early August.

SW

Maria and Doc sat alone in Maria's office after dinner on the day of the strike. She sat at her desk, piled high with medical charts and mementos such as small stuffed animals.

"I need to get away for a half hour. I'm beat. I can't help but think we've done something wrong, Doc, or else this strike wouldn't happen."

"Maybe you're right," Doc answered. He sat in an antique oak rocking chair at the side of her desk. He rocked slowly back and forth. "Yes, maybe so."

Maria had loosened her bun so that her thick dark hair cascaded over her shoulders. Her white uniform fit tightly over her breasts, and lately she had begun to keep her hemlines at least two inches above the knee.

The administrative office area was quiet, since most administrative staff were still performing direct service on the wards, in the kitchen, or in the laundry. The facility had kept going, despite the one-day shut down by the union members.

Fatigue drew down Maria's delicate face.

Doc said, "We got off on the wrong foot, Maria, but I hope that's behind us." Her shoulders were beautifully rounded as he viewed them from the side of the desk.

"Oh, Doc, that was a long time ago. Things are fine with us. I'm going over material for some articles in our newsletter. We call it the *Golden View Glitter*."

"What are the articles?" asked Doc.

"Well, one article is about two of our sweeties, Myra and Margaret. They don't give up. They fight on against big odds. Did you know that Myra was a tomboy? I interviewed her. She played with boys most of the time: Baseball, basketball, touch football–they couldn't touch her except on the arms and butt–and doctor-nurse. She liked the strength of boys, their agility and their speed. Most of all, she liked their aggressiveness. It allowed her to be forceful and assertive; no one noticed. She was one of the guys. At one point, she thought she'd become a teacher or a high school coach. But women coaches hadn't been encouraged in those days."

"I get inspired by those two," said Doc. He smiled tentatively as he added, "You inspire me, too."

"Well, Doc, I didn't think you cared," joked Maria. "You're divorced, aren't you?"

"Yes, our daughter died and the marriage died, too. You?"

"Nope, never married so never divorced, but I've made some mistakes along the way. By the way, Margaret's family had a huge lawn party for her and James on their sixty-fifth wedding anniversary. They sat next to each other in their wheelchairs, festooned with ribbons and balloons. They slept during most of it. Family kept saying `Don't they look great?' And, `they're something aren't they?'"

"Anything new about Myra's family?" asked Doc. He stopped rocking, got up slowly, and then stood behind Maria's chair.

"Myra's husband, John, has been gone for nearly ten years. Until the diabetes got to her feet and legs, she led an independent life. Her daughter, Trudy, always wanted her mother to remarry, or at least keep company with a man. Myra always refused. The first time was perfect, so you cannot improve on that."

Maria reached her arms around the back of her desk chair and held Doc lightly on the hips.

He trembled slightly. "Anything else about Margaret?"

Maria's hands and arms began to rub and caress Doc's thighs. Otherwise, she didn't move. "Well, you know that Margaret is more acutely sick than Myra. She has bladder cancer, which is spreading to other inner organs, and she can't breathe worth a damn. She was a restaurant hostess and waitress, has six kids, fourteen grandchildren, and three great grandchildren. Her breathing is the worst. She's horribly afraid she'll choke to death, and she relives an incident daily in which she nearly drowned in a pond at her family's farm when she was seven."

Doc bent over and kissed Maria's head and neck tenderly.

Maria said, "During coffee breaks, the nursing assistants compete in their praise and love for them. They say wonderful things. I wrote down some quotes for my story." She read them to Doc while he nibbled her back and shoulders:

"I don't know what we'll do if anything happens to Margaret or Myra." "It'll be like losing my mother." "She's like a sister." "They're the best people I've ever served here." "Those two are what makes it meaningful to serve others." "God is in that room."

Maria completed the family background update. "And Myra told me a secret. She has the right insurance mix–Medicare, Medicaid, and Medigap. A very clever tax lawyer in Cleveland has her inheritance in several trusts with the income going to other trusts. Her taxable income is negligible. Medicaid would have its hands full trying to disentangle the facts."

Doc opened the top button of Maria's uniform slowly and awkwardly from his standing position. His breathing change. So did hers. Doc undid the back of her bra. Her tousled black hair, the burnished gold of her skin, and the bright red lipstick were dramatically highlighted by the tight white starched uniform. She moved her hands away from Doc's hips, and unzipped his pants. She held him now. He was very hard.

"Just this once, Doc. Just this once."

Maria brought her arms down and swiveled her desk chair to face Doc. She held him tightly. His hands and lips ravaged her body. Their lovemaking was precise and expert, mindful of the risks, yet strangely wordless.

Afterward, Doc kissed her goodbye and left her office. They both needed to regain their composure. Maria would return to her nursing duties soon. Doc, catching his breath, perused the results of the staff survey.

One hundred and fifty employees had anonymously responded to the survey. Seventy-five percent–a high rate of return.

"How would you rate your supervisor?" Sixty-five percent said good or great. Doc figured that to be high–they weren't that pleased.

"How would you rate the entire management team?" Sixty-eight percent said terrible, poor, or average. The staff had a very dim view of the department heads, board, and administrator.

"Are you kept informed of the changes that occur within the facility?" Only twenty-nine percent stated usually or always. Most staff felt left out and uninformed of change.

"Are your concerns handled sincerely?" Only thirty-five percent said usually or always. When the staff voiced a concern, it was ignored or handled poorly.

"Do staff work together as a team?" Twenty-six percent said usually or always, while thirteen percent said never or rarely. Considerable dissension splintered the staff.

Judge Williams wore a rumpled, oxford gray, Brooks Brothers suit. "Morning gentlemen, good morning. How are you?"

"Just fine, your honor," answered Noel Crossley. "Good to see you again."

"I'm Gerald Greene from Cleveland, your honor, nice to meet you."

Judge Williams said, "Likewise, Mr Greene. Please help yourselves to coffee and rolls, gentlemen. This morning's proceedings will be quite informal."

Doc looked at Greene, a tall, bony man with long straight silver hair slightly tufted at the neckline. He dressed impeccably. Crossley was short, pudgy, and wore thick glasses without frames; he sported a shiny, grey polyester suit with an even shinier, two- dollar, grey tie from K-mart.

Ursula, Trudy, and Helmut sat stiffly together in chairs located about the middle of the room, underneath a framed print of a turbulent ocean holding a small fishing boat struggling to avoid capsizing. Susie hadn't arrived yet, nor had Margaret Princeton. Dr Ramantha and Doc sat together on the opposite side of the room. Both looked straight ahead and did not chat. A dowdy woman sat down quickly, poised to begin her court reporting duties.

Judge Williams cleared his throat several times. He glanced nervously at each attorney. "Good morning, everyone. We are here for Case Number 10012794. An injunction is sought by the adult children of Mrs Myra Gronbeck, a patient here at Golden View Rehabilitation Center. The injunction requests that all life-saving medical treatment cease immediately. Mr Greene represents the Gronbeck family, while Mr Crossley represents the home and the doctors. I request that there be no talking during this proceeding, except when you are a witness under oath. We want things to be as orderly and calm as possible. We must respect the frail and disabled who live here. I'm going to ask Mr Greene to present his ideas for a few minutes, next Mr Crossley, and then we'll call several witnesses. I must admit that this is an unusual request; the first time I've been involved with someone seeking an injunction like this. I guess we'll all learn something today." He blew air out of his slightly open mouth several times in rapid succession, barely moving his lips, like basketball players do before they shoot free throws. "So, Mr Greene, please get us started," said the judge.

Gerald Greene stood slowly and walked to the window. He pushed the drapes open as wide as they would go, and raised the slat blinds. Bright sunshine suddenly burst through the window, behind a clear, cloudless sky stretching to the horizon. Greene peered out the window without speaking.

Finally, the judge said, " Mr Greene?"

"Yes, your honor. As I view this fine day, I was thinking about freedom. Mrs Gronbeck deserves freedom now; the freedom to stop a losing battle; the freedom to cross-over in peace. She deserves the freedom to rest after living a full and productive life. Our injunction makes that freedom possible. If all life-saving medical attention–pills, machines, treatments–if these are stopped, then Mrs Gronbeck, God bless her soul, will be free to make that final journey home to everlasting comfort and peace."

The judge glared in confusion at Greene as he sat down. Greene's face showed no smile, no sign of a smirk, and not a hint of parody or cynicism.

"Thank you, Mr Greene. A very intriguing statement, to say the least. Mr Crossley would you like to comment briefly now?"

"Yes, thank you, your honor. May it please the court," Crossley began softly while staring at the stack of papers. He sat rigidly without turning his head to engage the judge or others in the room. "I'm quite shocked by Mr Greene's ideas. Golden View is committed to quality care for each and every resident. Dr Ramantha is an excellent physician and we rely on him for medical care and decisions, which are always made in collaboration with the wishes of the resident and their family. Doc is here today and he provides psychological counseling to our residents. We have excellent nurses and committed aides and dietary staff. There is no neglect or abuse at our facility. Living Wills or Orders Not To Resuscitate are respected, but *not* the idea that Mr Greene proposes." Crossley bowed his head further, as if he wanted to shrivel up and disappear into his shirt and tie, or preferably become the invisible man.

"Are you feeling okay, Noel?"

"Yes, thank you, your honor." He did not look up.

The judge stared at him, concern lighting his grey eyes. "Well then, thank you both for your opening statements, gentlemen. You have framed the issue for this injunction hearing very well. Mr Greene, would you please call your first witness?"

Trudy quickly moved to the witness seat at the end of the table, wearing a simple but elegant black sleeveless dress. Her makeup left her quite pale. She drummed her fingers on the table, but otherwise appeared to be at ease. She was sworn in quickly.

"Trudy," asked Mr Greene, "you are the daughter of Myra Gronbeck?"

"Yes, I know her very well because I've been the primary caretaker for her for the last five years or so. I love her as does my husband, Helmut, and my children. I know her as well as I know myself. I think I know what she wants out of life."

Mr Greene remained seated. He spoke softly to Trudy. "Please tell us your intention in being here today. Is it primarily to gain her assets?"

"We do want our inheritance. She has willed it to us. Yes, we need it. But, I want what's best for my mother. I'm not sure that the doctors always know best. Dr Ramantha hasn't known my mother for more than a year. How could he understand her true needs? Her psychologist, Doc, only knows her since she's been so sad and melancholy."

"Yes, go ahead," said Mr Greene.

"And she, herself, may not know what's best for her anymore. She's sick and old, and she feels depressed a lot of the time. Only those of us who have known her for our lifetime, and who love her, would know what's best for her. She's in no shape to judge things now."

"And what do you want for her now?" asked her attorney. He stood up and moved toward the sun drenched window again. "What do you wish to have the court do for your mother? What is your goal here this morning?"

Trudy readjusted her blonde bangs. She stopped the jittery drumming of her fingers. She wet her lips. She looked at Judge Williams as she answered, "Please let her die in peace. That's what I want. That's what my husband wants, and my sister, Ursula, too. Stop the treatment and let her cross over in a calm and dignified way. Hopefully, she can die in her sleep after we've all said goodbye to her."

The room became deadly silent. No one moved. No one made eye contact with the judge, except Trudy. Doc watched the judge look away again and scan the rust-colored carpet, the teak furniture, and the comfortable beige naugahyde furniture. The court reporter's machine was quiet, too, her hands completely still. Moments passed, which seemed like hours.

Mr Greene moved closer to the window again, and stared out with a soulful expression. "Yes, Trudy, we understand. Thank you. You want your beloved mother, Mrs Myra Gronbeck, to have the freedom to die with dignity and respect because her happy and productive life is over. There is zero quality to her existence. Is that it?"

"Yes, exactly. I hope everyone agrees that her family knows best. I speak for all of her immediate family who love her. I've been in charge, if that's the right word." The tears streamed down Trudy's cheeks as she sobbed during the last few words. She wiped them away with her fingers. She'd left her purse and tissues on the table near her other chair. Helmut reached over to push both of them toward her.

Mr Greene acted fast, too. “Fine, thank you. You’re excused for now, Trudy.”

Trudy stood up quickly and returned to her seat. She daubed here eyes, then wiped her whole face with tissues. She blew her nose several times. She held Helmut’s hand as he turned toward her.

Judge Williams finally spoke. “Thank you, Trudy. That was very honest and quite heartfelt. We are very moved by your statement and your request.”

The Judge looked at Crossley. “Why don’t we hear from Dr Ramantha, Noel. I know he’s swamped and needs to get back to work.”

Dr Ramantha moved to the witness chair. He walked slowly and held the back of the chair with both hands for a moment before he sat down. Doc knew he disliked these hearings. After he had sworn to tell the truth, the whole truth, and nothing but the truth, the questions began.

“Do you know Mrs Myra Gronbeck?” asked Noel. Again, he remained seated and only peripherally eyed the doctor.

“Yes, I do. She is my patient. For many months, since her surgery. I know her reasonably well.”

“Is there a Living Will which requests no life support or extreme medical efforts?”

“No.”

“Is there an ONTR?”

“No.”

“Has Mrs Gronbeck requested euthanasia or physician-assisted suicide?”

“No.”

"What is her condition?"

"She's old, frail, and quite ill. She's been increasingly depressed and receives medication for it, as well as psychotherapy to help her work through the depression. She doesn't participate in very much."

"Has she given up?"

"Not to my knowledge."

"Can she understand what's happening and judge for herself?"

"Yes, she can. She is competent and can think for herself. She knows she's very sick. She wants to go on. She wants treatment. She needs my help and wants it."

Margaret, who had been wheeled in as the doctor testified, said as loud as she could, "It's *her* life. *She* can decide. She wants to live, you people. Myra does not want to die yet. She even wants the machines to save her." Her face was beet red. She was trembling and her breath came in short, fast spurts. "Myra knows what she wants. She's sick this morning."

Judge Williams said, "Please, we must speak only when we are witnesses, only when the judge or attorneys ask questions."

Margaret's outburst had made its point, however. She had defended Myra's judgment and point of view; more importantly she had affirmed Myra's right to decide.

"Please, go on, doctor." said Noel.

"I forgot where I was."

"Would you consider stopping medical treatment–doing what the family requests?"

"No, not if I went against Myra. Not unless she was ONTR, or she was incapacitated and incompetent, and a judge ordered me. A lot of our residents have a limited quality of life and a lot don't. That doesn't mean we walk away and let them die." He squirmed in his chair and searched for Doc's eyes. He needed support, which Doc gave as best he could.

The judge asked, "Could you be negligent if you did what Trudy asks?"

"Yes, I feel I would be–legally and morally. I'm committed to helping patients, and curing them whenever possible. Or, making their lives more livable, if I can't cure them."

"Do you consult with families?" asked Noel. This time he stared directly at Trudy, then shifted his gaze to Ursula.

"Of course, every day. We value family support and family input on the resident's condition."

"Is this different? Why not listen to the family here? Maybe they know more than you do, or even Myra does." Crossley was being Socratic, stealing some of Greene's questions.

Dr Ramantha tried to be fair. "I'm sure they have good reasons. Obviously, they know her much better than we do, and love her, and care about her. It's hard to think they know her better than she knows herself, but that could be, too. As her doctor, I can't go against her wishes. I can't let her die when she has not requested it legally, or directly to me. People do change their minds, but she hasn't done that. She gives informed consent where it is required."

"Final question, doctor. Are you just doing what you want to do? Are you playing God here against the family's wishes?" Noel pushed his chair back, but did not arise yet.

Perspiration from Dr Ramantha's long, sleek hair had dripped down his shirt collar "I hope not, Mr Crossley. I hope not. I'm trying to help her. She wants my help, despite her grave condition. She is sad, but alert, when we meet, and understands what I say and what I'm trying to do for her. From a healthy young person's point of view, I can see where her life would look very, very limited. But it's her life. A moment ago, her roommate, Margaret, said it better than I could have. *Myra wants to live*. Her depression has not cleared to the extent I would prefer, but her judgment, understanding, and reasoning are sufficient for what she faces."

Crossley finally stood up. He didn't walk anywhere. Behind his chair he read from a note card. "I forgot that I had a question I should have asked earlier, doctor. In your opinion, is Myra competent to refuse an offer of euthanasia or doctor-assisted suicide?"

A stunned silence again filled the conference room. Doc feared that Margaret would faint, or worse, or that Dr Ramantha would become hostile and defiant.

The doctor drew air inwardly as he answered, "Yes, she's competent to refuse such an offer. In order to refuse such a questionable procedure, the individual would need to pass a very low level of competency. Myra's level of competency is much higher than that."

The judge said, "Let's take a ten minute break and then resume. Thank you very much, Dr Ramantha. You've been a very helpful and forthcoming witness today. You are excused from the hearing in order to perform your normal medical duties."

Margaret whispered hoarsely to Doc, "They only want the money. You know that. I know that. They don't care about Myra–especially that daughter from the west coast. She never calls or writes–just visited once. They don't care."

"Yes, I understand Margaret," said Doc. "You're probably right. It's hard to see it from the family's point of view. But they have children and their own needs. It's expensive in today's world. They see their money going down the drain on care for Myra, who's so ill. They need the money. They feel Myra is terminal and that the amount of time she has left is not as important as their quite legitimate needs. I'm on the same side as you, but many people would be more sympathetic to what they want than we are. Trudy feels she knows what's best for Myra right now, that she knows Myra, at least a sick Myra, better than Myra knows herself."

Margaret began to wheel herself to the door. She seldom did that anymore. "Doctors and shrinks, and roommates are not wrong about what's really in Myra's mind at this point."

Patterned sunlight now filled the room. The rear wall looked striped because someone had closed the window slats just enough to create lines of light and dark. There was very little talk as the room cleared. Judge Williams sat immobile, except for his hands., which scribbled furiously.

Doc watched Helmut hold Trudy's hand as they walked into the hallway. Ursula stood nearby and actually smiled warmly at her sister. "I hate to admit it, but I couldn't have done better. There's not much I can add, is there?" Trudy and Helmut hurried on without responding.

Both of her Margaret's daughters carried brown cardboard boxes when they entered her room. Some kind of a surprise lay within, but she couldn't guess what. Fine with her. She liked surprises, and was so happy when her daughter visited. She sat hunched over her table doing a cross-word puzzle.

"Hello, you two. I see those boxes. What's up?"

Joyce leaned over and kissed her on the lips. "Love you, Mom. You look better." Joyce, now forty-three, had three sons ranging in age from twelve to eighteen. Joyce was the baby, born in Margaret's forty-third year.

While Joyce put her box on Margaret's bed, her older daughter, cheerful, rotund sixty-one-year-old Shirley, placed her box at the edge of the table. "How about me? No kisses?" She bent down to kiss Margaret's forehead tenderly and hug the upper part of her body she could reach, since Margaret sat snugly in her wheelchair.

"You two are up to something. Skip the lovey-dovey stuff. What about those boxes?"

"You get right to it, don't you," Shirley said with a smile. "No hi, how are you, how are the kids, and all that? Right to the boxes."

More people streamed into the room before Margaret could defend herself. The husbands of Shirley and Joyce, each carrying in a great-grandchild in one arm and either an old leather briefcase or legal size folder full of letters and pictures in the other hand.

The two "greats" brought tears to Margaret's eyes. She held one, then the other. A boy, Joshua, six months old, son of Rebecca, her granddaughter. Four-month-old Amy was the daughter of granddaughter, Susie.

After a quick "Hello, you two" to her sons-in-law and an equally quick return kiss from each of them, Margaret played with the babies. "This is heaven. This is sugar. This is ice cream." She immediately felt guilty mentioning sweets in front of Myra, but peeking across the room, she breathed easier. Myra slept through just about everything these days, including visits such as this.

Her daughters and sons-in-law all smiled broadly, eyes twinkling, full of Christmas surprise and excitement. The boxes and folders needed explanation. Margaret felt torn between the sheer joy of fondling the infants and curving them into her chest versus her growing curiosity. She loved the attention. Joshua's sharp blue eyes reminded her of her husband. Amy had her nose and hair, of that she was sure.

To actually see the generations provided a tangible sense of continuity. She wept inwardly, ecstatic but also feeling the poignant sense of loss. She would never see these "greats" marry, graduate, or anything like that. She'd be in heaven, but they would remember; at least her children and grandchildren would. If only a way existed to imprint something into her "greats" so the name Margaret Princeton would conjure up feelings of love, respect, and kindness. She felt as though she'd been away for a few minutes. Oh, dear, had she fallen asleep with all the family around her?

"Now, Mom, it's time. The boys will take Amy and Joshua for awhile and go see Dad. Of course, he won't remember everything. We've got a job to do," explained Shirley.

As Joshua and Amy were handed over, they both cried. So did Margaret. She raised her voice. "Love you both. Gramma loves you, loves you." And they were gone, her daughters pointing their husbands out of the room. These were powerful women Margaret had raised, that indomitable spirit, a never-say-die will, and a make-the-best-of-it practicality that their men appreciated and respected. Sometimes, they could be formidable foes, too, in a worthy struggle over money or children.

Joyce put both boxes and the two cases on the bed. "We're here to do an annual calendar for you and Dad. There's a company that makes a calendar with a picture for each month at the top of it. It could be you, or you and Dad, or whomever you want. We've got plenty of pictures to choose from." Her hands moved gently over the boxes like a QVC salesman on TV.

Margaret almost gasped, hoping the choices of pictures would be hers. "How much does it cost? A calendar. I hardly know one day, or even one month, from another. I'll bet it costs way too much."

Both Joyce's and Shirley's blue eyes widened, and then Joyce simply said, "Not to worry. We're all sharing the cost, so it's not much for any one of us. You do have six children and fourteen grandchildren, and now you even have two `greats.' Please don't worry about the money. You and Dad mean everything to us."

"Well, if you say so. So, what kind of calendar is it?" asked Margaret.

Shirley answered, "In addition to one large picture for each month, the days and dates of the month can identify birthdays, memorable events like wedding anniversaries; upcoming special times like parties, weddings, or graduations; and smaller pictures."

"God knows we could fill it with birthdays, anniversaries, and communion dates," Margaret said. She ran her fingers over the typed list she kept on her table. Recalling everyone these days wasn't easy. The list of grandchildren was studied before visits or phone calls, even when she read their cards or letters. First the girls: "Bobbie, Toni, Karen, Cindy, Susie, Anna, Vickie, Carla, and Rebecca," and then the boys: "Joseph, Michael, Adam, Richard, and Marvin."

Shirley opened a cardboard box and laid the contents out on the bed: a white leather picture album, two old audio tapes, a guest sign-in book from James and Margaret's wedding, and newspaper accounts of most of their children's eight weddings–two had remarried. Three high school year books covered the time when all six kids went to either St. Jerome's or Sisters of Concordia. Tuition money wasn't easy to come by in those days.

Margaret trembled inside. She and James were still so important to them that they wanted to establish a gift to reaffirm the family on a daily basis. She'd see the dates of weddings, birthdays, communions, and parties. The family would be united on each day of the week, each date of the month. The history of her life and her family would be on the calendar. She'd be reminded of all the happy events, all the joyous and memorable circumstances of her life, with those most important to her named and in pictures before her eyes. The feelings and emotions left her overwrought. She wasn't sure that she had the emotional energy to look through picture albums. The flooding of her mind might be too powerful.

"Mom, you with us? You okay?" asked Shirley.

"Yes, I'm fine," said Margaret, not wanting the excitement to stop.

Joyce opened the leather album and sat on the bed near her mother. Shirley stood at the side of Margaret's chair.

"I love this wedding picture of you and Dad," Joyce said, tears in her big blue eyes. "I feel so proud to be a part of you both and our family. I was lucky to come along when I did because I got so much attention from everyone."

"Mom?" asked Shirley. She grinned sheepishly. "Do you remember your other four kids? I see you've got a list of the grandchildren."

"Am I still sane, is that it?" Margaret asked, kidding her back. "Well, I've got two daughters and four sons–James, Jr., John, Steve, and Bill. So there, how's that? Two of them got divorced and married again, but I have trouble keeping that part straight, don't I?"

"Very good," Shirley said, clapping. "Your memory is as good as mine."

"Well, you're over sixty yourself, if I remember right," said Margaret. They all laughed, hearty and deep, but Myra still did not stir. "That feels good to me. I haven't had such a good chuckle for weeks. Myra and me, well, it's not so much good anymore."

Joyce suggested, "Let's look at these," as she thumbed through the white photo album. "Many of the best pictures are here. We could have pictures of you and Dad, you and each of us kids, and the pictures with grandkids as the main thing on the calendar for each month."

"Yes, that would be good," agreed Margaret. "Were you always so organized, Joyce? I don't remember things that way. That wedding picture is so sweet. I want that for January."

"That's fine," said Shirley, sorting looking through another set of photos, some blurred by time, crinkly, or cracked around the edges, probably done with a Baby Brownie. "Here are some, Mom, that weren't such good quality pictures. But they're interesting."

"Yes, yes," offered Margaret. She glanced at a picture of herself and James with four of the children taken on a sandy beach in bright sunlight. "That was at Twin Lakes, not far from town. You kids–well, at least four of you–were under twelve, it looks like. Yes, it was someone's birthday; see the picnic basket. I remember the cake, a big angel food cake with chocolate icing, but not what we ate for lunch. Dad took you kids in the water. He was a better swimmer than I was. And you know James, Jr. was on the swim team in school. You girls liked basketball better. I used to wonder sometimes if the boy genes and the girl genes got mixed up inside of me. None of the boys got Varsity letters in football or baseball. It was golf, tennis, and swimming, sort of sissified is what I used to think, but I never said it. I'm sorry to go on like this, but I do recall that afternoon. They pulled a dead horse out of that lake, and we never went there again. I don't know if we ever told you kids why we didn't go back." Winded after this outpouring, Margaret put the oxygen nosepiece back into her nose right away. She often let it slip out because she didn't like the feel of it, or the way she looked with it covering up the bottom of her nose and her upper lip. She feared it made her look like a hospital patient.

Shirley remarked, "Mom, your memory is fantastic. I don't remember any of that." Then she smiled and asked, "Is that all true, the dead horse and all?"

Margaret just chuckled.

"Look at this one. It's the four boys with you and Dad," said Joyce. "Too bad it's so discolored, and you can barely see the people."

Margaret could see the figures clearly, however. She remembered that she and James tried to do different things with the girls than with the boys. Maybe it was a mistake, but that was their thinking back then. She explained, "We always took the boys fishing together, and James would take them hunting. I never hunted, always hated shotguns. Well, we went fishing once in a lake that was supposed to have large-mouthed bass in it just waiting to jump into the boat." She stopped for a moment to catch her breath. "Your Dad knew the man who rented the boats and owned the bait shop. He always gave us hot tips on how to catch fish. One afternoon, the sky was pure blue. There wasn't a cloud for miles, and it was very hot. He told us to use some minnows on a new huge spinner and to cast our lines into the lily pads. We had three small rowboats. Your Dad and I were in one, and two of the boys were in each of the others. We went to the spot the guy told us about. We tried all afternoon. The Cokes and sandwiches were good, but nobody caught a big large-mouth like we wanted. We wanted a trophy fish to stuff and hang in the living room at home. We were getting ready to leave and go back to our cabin when your youngest brother, Bill, caught his line in the lily pads and around one of the oar handles. It took us at least a half-hour to figure out whose line was whose and to unravel the line and save the dumb spinner and bait. I wanted to cut the line off, but your Dad wanted to teach the boys patience. To make a long story short, somehow, in all the excitement, confusion, and yelling back and forth, a huge twelve-pound large-mouth bass had been hooked on the end of the line. It had exhausted itself while we worked on the line. We didn't even know it was there."

"Some brothers we have," Joyce said, smiling. "They didn't improve much, did they?"

Margaret gathered enough energy to finish. "Your Dad wouldn't let them keep it. The fish was a beauty. Dad was a stickler for honesty and told the boys that they hadn't caught it fair and square."

"I'll bet the boys were as mad as they could be, weren't they?" asked Shirley. "Bill must have been fit to be tied."

Another round of laughter came at the boys' expense. The humorous sarcasm in the family had lasted a lifetime, as the perennial girls versus the boys still lingered on, far past whatever function it had served, if any. James and Margaret had always had plenty of love, support, and respect for their kids, whatever shortage of money existed from time to time.

By this time, each of her daughters sat on the bed with Margaret's chair between them. After she put the fishing picture back in the pile, Shirley and Joyce each took one of Margaret's hands and simply held it. No one said anything in the rich silence. They had always been close. Margaret was not forever; even the pictures were crumbling. Nothing lasted, but they had memories to nourish them, and they had this moment.

Margaret weakly said, "I need to rest now, girls." She added, "I haven't talked this much in weeks. We'll finish this another time." She fell instantly asleep in her chair.

Carl was very bothered by the strike. His family had never thought of him as particularly sensitive to feelings or ideas, but he did scare easily. He'd been a gruff, cranky dad to his three kids, and a demanding husband to his wife, Norma. She didn't hate him, and she didn't love him. She had lived for most of their marriage in sort of a half-numb state somewhere between love and hate, where she breathed more easily once he'd had dinner, a few beers, and fallen asleep in his pale blue velveteen Baracalounger at position-three watching pro sports on TV.

Norma knew the rumors of the strike, all that this would imply for him and his wife, had affected Carl deeply. He'd picked this facility. Lukewarm about it, she'd gone along with his decision. They had reached a *modus vivendi*, a comfortable and secure way of life there. He didn't want to change anything. He liked Jeremy and Johnnetta in particular, especially when they rubbed his back with oil after his bath. He felt good in his room, now that both of them were together. He felt as though he were not so alone. In the rehabilitation unit, he'd felt more scared and lonely. His children wanted them both in the more expensive private facility, figuring neither would last that long anyway.

So Carl became more worried about his life than he ever had been, even more concerned than he'd been during the months when he was acutely ill. He didn't cope well with "this case of the nerves," as he put it. He had no experience with the level of tension and anxiety that engulfed him, especially the vague sense of terror that he said gripped him in the dark at night when he heard Norma's gentle, rhythmic snoring. If he could have said it, he'd have said he was "scared shitless." He never spoke of death. He didn't talk about life much either, so he played no favorites. "You were born, you lived, you died." Carl was a practical man.

He simply didn't wake up on the day after the strike. He'd always wanted to keel over or die in his sleep. He didn't want to know when, where, or how it would happen.

Norma knew what to do. He'd planned it, picked his clothes and the casket. She couldn't understand his choices or preferences for the new clothes, but what the hell? She could handle problems much better than he could. So, the psychoneuroendicrinology of his being–

he'd agree to the term "soul"–said goodbye to its earthly temple and let Carl die in his sleep.

Dr Ramantha reached Carl's room where Norma sat near the door. She was crying. He said, "You have my condolences, Norma. He was quite a guy."

Through her tears, she mumbled, "Thank you. We disagreed on everything. I loved him."

"He died in his sleep, so I see no reason for any investigation or an autopsy, do you?" asked the doctor.

"No, I don't either. He was just so worried by everything here. He was worried they'd close the home, or that we'd have different staff. Carl was such a worrier."

"Yes, yes," replied the doctor. "We have to sign a death certificate. Then his body will go to a funeral home nearby."

"That's fine," she replied. "I want to be alone with his body for a few minutes. I want to pray. I guess I'm in shock. It doesn't seem real to me yet."

"Please let me know. I understand completely. Take your time. It will be your decision whether he is buried or cremated."

"Oh, he hated the idea of being burned up."

Norma tried to understand. Was it stress? The strike? Did it all overwhelm him? He'd been a tough old geezer, but he'd been scared to death.

Due to the poor breathing, lousy oxygen tanks, and months of being bedridden or in the chair, Norma was immobile much of the time. She felt slightly euphoric, nearly a little drunk when she moved her head from side to side.

The angels had returned the night before, and she still thought about them. They hadn't spoken, but their beauty was overwhelming. They wore pure white ballet dresses, sheer white hose, and no make-up. Their eyes were clear and trusting. Their skin was almost snow white and unblemished. Small wings adorned their shoulders, unobtrusively fluttering while they hovered at a near standstill around her bed. Several came, but she couldn't get an accurate count. Her mother had told her, as a young woman in South Carolina, that when the white angels come for a visit, death is nearby.

With Carl gone, death was fine with her. Death was a friend. She never had been afraid. Her belief in the Lord helped, but she knew she wouldn't have feared death even if an agnostic or an atheist. Her lack of crippling anxiety probably helped her live longer. She'd beaten the odds, outlived the doctor's forecast. But that was only a temporary victory. She didn't want to leave the earth and stop living, but if the Lord wanted her, she had made her peace. She had forgiven herself of her sins, limitations, and insensitive behaviors. She would say something impulsively to people, occasionally blurt out a remark that hurt another's feelings. She was sorry. It just happened.

She had forgiven her first husband, Gerald. He wanted sex twice a day, fresh baked bread every day, and then, after two kids, he'd gone off with a real piece of trash. She'd forgiven, but she'd never forget the bastard. It had only lasted two years. But if Gerald hadn't been a lousy husband who never gave her a penny to help raise the kids, she would never have met Carl.

And those decades with Carl provided the best years of her life. She'd been a cook and run a store. He had a good job working in town, too. He loved the kids. He was a good father, and as good a provider as he could be with a fifth-grade education. They lived in a doublewide trailer and paid their bills on time. He drank too much beer, but he never hit her or the kids. They had two TV's, so she got to watch her own programs. He wasn't selfish.

He only spent wildly once. Just after his first heart attack, but before the stroke, he planned his funeral. He bought a two hundred and fifty dollar blue suit, a new shirt and tie, and new shoes. She tried to stop him, arguing that he already had two suits. And why did he have to have new stuff to be buried in, anyway? He insisted, comparing it to when she had written two songs for her funeral and picked out organ music. He just wanted to be buried in new stuff, didn't care if the casket was open, but he wanted brand new stuff. She still smiled at all that, but he got his wish. He looked good, too. He was a good man.

When she had passed out the other day in the lounge, the nurse told her she'd fallen asleep. She knew differently. She had been allowed to sit in her chair for fifteen minutes in front of the big TV in the lounge. She felt dizzy, then her eyes closed, and the next thing she knew, she was being yelled at, "Wake up, wake up," and one of the maintenance guys was shaking her gently. She knew right away that she'd passed out. He clearly thought she had passed on.

He asked her point-blank with no sugar-coating of any kind, whether she'd seen bright lights or been in a tunnel with a light at one end of it. He told her he was sure she had died when he saw her. He apparently wanted to know in the worst way whether she had a near-death experience. She couldn't recall a thing except for feeling dizzy. She hated to disappoint him. The more she thought about his response, the more scared she got. Until she reminded herself, "If I had died, it would be all right. Carl and I would be together. If I came near death and then returned, that's all right, too."

She feared much more for her memory. Her daughter Monica's young daughter had visited with family members over the weekend. A very beautiful child of eleven or twelve, Cheryl had blonde hair to her shoulders and brilliant wide-set, blue-green eyes–a potential heart breaker. She lived in Houston, so they weren't well acquainted. In fact, she didn't remember her when she said, "Grandma, don't you know me?" No truthful answer existed except, "No, sorry, I don't." Was she losing her memory? She'd have to study the snapshots. She'd have to review the family tree. She thought she had her picture board arranged perfectly.

To forget a granddaughter had to be a cardinal sin. The poor child could be marked for life, never forgetting that even her grandmother didn't recognize her, that she had no identity at all with the matriarch of the family. Grandma is old. Grandma is sick. Grandma forgets, so please forgive her. Please. Please. Please.

Chapter Fourteen

To Staff:

August 1, 1995. Weather report is for the end of the several days of rain, with warm, dry, sunny weather ahead. Lo 62, Hi 90. Census at 147, with one expiration. Administrator, department heads, and all board members will be in today. Crime report: theft of one table and two chairs from the storage area. Enjoy the annual Bar-B-Que.

SW

The maintenance crew began preparations for the annual staff-resident-community Bar-B-Que several days in advance. They swept and cleaned the rear parking lot. Next, they put on the yearly thin coat of sealer over the cracking black top, covering up the imperfections and making the lot more presentable. They erected a wire fence about four feet high to encircle the lot. On the day of the Bar-B-Que, the staff would run red, white, and blue crepe paper streamers through the fence links, trying to create a festive atmosphere. Finally, they cleaned the large butane grill, removing the rust spots and oiling all the moving parts. The old grill, seldom used, worked well. Millie and her crew would cook ribs and chicken on it.

Susie wanted this year to be special, so she had asked the kitchen and dietary staff to roast a whole lamb. They designed a fire pit to hold charcoal briquettes in an aluminum shell mounted on a bed of stones. The lamb would turn on an electrical spit that the home borrowed for the day from a local Greek restaurant. Coleslaw, garlic bread, fresh corn, and grilled potatoes topped off the menu with ice cream bars for dessert–chocolate over chocolate or chocolate over vanilla.

The home knocked itself out for the event, which included not only family, residents, staff, providers, and representatives of referral sources, but also guests from the nearby community. As many as three hundred people might attend over a four-hour period, between eleven a.m. and three-thirty p.m., weather permitting. An acapella choir from the home would sing shortly after noon. There would be door prizes and candy canes for all the children under twelve. All of it given freely to everyone who attended. John Anderson used to do the barbecuing himself and would invite his wife to co-host. It had become a tradition for the two of them to greet everyone and serve their meat or chicken course.

Susie wanted to make her presence felt. At the same time, she thought it would be polite, reflecting on the close collaboration of the administration and Board of Commissioners, to ask Jack Wheatley to co-host this year. Susie would slice and serve the roast lamb. Jack would lead the way with the barbecued ribs and chicken. The kitchen staff would do the bulk of the work.

If rain developed during the food preparation, large beach umbrellas sat handy to protect the cooking meats and potatoes. However, if rain came during the eleven to four period, seating rotations would be provided inside the home, using both of the large dining rooms. They also rented picnic tables, placing them around the perimeter of the lot. At least one hundred people could be seated at one time outside, while one hundred and seventy-five people could eat in the two dining rooms at the same time.

The Bar-B-Que, now in its eleventh year, had never been rained out. For that one afternoon at least, the gods smiled on the home. Snapshots of residents in their chairs eating barbecue, talking, and sunning themselves lined the activity room wall, and bulletin boards for weeks following the event. The variety of foods, so different in type, aroma, and taste from the home's ordinary fare with its hospital-type simplicity, provided a treat for all, and the sounds and smells lingered in the residents' collective memory for weeks after the event.

Millie beamed at the quality of the vegetables and meat. The corn was sweet and bi-color with bright yellow and snow white interwoven kernels. Even the cabbages for the coleslaw looked delicious, deep wine colors for the red and frosty green for the others. The corn, bubbling with momentum in huge vats, gave off a mild sweet aroma that gradually gained strength; then thick pats of butter were applied just after cooking. The mayo and seasonings for the coleslaw were a delicate blend, contrasted with the pungency of the barbecue sauce. Millie had used her secret recipe for eleven years and told no one, not even Tom, the mix of her critical ingredients. Her trick was to keep it balanced between sweet and sour, using plenty of lemon juice with cane sugar and maple syrup, along with the tomato-based sauces. She called it "bittersweet barbecue sauce." It was sweet, but sad, like life at the nursing home.

The preparations went well, and Susie felt confident on the morning of the event. So much pressing business loomed that she didn't know if she would be there at the beginning of the festivities. Board members would be present, and some of the union people from Cleveland would probably drop by also. She wanted to cut the lamb, even if she didn't have time to baste it every ten minutes as suggested while it roasted on the spit. She figured that Lieutenant Grocchi would probably be coming too, both for his continued investigation, which had a zero yield hence far, and for his love of huge helpings of barbecued meat and chicken. He couldn't miss.

She took her first telephone call at five after eight in the morning from the Crossleys, the local lawyer couple. Both were on the line.

"Morning," said Susie.

"It's not good," Noel said.

His wife, Joanne, explained. "At least five more families want their kin out, even if a further strike threat disappears. Not good. We can't explain or negotiate it. Is there any way to reduce costs as an inducement to stay?"

"No," said Susie. "No way. Thanks for the update. Keep doing your follow-up on the big meeting. No other facility around here will take them until the new union contract is signed. Did you get your check?"

"Yes, thanks," the lawyer couple said in unison.

At eight-ten a.m., Susie made a brief note to explain the news to Jack Wheatley.

Maria knocked on her door at eight-fifteen, and Susie invited her in. She was the only staff member with that privilege.

Maria smiled and flashed her very bright, perfect teeth. "Cas is a mess since Elizabeth died. He's been hallucinating. They've put him on Zyprexa, after the Risperdal failed, but it doesn't seem to be doing it. Dr Ramantha says that he has to play around with the dosages, but maybe we need a shrink to evaluate him and prescribe it. Doc says he's not sure if Cas is truly crazy or if the hallucinations are secondary to the severe depression. They had to take him off of Prozac, discontinued it two days ago because his hands and arms started shaking. Doc remembered hearing somewhere that Prozac can increase extra-pyramidal symptoms in the elderly who have Parkinson's. Sure enough, we checked his history, and Cas had a Parkinson's diagnosis, but no treatment, some three or four years ago. We didn't know it. So, no Prozac for now. His blunted affect could be from the depression or the Prozac. How do you like modern medicine?"

Maria seemed relieved to be able to share the complexity. Her friend didn't like this kind of ambiguity in treating the elderly, with so many adverse effects or paradoxical effects of medicines in elderly patients who had so many dual or multiple disorders simultaneously. And the doctors seldom visited the home in person, often only once per month. She really couldn't always trust her nurses or herself to present an accurate portrayal of the symptoms over the phone. Maybe video conferencing would improve the situation. They could see and hear the doctor, and he or she could see and hear the nurse and the resident. Time would tell.

Cas had been wandering the halls aimlessly. Maria reported he tried to take off the wander-guard ankle bracelet. When asked why he wandered ceaselessly, he said that he was looking for something. One of the nurses gave him a single goldfish in a small bowl full of water, but nothing else. When he was too tired to walk the halls, Cas sat in his room and observed the goldfish wander in the bowl. He began referring to himself as "just another fish in a bowl" or as "another fish swimming upstream."

He agreed to a behavioral plan in one of his more rational moments. Doc had told her he'd offered Cas a reward for each hour he didn't walk the halls. Originally Cas agreed, and then backed out.

Cas was powerful in his way. The discontinuance of the Prozac may have contributed to his agitation, but Zyprexa should have reduced it. He was undoubtedly grieving the loss of Elizabeth, and told Maria that he wanted Elizabeth's jewelry. She had told him that if anything ever happened to her, it was supposed to be his. Maria had checked with the office, they had no jewelry in the home's safe, and no record of a bank safe deposit box that held jewelry. Elizabeth was severely disturbed, but no Power of Attorney existed, even for medical decisions. She was legally competent and, in the absence of a written will, Susie felt that maybe Cas could still have a valid claim. Golden View's attorney would consider the possibility. At any rate, Maria and several

LPN's had gone into Elizabeth's room and searched through her effects.

"You can't believe what we found," said Maria, eyes flashing. "It was a gold mine. Well, a jewelry mine. She had five boxes under her bed."

"What was in them?" asked Susie.

"All kinds of jewelry. Some junk, some real, a few with real gold or silver, and one genuine diamond ring. It is part of her estate, and the lawyer says that it will have to be appraised first. Then if Medicaid says it's not too valuable, I guess over fifteen hundred dollars, then it could get passed on to the county, or if there's a will, or a valid bequest, it could be a valid gift to Cas. But he wouldn't see the stuff for at least a year or so. Could take that long. He took a ring while we looked through the stuff, looked like something Elizabeth got at a carnival, and said it was his gift to her, but he was lying. The poor guy must have cared a great deal about her."

Susie thought out loud. "Interesting about her hoarding all that stuff. No one saw it, and she hid the entire experience from staff. She probably took it out at night and got satisfaction and a sense of security from it. She was so frightened and insecure behind that mask of anger and craziness. God, I'm starting to sound like Doc, aren't I?"

"The good news about the whole thing with Cas," said Maria, "is that he hasn't talked about going AWOL or suing us for Elizabeth's death. At least he's put both of these aside for the moment, maybe for good. The downside is his behavior, which is tough to manage for my nurses, and the medicine he takes. We'll do it though. We don't just help the 'sweeties' here."

"Speaking of sweeties," Susie said as she got up from her chair and wrung her hands, "that pair of sweeties, Helmut and Trudy, are due here at nine for the meeting. I invited Doc and Dr Ramantha, but I don't know if I should have. They never did replace either of them, so both are still officially working with Myra, although there have been some second opinions."

Maria pushed back her chair, smoothed her uniform, and stood up. "Fine, I'll take a breather and be back at nine o'clock." She paused a moment and tilted her head. "Thanks for listening."

Outside in the parking lot the choir practiced. The sweet and sour aromas of charcoal and the ribs cooking wafted in, and she could see the smoke from the fires. She objected to the *Kool-Aid* being served, but you can't win them all.

Doc entered Susie's office with the rest of the group and sat at the table. Underlying resentment, bitterness, and disappointment bubbled close to the surface.

Susie waited to raise the window and soak up the cooking barbecue aroma. The sun shone bright and clear.

Trudy lowered herself into her chair. Before the niceties began, she spoke coldly and abruptly. "We're definitely going to sue you people as individuals, the home itself, and the county. You've screwed us badly, as if that Judge Williams hadn't done enough to us by denying the injunction."

"Trudy is very upset," said Helmut. "We've heard about the change in Myra's will. Ursula told us. We know she would have never done this on her own. You've turned her against us. She even gave Barry the Bear to Margaret. Barry was her prized possession."

A brief smile crossed Maria's face. No one else even blinked.

Doc said, "You're both upset with all of us and the facility. We understand that. You blame us. What exactly is the change in the will?"

"As if you all don't know," Trudy answered. "Margaret, that bitch, that sneaky gold-digger gets half. So, Ursula and I only get half of what's ours. It is ours. We're her children. We need it. We've waited so long and have been so patient."

Doc swallowed a smile, so proud of Myra for her good judgment, and happy for Margaret and her family, but of course. "Some blow to you. Some change."

"What a shock," added Susie. "I can imagine what this felt like to you."

"Did she try to kill herself?" asked Trudy. "She told me about pulling a tube out of somewhere in her body, but I couldn't tell if she was delirious or if it was true."

"We have no nursing report of suicidal behavior," answered Maria, cool and inexpressive. "Nothing at all."

"Well, if she's so depressed, she might kill herself here. Shouldn't her medication have been changed?"

Dr Ramantha loosened his tie and asked softly, "What about the second opinions? You haven't replaced Doc or me yet."

"You got lucky, both of you. They said the same thing, but still, if Mom is so depressed, shouldn't her medicine change?"

Susie explained that no nursing report existed of suicidal behavior and no psychological report of suicidal intent. "In addition to your second opinion, the facility had a local Doctor of Clinical Pharmacy review Myra's medication history, and she agrees with Dr Ramantha's decision and Myra's specialists. I guess we're all on the same wave length now."

"Oh, no. Oh, no we're not, young lady," shrieked Trudy. "Not one bit. I don't trust the other doctors, or you for that matter. They're all in cahoots with each other. You people have turned my mother against her family and are cheating us–Helmut, me, and my sister–of a million dollars. It's called conspiracy. You have also given her improper and unacceptable medical and psychiatric treatment. She has become suicidally depressed with no appreciable change in her medication or otherwise. And you've gotten several other fraudulent doctors to make it look like it's the proper and correct thing."

Dr Ramantha had the good sense to simply look at the conference table. Maria reddened and perspired. Susie adopted a blank stare.

Doc looked out the window wistfully and, with as much sincerity as he could muster, said, "We hear you, Trudy. We hear you."

Silence. Obviously, so much was left to say that no one knew how to say it without bedlam. Doc concluded with, "Dr Ramantha and I will continue treating Myra until you remove us. We'll do our best. See you all at the Bar-B-Que."

Susie jumped up to answer the phone at her desk. The others arose, avoided eye contact, and went out the door in single file. Doc, who stood and closed the door, stayed, listening to Susie on the speakerphone.

Susie said, "Hello, this is the administrator's office."

Noel Crossley answered, "Hi there, Susie. My wife and I are putting together another report on what will happen if the strike is prolonged, or happens again. How many empty beds? The costs to be incurred. All that sort of stuff based on follow-up interviews and phone calls with relatives and some staff."

"Sounds good," she said. "Incidentally, Myra Gronbeck has left half of her money to her roommate, Margaret Princeton. Myra's family is threatening havoc. It's a million."

"Did she have a lawyer draw up the will? That's a lot of money."

"Yes."

"Does she have a POA for health care or a guardian?"

"No."

"Then the only question or problem will be Margaret's. Myra's family will just have to accept it." His voice became deeper and more reassuring. "Margaret would probably like to shield the money from Medicaid and the IRS, to the extent possible."

"Yes, if she understands," replied Susie.

"You could suggest a good Cleveland tax lawyer. She might transfer it directly to her kids or grandkids in trusts. You know, find a way to keep Medicaid off their backs. Or, they could buy their own fifty-bed nursing home and have a facility just for themselves."

"Thanks, Noel. You lawyers are really something. Talk to you soon." Susie hung up the phone, rearranged her hair, and checked her earrings.

"You don't trust Noel's judgment, do you?" Doc asked.

Susie stood up, sighed several times, and then took a deep breath. "Right now, it's all we've got."

Lieutenant Grocchi's folding chair barely held him. Tony Dee and Lou Giordano sat at the same table as the Lieutenant. Lou, even larger than Grocchi, was better proportioned and more athletic looking. Susie joined them, smiling at Lieutenant Grocchi.

"Good morning, Lieutenant. Beautiful day. Glad you're here," began Susie.

"Morning. You know Lou and Tony from the union in Cleveland? This is Miss Wilson," responded the Lieutenant.

"I prefer Susie. I'm the administrator now that John Anderson is no longer here."

Tony Dee offered his hand. "Nice to make your acquaintance. Heard some very nice things. Getting it all fixed up, I see. Just beautiful."

Lou tried to offer his hand to Susie, but he knocked over his *Kool-Aid*. The table was crowded, and Lou was not as athletic as he appeared. He wiped it up. Then he explained, "Nice to meet you in person, Susie. I'm Lou

Giordano, the attorney. We talked on the phone a few times."

"Oh, yes," said Susie. "I recall you quite distinctly."

Lou leered and said, "Nice to meet you in person. Your neighbors and the families seem to love the place. I hope our one-day walkout wasn't a problem for you. We just wanted to make our point."

"No, we survived. There were several deaths that may have been hastened by it. We'd like to end the dispute and sign a new contract when you're willing to do that," stated Susie.

Lieutenant Grocchi fidgeted, his chair straining. "I just met Lou and Tony here, so I wouldn't have to go to Cleveland. They know I'm a detective, and that I'm suspicious. Did the union do any of this stuff at the home–the fire, the graffiti, the break-ins–and were they in bed with the remodeling contractor in any way? Pardon me, Susie; that's the way I talk. I guess that's the way I think, too."

"No problem, Lieutenant. I've heard worse." Susie reassured him. She sat up straight in her chair.

Tom and Millie walked over to pay their respects to Lou and Tony. Awkward greetings of, "Hello, how are you?" and "Hi, Lou, how is it going?" filled the air. Lou and Tony did not ask them to sit down, and they sauntered off quickly, saying they'd return later.

Lou quipped, "As I was about to say before we were so rudely interrupted, our union absolutely does not do that stuff. Right, Tony?"

Tony replied, "At least to our knowledge. Some union members do their own thing."

"I'm holding two ex-cons in the tank downtown. We arrested them last night not too far from here. The car and the guys pretty much match the description of some guys seen here in the early a.m. on the day of the kitchen fire. It was too late at night for them to call their attorney, but we said they could do it this morning. He's a Louis Giordano of Cleveland, Ohio. That's you, isn't it, Lou?" Grocchi went on, "Susie, would you excuse us for just a moment? I want to give the boys here every opportunity to be relaxed and answer me truthfully. It's kind of a suspicious turn of events."

Susie got up and started to walk over to the lamb rotating on the spit. "Gentlemen, don't forget the lamb we're roasting. There's a special rice pilaf that goes with it. Just for my friends." She winked at them as she walked away.

"Well guys, how about it?" asked the Lieutenant.

Lou finally said, "I don't know who they are. I've got many clients. Can't discuss my clients anyway. You know I'm like a priest in that regard. My lips are sealed."

Grocchi said, "That's not funny. And you're no fucking priest. You're a mob mouthpiece. And Tony runs the union crap in Cleveland. We're not fools here, you know."

"Please, Lieutenant, don't misunderstand. We have the greatest respect for you. This facility is great. We give a lot to the local youth program. Lawyers can't talk about clients. Who are the two men?" asked Tony.

"Can't talk about my prisoners either. You guys know that. When there's an arraignment, you'll know, and we'll know. How would conspiracy to commit arson and attempted murder do for starters? They got a little testy, so we could add resisting arrest. One of them had a gun, so there's a carrying a concealed weapon charge to add to the list. Phone numbers for a 'Lou G.' and a 'Tony D.' were among their possessions. I think a stolen Rolex was in there, too."

Unable to keep his massive frame on the card-table type folding chair any longer, Grocchi finally stood up. He loomed over the others. His height and girth were impressive. Lou started to stand and then stopped as Grocchi walked over to the roasting lamb.

Jack Wheatley walked by Susie's roasting lamb as he went back to his fresh batch of ribs and chicken on top of the charcoal. "Nice party, Susie. Congratulations."

"They love it, Jack. They love the ribs. The sauce is better than last year; they all agree. Wish it could be like this more often, don't you? More fun and excitement, and more pleasure for our residents. We've always got one big crisis after another. Is it like this in your car business?" Susie asked.

"Well, I've got a philosophy that keeps me going. We've got problems, but I don't let them get to me. I try to attack other people first. I always figure that if I let my guard down, they'll get me. So, I try to get them first, before they know what hits them. You should try it."

Susie wasn't entirely sure she understood him. The more she saw of him, the less she cared for him. She shifted back to the barbecue. "Thanks, Jack. I hope we build some goodwill today. We need it."

"Well, I think we're going in the right direction. This whole union thing may work out. Golden View could have a new contract."

"You act like you know something," she said.

"I do," he answered, smiling.

"I hope so. I don't mean to shock you, but I'm planning to resign. It's all just too much for me. I feel horrible about the strike, and guilty about the deaths and Mabel. You'll find someone who's better at it."

"Oh, now, don't you worry, young lady. You can't blame yourself. Things will get better. Just hang in there. We'll talk more after the next board meeting. I've got some good news for you."

"I mean it, Jack. I'm leaving. I do blame myself. I'm finished." Susie walked quickly to a table of residents. It relaxed her to talk to them after the harrowing discussions with Jack and the Cleveland people.

Jeremy was helping Dorice eat. Her condition had deteriorated. She now had periods where she talked ceaselessly, and much of it was gibberish. She could not feed or bathe herself, or even brush her teeth, and she had become more confused and aggressive. She had just hit Jeremy with a pork rib, and he was cleaning the front of his nurse's shirt when Susie arrived.

"Hi, Jeremy. Hello, Dorice. Good to see you," said Susie. She did not know what to expect. Dorice's hygiene was good, except for the right side of her hair, which had imprints of a handful of barbecue sauce in it. Jeremy would clean it later when Dorice was more calm. He'd give her both a bath and shampoo.

"I want oatmeal. Where's my dish?"

"Yes, Dorice, you want oatmeal," echoed Susie.

"She changed her mind," said Jeremy. "She changed her mind. A minute ago, she wanted ribs. Then she threw one over the fence, hit me with another, and rubbed the sauce in her hair. She's more calm now."

"Thanks, Jeremy, you're good," said Susie. She moved on. "Dorice has seen better days. Make sure she's strapped in nice and tight. She's a good wiggler, and we don't want her to fall, especially now that she's so frail."

Agnes, Norma, and Ralph were in their chairs, arranged at the table so that the bright sun did not shine directly into their faces. Agnes and Ralph did not talk to each other. Norma wore sunglasses and what looked like a new kelly-green pantsuit.

Susie said, "Norma, you look marvelous." She then pulled up a folding chair next to her.

"I'm doing better. Guess I missed Carl more than I thought. The picnic reminds me of that dinner we had when he stopped eating. My breathing is better now."

"Glad to hear it," said Susie with a smile.

"And Monica is going to come today. She's in town with two of her kids. The family is all that matters to me," explained Norma. "Of course, my new roommate is great. Just like Carl, she is. We disagree about everything–hot and cold temperature, loud and soft music, TV, lights on or off–just like I did with Carl. It's really working out perfectly for us." She chuckled smugly.

"Sounds good," said Susie. "I'm so pleased you're doing well. Your Carl was quite a guy. He'd be proud of you."

Susie stood up and slid her fold-up chair over between the wheelchairs of Margaret and Myra. "How are you both today?" she asked.

"Margaret says it's pretty with the colored paper and the balloons. Smells good. Music stinks. She drove me nuts, but I miss Mabel. I've felt better for the last day or two," Myra said, somewhat breathless from the effort.

"Yes, now that she's awake longer, she wants to visit her cemetery again. How's that for a celebration?" Margaret quipped. "She's a fun gal, my Myra."

Susie smiled and said, "You both look very pretty today."

Johnnetta, who sat near them to help feed Myra and readjust Margaret's tank, had taken extra pains to get them ready for the Bar-B-Que. Myra's silver hair was curled and set. Though noticeably thin, it looked shiny and lustrous. Margaret had on a new light purple and blue smock that highlighted her blue-gray hair, which had also been permed recently. Both had manicures topped off with bright red polish. Johnnetta had cut up the rib meat for them, and both had plates of baked beans and coleslaw, along with the meat. Myra hadn't touched hers. How very thin and frail she was, her skin showing a slightly translucent, waxy quality.

"You are both very special to us. I hope you know that. We even call you M&M's–you are two sweeties." Susie leaned over and kissed each gently on the forehead. "Very special to us. How do you both feel about the strike, and Elizabeth and Mabel?"

Myra answered first. “It was a surprise. We’d been with Mabel just before she walked out. There wasn’t much left of her.”

Then Margaret said, “Yes, but I recall her better days. She was a good organization person. She belonged to clubs. I’ll miss that Mabel.”

Susie nodded. “Me, too.” As she sat down, she said, “I wish she hadn’t walked out. I wish it had never happened. She was about to go into the locked unit.”

Margaret turned in her chair so she could look directly at Susie. “It’s a different story with Elizabeth. She was hard to like. She never let up. She was real mean and real crazy on the outside.”

Myra added, “And we never got to know what was on the inside. She wouldn’t let anybody know her.”

Susie said, “Yes, but Cas got to know her. He must have seen the good parts inside of her.”

Myra finally took her handkerchief out and wiped her face several times. “Could you turn me so I’m not directly in the sun?”

As Margaret turned her, Myra waxed philosophical. “You know, Susie, you’re young, but we’re old.”

Margaret said, “That’s brilliant. That’s really brilliant.”

“Well, I’m not finished,” said Myra, feigning annoyance. “Young people think you should mourn and grieve and carry on for days and months, or even years, when someone you know dies. When you get used to death, it’s like anything else. You get used to it.”

“Yeah, you’re right,” said Margaret. “You get used to it, except for very special people. You know, like husbands.”

Susie stood up. "I see what you mean, although I don't really feel that way. I'm still sad about the loss of both Elizabeth and Mabel. I wish we'd been more careful with Mabel. I wish she'd been more careful."

"It's a real nice Bar-B-Que, Susie," said Myra. "Real nice. Thanks. You're real nice, too."

As Susie walked away, Margaret said, "She's awful nice, isn't she? Why would she want to work with all of us old biddies?"

Alone now, they could talk more comfortably.

"It's been such a long time since I've been outside," said Myra. "I don't feel alive in that place. I know I'm closer and closer to crossing over." She smoothed the blanket over her stumps.

"I know what you mean. So much death in there," answered Margaret. "We got through it all."

Myra thought for a moment before she said slowly, "Yes, you're right. We made it."

"Do you believe in life after death? You've never told me if you do or not."

Myra pursed her thin lips and paused before answering, "Sometimes I do, and sometimes I don't. Sometimes I just think I won't be here. That's all."

Margaret asked, "Where will you be?"

"Maybe my soul will be around somewhere. You'll remember me, won't you?"

"Of course," answered Margaret. "Of course, I will remember you. That is, if I'm here and you're not. Who knows with any of us?"

Myra said, “I know you’ll remember. That comforts me. I wasted a lot of time. I didn’t realize how little time there was.”

“It goes faster and faster, doesn’t it? You couldn’t convince a young person, though. They’re always in a rush, but they think there’s plenty of time to kill.” She chuckled.

Myra tilted her silver head towards Margaret, turning her delicate face directly to her, almost as if she could see. “I would have been gone months ago without you. Maybe my kids could have even gotten the doctors to let me die. You spoke up for me. My kids can’t see the value in hanging on. I don’t blame them.”

Margaret looked into the sunglasses, imagining Myra’s pale blue eyes. “My kids have kept me going, and my grandkids, too. I’ve been unhappy with your family. Even if they thought you had no life, they should have agreed with you. I don’t approve.”

Myra perspired, but didn’t complain. “Be patient with my girls later on. I’ve forgiven them. They’ll be unhappy over the money, but that’s the way I want it–half to you. If I was still as angry and disappointed with Trudy and Ursula as before, I’d have given you all of it.”

The talk made Margaret twitch, fearful of being alone. “Do you want more of this sweet punch? It’s good, isn’t it?”

Myra didn’t answer. Her head had slipped to one side. Margaret stared at her and, for a brief moment, thought she was gone. Then, Myra’s hands jerked involuntarily as one of the nursing aides brought out a cage with two love birds for the residents to admire. Myra’s hands moved again, more gracefully this time, as if flying into the heavens herself. She was asleep.

Later that day in their room Myra asked, “Why do you think we’ve gotten along so well?” Her face was pinched with the pain and annoyance of the itching stumps. “We had similar husbands, I know that.”

Their intimacy helped to blot out Margaret’s constant physical pain as well. She wanted to hold Myra’s hand. Instead, she moved her wheelchair to face her friend. She was getting an oxygen treatment, and even surprised herself when she pulled out the mouthpiece and abruptly turned off the machine. So what if the nurse didn’t like it. Myra wanted to talk about important matters.

Margaret began, “I like to be needed. I need someone to care about.” She paused, not wanting to offend Myra, but needing to say it. “I hope you don’t mind me saying . . . someone to love.”

Myra nodded. “Yes, you surely are needed. An old, blind cripple like me needs you. That’s for sure. But yes, it’s more than that isn’t it?” She added, “I wish I could stand, just for a moment. I’d like to walk over to you, to see your face, and to look into your eyes.”

“Oh! I wish you could,” Margaret agreed. “We’d be friends, really close friends, even if we weren’t old and sick. I just know it.”

For Margaret to move closer to Myra’s bed had become a habit. She wheeled over, rearranged the bed covers and handed Myra her glass of water and straw.

Myra sipped slowly. “I think our men make us closer too, don’t you? You, our friendship, keeps me alive. It tells me I’m still alive. But our men . . .”

Margaret nodded. "Yes, yes. Maybe we're queers. Isn't that what they'd call us? Well, not really." They both screeched. Margaret coughed and then spoke again. "The men. Oh, the men. My James never did say much. We had the kids. We raised them. He was a good father. But at night he'd just eat and go to sleep. He didn't start the heavy drinking until we'd been married for many years."

"I know. I understand perfectly. I loved John till the day he died. I truly loved him. It was feelings he couldn't handle. Just feelings. But he was a good husband, a real fine man till the very end." Myra squinted hard but a tear escaped anyway. "He could never talk like this. Just talk about *us*."

Margaret felt so warm. "Even before he drank or had a stroke, James and I didn't talk like this. You're right. It was feelings. Do men have the same ones we do?"

Myra tried to shift her position, but with both legs gone that always proved difficult. She answered, "If they do, it's not so you'd notice. No ma'am."

"Do you smell smoke?" asked Margaret. "Like when we put water on a campfire. A smoky, sooty, charcoal smell."

"Yes, do you think the home is burning?"

"No, I'll check the bathroom." Margaret rolled her chair quickly into the bathroom. "No smoke. No fire."

"Look around," suggested Myra. "Be real careful."

"Oh, yes," answered Margaret. "Here's a cigarette butt in the toilet bowl. Did you smoke it?"

Myra's sunken face contorted. "Very funny. One of the aides must have smoked in there and left it." She shook her head. "This place gets me down."

"Yes," Margaret said, wheeling back to her bedside. "Me too. But at least I've had you with me all these months. And you know, to think that people will say I talked you into giving me that money makes me laugh."

"Me, too!"

Again, both chortled, not so much that Margaret had to turn the oxygen back on, but enough that she wheezed a bit.

"Especially," Margaret added, finally settling back, "when you can flip a coin as to which of us goes first." She paused and breathed, trying to get more oxygen into her lungs. They were playing out. "I've had many a good laugh with you, Myra."

Myra nodded, almost asleep again. Her waking moments proved shorter and shorter. But a lightness had crept into her, a fluttering of butterfly wings. No, not just butterflies, Monarchs, the mottled quality of those wings lifting Myra's paper-fine skin.

"I can't wait until tomorrow," Myra said, startling Margaret.

"Yes. How nice of Doc to take us to the cemetery. I hope James' and my plot is as pretty as I remember."

"And I can see John again . . ."

She drifted completely off this time, into a snoring slumber. Not exactly a peaceful sleep, but that kind would come soon.

How lucky I have been, Margaret thought, having two great loves. Oh, and the children of course–how rich they had made her entire existence. But Myra had been a gift, Margaret's last one of this life. A gift from wherever eternality was.

She closed her own eyes as the whisper of white wings sang her to sleep.

9 781928 704102